Alex Wheatle was born  London. He spent most of his childhood in a children's home, which he left at fourteen to live in a hostel in Brixton. At eighteen, he was involved in the Brixton uprising and went to prison for three months. On his release, he continued to perform as a DJ and MC under the name Yardman Irie, moving in the early '90s on to the performance poetry circuit as The Brixton Bard. His second novel, *East of ... ne*, won the London New Writers Award (2000). *The Dirty ... is* his sixth novel.

THE DIRTY SOUTH

ALEX WHEATLE

A complete catalogue record for this book can
be obtained from the British Library on request

First published in 2008 by Serpent's Tail,
an imprint of Profile Books Ltd
3A Exmouth House
Pine Street
London EC1R 0JH
website: www.serpentstail.com

ISBN 978 1 85242 985 0

Designed and typeset at Neuadd Bwll, Llanwrtyd Wells

Printed and bound in Great Britain by Clays, Bungay, Suffolk

The paper this book is printed on is certified
by the © 1996 Forest Stewardship Council
A.C. (FSC). It is ancient-forest friendly.
The printer holds FSC chain of custody SGS-COC-2061

10 9 8 7 6 5 4 3 2 1

To all those who have suffered the ultimate loss

Acknowledgements

Shout outs to Laura Susijn, Nicola Barr and to Pete Ayrton and all at Serpent's Tail for believing in me and venturing where others feared to tread. Honourable mentions to Kolton Lee, Clint Dyer (let's make that bloody film!), Catherine Wearing, Jonte Richardson, Courttia Newland, Stephen Thompson, Anjela Lauren Smith, Simone Pennant, Clyde Minott. Respect to Raymond Stevenson, Lucia and the rest of the crew working on the Don't Trigger Campaign. Salutes to Blacker Dread and the other organisers of the Brixton Summer Splash. Polite bows to all those people, including the police, who work hard to make Brixton a safer place. Shake of the hand to all at the Streatham Youth Community Trust. Big respect to Charlie and the rest of the Burru drummers who backed me at that memorable night at Brixton Library. Respectful nods to Henry Bonsu, Devon Thomas, Tim O'Dell, Michael Groce, Julia Jacobs, Mark Norfolk, Vanessa Walters, Dreda Say Mitchell and to so many others.

Last but not least a special thank you to Veraldo Barnett, DJ of Radio Mona 93fm, located at University of the West Indies campus, who allowed me on a steamy Kingston night to play whatever reggae I pleased for an hour. One of the best nights of my life.

...so don't you forget, no youths, who you are
And where you stand in the struggle...

Bob Marley

Chapter One

BRICKY

My name is Dennis Huggins and I was born in 1983. Right now we are, as my granny would say, in the year of our Most High 2006. I'm in Pentonville Prison in North London. They say there are more black men behind bars and in mental institutions than there is in universities in England but I reckon it was a white man who researched that shit.

The English tutor said I should write my tale and she offered her help. But burn her help, I don't need it. Patronising bitch. 'Cos I am black she didn't think I could write too good, didn't think I had an academic brain. When she finishes her shifts she probably wants to tell her white friends and family how she's helping poor, ghettoised black brothers with their English. Burn her! The only way she can help me is leaving me alone so I can get on with my tale.

So I'm gonna write an honest account of what's really gone on in my life, the mistakes I've made, chances I had and why I ended up in this grimy place. I just hope that my mother doesn't read it.

Before all you know-it-all pussies start thinking that this is the story of some young black guy who didn't know his paps and lived in a Brixton ghetto – you're wrong. Yeah, I lived in Brixton, or Bricky as we call it. But in a nice street. Leander Road, just behind Tulse Hill estate. Bricky does have decent streets but with all that fuckery stereotyping and media shit, you well-booted living in Berkshire and wherever wouldn't know that... Actors, bankers, librarians, secretaries, doctors all live in my road. Even gay people or chi chi men as we call them on the road. So I ain't the product of a grimy sink ghetto. Nor the product of a single mother family...

Sure, Bricky does have its ghettos. Tulse Hill estate where a trailer load of eastern European people and white trash families live. At night you see their whores stepping for trade on Upper Tulse Hill Road. Myatts Fields estate where all the crack houses used to be; fuck knows where they all are now since the Fed clamp-down. Angel Town where every second brother seems to be packed with a gun. Stockwell, where the rude boys show off their guns in the local youth club and Vauxhall where the Portuguese shottas sell the best hash in London while dodging the moves of the chi chi men who prowl and hang around in those ends. The Camberwell end of Coldharbour Lane where so-called Muslim gangs cruise and jack any shottas and run protection rackets.

I didn't start off my life in a three-bedroom terraced house. My family lived in the Palace Road ends just off Streatham Hill until I was five. I don't remember much about that place save one time when my mum took me to the corner sweet shop for a treat. Mum was taking out her P's to pay for my crisps and a chocolate bar when two brothers ran into the shop armed with long shanks. I remember the shopkeeper's reaction. Mum was all upset and by the time we got home she was bawling and shit, hugging me to her chest and asking me if I was alright. I wasn't really scared, just buzzing to see them two brothers in action. After that, my parents were proper determined to move into a house and away from an estate. Many of my parents' old friends had moved to Croydon and Thornton Heath, which we now call 'Little Bricky'. But Mum didn't want to move too far from her own parents – even though they never approved of her marriage – who live in Elm Park, just a two minute walk away from our gates.

My mum is now a legal secretary and she works for some solicitor firm in Clapham Junction... When she gets home from the office she's always bitching about the white people at her workplace and how she has to be better than them just to get equality... Fuck equality my paps would say, he wanted justice. Anyway, I've never seen any of Mum's white colleagues step through our front door nor any of my paps' work bredrens. Mum earns about twenty-five grand a year but she was always cussing me about wasting the odd potato or a spoonful of rice from my dinner plate. When I was a kid she always checked me from scalp to toe making sure I was neat and shit to go out. She still would if she could find a way to see me every morning in prison. An unwashed mug in the sink was a worse crime than chatting back to my teachers in my mum's universe. I might have given my mother a world of grief and frustration but I have never sworn at her, not like how those white trash kids swear at their mothers. Got too much respect for her. Despite the life I have chosen to live she's a good mother and I don't wanna hear no different.

My paps is a librarian at the Lambeth archives. He has to use a walking stick after some accident he had when he was eighteen. He's never talked about it but I know he was a shotta of some fame back in his day. In Bricky it seems that every black brother between the ages of forty and fifty knows my paps but it always fucks me off when these brothers don't wanna spill the shit about him. Once, Uncle Royston told me a little when he came around my gates and he had too much to drink. Apparently, Paps' so-called accident was the result of an encounter with a Bricky crime lord who ended up dead. I thought all this was so heavy and my respect for Paps grew. I wasted no time in telling my school mates. 'My paps used to be a famous shotta! What did your paps do? Fuck! You don't even know your paps, you sad pussy!'

'Fuck you!' they would say. 'Your paps is Bricky's version of Stephen Hawking with his fucked-up legs and hop-along shit. I wouldn't want no paps if he was a spastic.'

'At least I know where I come from,' I would retaliate. 'Them fucked-up alcoholic men who hang outside Bricky library and beg old white women for twenty pence could be your paps, you fucking fatherless pussy.'

My own paps can lecture a bit though. I always preferred Mum's five minute screaming and then the slamming of doors whenever I did something wrong. Paps would sit my black ass down and talk all calmly and reasonably, making me feel as stupid as a dumb-ass ghetto brother faced with quantum physics. He lectured me for two hours after I jacked this new Kosovan kid's dinner money at school; the boy couldn't chat no English so I thought it was an easy jack. I was eleven at the time and I didn't need the money... It was the buzz, the adrenaline rush. Simple as.

Behind his back I always call Paps the preacher. Forever going on about what it was like for him when he was seventeen or eighteen, but refusing to chat about his life as a shotta. If he talked about that I would have paid attention like a dick in *Destiny's Child*'s dressing room. I was never going to be interested in the numbers of young black unemployed in 19 fucking 80, long forgotten riots, funny-named TV characters like Yosser Hughes, crazy garms like silk flower shirts, fucked up afros and how Margaret Thatcher messed up the country. Burn that shit.

I didn't really have a bad argument with my parents until I left school at sixteen. Paps was vex at the time, waving his walking stick in my face telling me 'education is the key', trying to convince me to go college. He's always told me that education is the key phrase as far back as I can remember. I can recall Paps introducing me to this one-eyed rastaman. Jah Nelson his name was, and he tried to give me some extra black history lessons. He was around for over two years in my early days. I can't remember what he taught me but I definitely remember his face scaring the fuck out of me.

'Education is the key, education is the key': that was Paps' mantra. I'm sick to death of it now. I felt like hitting him many a time but how can you strike a man who you have seen almost every day of your life struggling up the stairs? Clump, scrape, clump. Clump, scrape, clump. It was proper embarrassing when friends were around. He's stubborn too. If you asked him if he needed help he would put on his screw you face. I hate to admit it now but there were a few times when I wished he would fall down those motherfucking stairs. Mind you, we had some deep pile carpet on those steps so that would have cushioned any blows.

Life was comfortable growing up. I always got the Nike trainers I wanted, which was the important thing and I didn't have to queue up with the free dinner ghetto kids at school. If there was a film I wanted to see at the cinema I didn't have to wait outside the side door at the Streatham Odeon with the rest of the ghetto brothers to be let in.

And we had Sky TV. Schoolmates, whose parents couldn't even afford a TV licence, would come around to my gates after school and we'd sit on my couch watching Puff Daddy videos on MTV Base and all the fit gyrating chicks in them while we killed out all the crisps Mum bought for the month. We fantasized about wearing heavy gold chains and fur coats and driving them rides that bounce up and down on road. That was the bomb.

It was about that same time I stopped having white friends. Nothing racial about it. It's just that we have different musical tastes. Most of them like Oasis, Coldplay and shit like that, you know, music that don't require getting up and dancing to and instead they'll do that air guitar fuckery. We like R&B, hip hop and dancehall reggae. One or two other white brothers liked that shit too but it wasn't cool to hang with them. The fact of the matter is that most white brothers I know can't dance, just like most black brothers I know can't swim too good. Simple as. When I left school I might nod to a white brother in the street who I knew from school days but up to the time I was sentenced I didn't have any white bredrens. So burn the mayor's theory of a cool London multicultural society. It ain't real.

During my growing-up years Paps made me go on family trips to museums, castles, sites of historical interest, all that shit. My paps said it was good for my education… It bored me senseless but my sister, Davinia, lapped it up though. She's three years younger than me and was a proper Lisa Simpson from the day she was born. I would get excited by a new bike and Davinia would get all overcome like when my parents bought the entire World Book

Catalogue. When I had no homework to do my parents would suggest reading through book 'A'. Burn those books!

School was boring. Never had no problem with the work. The teacher would tell the class what to do and I would be finished within ten minutes or so. Then I would have to wait for some of those no-brain ghetto kids who didn't even know how to spell their own fucking name. They would sit at the back of the class with their stressed-out mentors, wondering what the fuck they let themselves in for while their charges were trying to string a sentence together. Dumb as shit they were. The funny thing was that the parents of the dumb fuckers were the first to come to the school and cuss the headteacher about being a racist and how their little darlings were not getting on 'cos of being black, but the same ignorant parents didn't give a shit about their little darlings doing homework…

While I was waiting for the idiots to complete a task, I would create a bit of mischief, start an argument or something, swapping insults about our mothers. Every kid did this to test how far could you go, how much could you tolerate before switching… Now and again, kids switched big time. Geoffrey Allen, a fat West Indian boy in my class, was brushed about his weight by Kole, this African kid. There was always beef between Jamaican kids and Nigerian kids. I didn't like the way Nigerians would go on all superior.

'Geoffrey, you're fat like a footballer's wife shopping bag. How you get so fat, man?'

''Cos every time I fuck your scar-faced, bruised-legged, droopy-titty mum she gives me a fried dumpling.'

Kole proper switched. Leaping on Geoffrey, kicking him, punching him while tears were running down his face. The rest of us collapsed in laughter. Geoffrey always had lyrics but then he had to have lyrics. He was fat and butt ugly.

The only part all the boys loved was Games. In my first year at secondary school, during the warmer months, our teacher, Ms Trevor, took us in the school van to Tooting Bec Athletic track. We threw the javelin at each other, tried to drop the shot on people's toes, see if we could piss in the long jump pit from the jumping board, hit each other with hurdles and ripped the shit out of other kids who went to better schools; given half the chance we would jack them too. And it was at Tooting Bec Athletic track where I first saw my life's obsession. It was like me sitting and chilling watching one of those MTV Base videos and all of a sudden one of the chicks just climbed out of the TV.

I was strangling a bredren with a tape measure when my MTV video queen burned past us like some rapid shit in a PlayStation game. I relaxed my grip around my friend's throat and just watched her. She must have done two laps before she rested on the grass near the track. Her hair was in long plaits, decorated with red, gold and green ribbons. She was taking in deep breaths and she was wearing this blue Nike tracksuit. She had this elegance about her, even when she ran. She wasn't muscular but petite and slim. She was the prettiest girl I had ever seen and I wanted to pack her away in my kit bag and take her home. She's gonna be my girl, I said to myself.

So every Friday afternoon for two years I picked a spot near the finishing line of the track just to see her run by. I would pretend I was performing warm-up exercises but really I was watching her every move, every step, every stretch. Even if I didn't attend school on a Friday I would still make my way down the track just to see her. In all this time she never once noticed me or acknowledged me. I found out from another boy that her name was Akeisha Parris. And that her PE teacher reckoned that one day she would run for her country. And judging by the determination on her face you had to believe it.

One time, watching Akeisha compete in a 800-metre race, I saw something drop from her wrist... She went straight on to the changing rooms and when I was sure she wouldn't come out, I went to see what had dropped off her arm. It was a simple wooden bangle, with a gap of about two inches from either end. It was neatly made and carved on it was the head of a lion, a pyramid, a bird with a long tail and the word 'love'. It was smooth all the way round, warm to the touch... I closed my eyes and imagined Akeisha's pulse vibrating through it. I then pulled it on. It was tight to my wrist and the gap of two inches was now three.

I knew I should have waited for Akeisha to come out so I could give it back to her but I wanted it for myself. I may have been too scared to talk to her but at least I had something of hers. So I took the wristlet home, cleaned it and polished it. The next day I even took it to school and instead of paying attention to the teacher in woodwork class, I sandpapered my bangle to make it even more smooth. I then gave it a light varnish and I remember the teacher was all shocked-like to see me fixing up a piece of wood. At home I placed it at the bottom of my wardrobe underneath the sheets and blankets. In private I would take it out now and again to look at it, thinking of her.

In my third year at secondary, Akeisha disappeared from the Tooting Bec track. I asked one of the groundsmen if she came on a different day but no, he hadn't seen her since last summer term. This news really distressed me 'cos my highlight of the week was watching my video queen run. On weekends I took a bus to the track and hung around for a few hours just to see if she would come. She never did. Some might say it's a bit over the top if a fourteen-year-old is suffering from depression but I really was. Mum and Paps didn't have a clue what was wrong with me as I spent sulky evenings up in my bedroom. I would take out my bracelet and look at it for hours, trying to picture Akeisha running around the track, red, gold and green ribbons flying out behind her. This went on for weeks but slowly the memory faded and the bangle remained at the bottom of my wardrobe.

Apart from Games, English was my favourite subject at school. Only because of the teacher Miss Blaine. Fit she was. She had a Hollywood eye candy thing going on and I liked the way that no matter what sweater, blouse or top she wore, you could see her nipples poking through. All the brothers behaved in her class and I reckon quite a few bishops were choked in the boys' toilets after her lessons. I noticed that she read black fiction, writers like Iceberg Slim and Chester Himes. She told me once she liked listening to R. Kelly and Usher. She even told me she always went to the Notting Hill Carnival. I guessed she was into black men so at every opportunity I eyed her up, staring at her breasts, her behind, into her eyes and I didn't care if she caught me. She would blush and turn away… I wanted to give her a wok so bad it hurt.

In one of Miss Blaine's lessons we had to do some shit about *Romeo and Juliet*… I wrote a piece about a black man going out with a white woman in 1970s Brixton… It was the only homework I ever did that took me more than an hour. I even asked Mum and Paps to help out and they told me what it was like for mix-raced couples back in the day. Miss Blaine loved it. She even wanted to type it out and display my story outside the Head of English office. Burn that idea. I just wanted to give her a wok. Not that I had given any girl a wok up to that point in my life, though I had had untold wet dreams about Akeisha Parris.

My chance came when I asked her if I could borrow one of her books to take home and read. She told me to wait behind after class and I sat through the entire lesson with an erection. When everyone filed out I remained seated at my desk. She was rubbing out instructions on her white marker board and for a minute or so, I just watched her shapely behind doing this Beyoncé thing in her smart black slacks as she erased away. She went to the store-room to put away some papers and text books. I followed her in and stood behind her not quite knowing what to do. She turned around and smiled. 'Can't you be patient, Dennis. I'll be with you in a minute.'

I just stared deep into her brown eyes feeling uneasy about my first move. I didn't know how to kiss so I kind of raised my hands and touched her breasts… Or I should say brushed her breasts. I was still peering into her eyes. She then turned around, her back facing me. She kicked the door closed, took hold of my hands and firmly placed them on her breasts. I couldn't believe what was happening. I kinda squeezed and groped for the next minute or so until she grabbed my right hand and placed it between her crotch. I wasn't really doing anything. She was moving my hand up and down and I could sense her growing excitement. I freaked and ran out of the cupboard.

When I got home that evening I took out my bangle from the bottom of my wardrobe, looked at it and then wiped the dust off it. I closed my eyes and saw Akeisha Parris running around the bend, her balance immaculate, her speed impressive and that gritty determination showing itself upon her face. Would I ever see Akeisha again? Where am I gonna put my face when I'm in Miss Blaine's lesson? Why did you run out, Dennis? You pussy! Got to see Akeisha again. Maybe she'll like that rubbing the crotch shit? I just wanted to see her so bad. Maybe I could just hang out by her school but what would I say if I saw her?

When I look back on the store cupboard shit with Miss Blaine in the store-room, it was one of the best and worst of my life. The worst 'cos I didn't have that experience with Akeisha. The best 'cos that was my first sexual experience. It could have been a dream for a fifteen-year-old boy, but I didn't get to give her a wok. I never told no-one about it 'cos I knew she would get into trouble. It only happened once and following the incident she hardly acknowledged me, refusing to return my stares... So I started to make trouble in her class, throwing things around and flinging books in the bin. She ignored me. I even started a fight with this Arab kid but she went and got help from another teacher and she blamed me more than the Arab brother. That really fucked me off. Because of all this shit, my written work for her suffered. She didn't say much, she simply marked my work with C pluses and Bs instead of the As I had been getting. Thinking about it, I haven't enjoyed English since – not until I started writing this at least.

At the end of that term, Miss Blaine left our school. I think she moved to somewhere like Guildford and taught there. Burn Guildford. When I think about it though, what bright young talented teacher with ambitions is gonna want to teach in a Bricky school? I wouldn't.

At this point I could just about get on with my life without Akeisha's buff self invading my mind. But there were moments when she was there in my head and I could do nothing about it. She would pop into my head when Mum was asking me how was school today or when Paps was telling me about some weird book that I should read... She was always there when bredrens chatted about busting their virginity and whenever I flicked through the pages of porn mags. Sometimes I would just 'surrender' to the bangle and take it out, giving it a clean and simply look at it for longer than was sane. It was as if my video queen was forever performing her shit in my brain.

History was an OK lesson. Mr Fletcher was the teacher, a long white guy who came from Poole in Dorset. I think our school was his first posting. In his own words he wanted to see 'integration in action'. He had been on anti-Nazi marches and read the autobiography of Malcolm X. He liked Gil Scott Heron and Curtis Mayfield and he said he admired Eldridge Cleaver... What a motherfucking fool! He didn't have a clue about black people. Brothers would say to him, 'Hey, Fletch. I wanna give your mum a wok.' And Fletcher would reply, 'That is very thoughtful of you but my mother has all the large frying pans she needs.'

At first Fletch tried to teach us all the normal shit. Like William the Conqueror, the War of the Roses, Queen Elizabeth I, Walter Raleigh and his fucking potatoes, Henry the Eighth and his six hos, crop rotations, Agincourt, Waterloo and all that fuckery. We all took the piss and no-one did any work. Not surprising as only four kids in our class were white and one of them's paps was rumoured to be in the IRA. Burn all that white history shit. Fletch panicked and, quickly realizing that hardly anyone in his class was GCSE material, he decided to ask us what issues of history we wanted to learn. It was uproar.

The few Hindus in our class wanted to write about how the Hindus kicked the Muslims' asses in India just after the Second World War. The Muslims wanted to write about how they kicked the asses of the 'Imperial West' during the Crusades, a couple of Eritreans wanted to write about their issues with Ethiopia, three South Africans wanted to learn about Shaka Zulu and his *fuck you* stance to the English, the Irish boy wanted to write his shit about the Irish potato famine and one third-generation Jamaican, me, was well happy to write about the Maroon wars in Jamaica and slave uprisings; it was so embarrassing that none of my fellow Jamaicans in my class knew my shit. Anyway, everyone got writing on their own particular projects, peace was restored to the classroom and

Fletch was going on like Hollywood might make a film of his 'new teaching' shit. Even the mentors sighed their relief and were happy to take longer cigarette breaks in the playground. The only losers were the Kosovans and one Vietnamese kid who didn't know a fuck what was going on 'cos they didn't know English.

The only problem was that in one lesson the Hindus and the Muslims kicked off big time and parents were called in but that only made things worse. It was proper funny to see those Asian parents fighting in the headteacher's study... Shortly after that, Fletch resigned and it was back to Kings and Queens of England and how they kept their power or lost it. The only thing that remotely interested me was the alleged assassination of Edward II, a chi chi King by way of a red hot poker up his bottom hole. To salute the memory of Fletch, me and Noel Gordon ceremoniously burnt our shared textbook which met with the approval of everybody in class, save our new teacher, Miss Irene Manning. She quit within a term but none of the brothers really cared 'cos she was ugly.

Chapter Two

NOEL GORDON

Noel Gordon had been my best friend since primary school. He used to live in Tulse Hill estate in one of the blocks on the third floor. His next door neighbours were this Somalian family with a look of war, grime and shit about them. Put a smile on! I used to say to myself when I passed any of the Somalis on the balcony on my way to Noel's gates. You're in England now where we have running water and men wear socks, you sad bastards.

Dirt poor was Noel, always coming to school in beat-up Gola trainers, Nine Elms market trousers and Bricky market shirts. He had three younger brothers and his mum worked as a check-out lady at the supermarket. Fuck knows where his paps was. Never saw him. But his mum had her share of men. None of them lasted though, what with her Brixtonian-fish-wife cussing and nagging.

Noel's flat was just proper basic. There was this tiny kitchen and the cooker was kinda stained brown like bad, fucked up teeth. All the woodwork was peeling and the walls inside the flat had nuff bruises and marks on it. You could always tell when the family was struggling for money when Noel's mum cooked only bully beef or pilchards and rice for a week before she got her monthly pay. During weeks like that they had the same shit for breakfast.

Unlike my yard, where my parents had shelves of books all over the place, there wasn't a single book in Noel's flat. He and his younger brothers would get home from nursery and school and just watch TV. Before I reached ten years of age, most times my paps would turn off the TV and take out a game for all the family to play. Monopoly or Ludo, with Mum's home-made board and Davinia played it like it was life and death. Noel had no shit like that. His mum had that constant 'how am I gonna survive through the week' look on her face. Her expression only changed when she was watching her soaps and if anyone made any noise while she was watching that shit she would cuss bad-word through her cigarette smoke and lick her younger kids... Now and again, Cara, Noel's mum, would arrive at my gates and ask Mum for money for her gas card or electric key. She would come inside my yard, look around and feel like shit, not wanting to stay too long. When Mum made her coffee she always sipped it too quick, scorching her lips. She'd always ask for fifteen pounds, ten for her meter and five for a packet of Benson and Hedges. Ever since I've always wondered why is it that the dirt poor smoke the most?

It was while we was both still at primary school that I first witnessed Noel shoplifting... I have to say most of it was my fault. Mum would always give me pocket money to go to school with that I was meant to spend on the way home. But I spent it on sweets before registration specifically to wind up the ghetto kids who didn't have shit. Noel took this kind of thing to heart and most times chased me around the playground saying he was gonna jack me. One morning I teased Noel with an extra long Mars Bar and a packet of extra-cheesy Doritos. He ignored me. Back in class I made as much noise as I could with my Doritos bag but Noel still ignored me. This really fucked me off. On the trod home Noel was all quiet and shit. Then all of a sudden he ran into the sweet shop in Elm Park, grabbed three packets of barbecue-flavoured Golden Wonder crisps and ran like Linford Christie with a firework up his black ass. I was proper shocked...

The theft was kinda stupid though. Noel and me had been in that shop nuff times and the Asian people behind the counter knew our parents. Bastards. It was where Cara bought her cigarettes. While Paps lectured me about the importance of paying for what you own, Cara was licking Noel with a Dutch Pot and a steel ladle. I said to my paps at the time, 'Why you lecturing me? I didn't t'ief nutten.'

Two days after the sweet shop robbery, Noel came back to school with a cheap plaster on his forehead and for the first time I saw a bit of coolness in him. The lickings from his mother didn't put him off and we made plans to 'hit' other sweet shops that were further away.

By the time we were at secondary school, nicking sweets from local shops had got a bit boring. The buzz wasn't the same. So we started to go up west after school in the hunt for clothes. Before we hit the shops I would lend some of my garms to Noel because I didn't want him to walk into any clothes shop looking like the ghetto sufferer he was. We would try on a top or a pair of trainers and then we would simply leg it from the shop, jumping on the nearest bus. The security guards were mostly African and one or two of them would chase us for a while to look the part but give up. Once we got home, Noel had to hide his new garms and trainers under his bed 'cos if his mum found out it would have been Dutch Pot time. As for me, 'cos the inside of my wardrobe was looking sweet already, Mum didn't notice my new garms. Davinia did though and I had to threaten her on a few occasions to keep her beak quiet. If Paps found out he would have lectured me 'til doomsday.

On weekends, Noel would take his stolen garms out from under his bed, put them in a bag and come over to my place to put them on. Then we'd head out on road, looking buff in our garms and chirpsing chicks. We were only twelve or thirteen but it's amazing the confidence new clothes can give you. We would hang out at Stockwell and New Park Road Youth Clubs, posing like we was in a hip hop video and tormenting those ghetto kids who were still wearing beat up trainers and cheap market clothes.

'Where you going with your cheap under-a-fiver jeans?' Noel would tease. 'They should make a law banning brothers wearing that shit on road and confining your cheap black ass to your flat where your shit-poor mum can't afford the motherfucking rent! You fucking pussy!'

But we wanted more.

As far back as I could remember, Noel's mum smoked weed and so did my paps. Growing up I never thought nothing of it and it was normal to me as drinking a cup of tea or seeing a Kosovan kid get jacked. I didn't even know it was an offence 'til I was fourteen. When I questioned Paps about his weed smoking he would say it was to ease the pains in his legs. I knew that was fuckery. Anyway, Noel and me, we wanted to try it. At school there were some older kids who smoked weed and they used to wrap their fat-heads in the toilets at dinner break. We thought they looked so cool with their red eyes and that Snoop Dogg 'don't give a fuck' look. Anyway, these cool kids would leave their fat-head butts on the toilet floor and we would pick them up and roll a skinny-head in a single cigarette paper. First time we did it I took one inhale, it didn't affect me. I took a second and my head started to feel warm, kinda like how a suit feels when its dry-cleaned with all that steam and shit. Then I had this kinda rushing sensation in my head. With a messed-up grin on my face I told Noel, 'This is good serious shit.' Noel, in response, offered me a fucked up nod.

It meant our afternoon lessons were kinda compromised. We would turn up at IT and giggle at everything. We just couldn't stop. Especially when this new Vietnamese kid turned up in the lesson wearing grey shorts, sandals and a refugee haircut. We laughed so hard that suddenly the kid burst into tears and ran out of the school. Noel and myself got detention for that shit but we still hadn't shrugged off the effect of the weed. This was all clear when the Vietnamese parents turned up, obviously stressed out at their missing son, with a stush-looking interpreter. Shouting in their language they were, hands going everywhere. The interpreter tried her best to relate what they were saying to the teachers. While all this was going on, Noel and myself collapsed in giggles yet again. That evening Paps gave me another lecture but he really got annoyed at my fixed grin. 'Don't smile at me while me trying to tell you some truths and rights!' he barked. I just couldn't help it. Noel got the Dutch Pot treatment and afterwards he was thinking about reporting Cara to the social services, but gave it up when he realized what his mother would do to him if she found out he'd reported her… It was at this point Mum warned me about walking with bad breed boys and about their unhealthy influence on me. Kinda hypocritical 'cos when Cara turned up at our gates Mum was all polite and shit.

Chapter Three

RED EYES

It was after Noel and myself had just turned fourteen that we decided to go into business... We had a hundred and ten notes between us, saved from our jackings at various corner shops and clothes stores. One of Cara's ex-boyfriends, Lester 'Red Eye' Davis, was shotting out of a flat in Myatts Fields North. The estate Lester lived in is like a maze and he never liked the hordes of Africans who had moved in there. 'How can they get a flat so easy while I was on the housing list for thirteen years?' he whinged. He was a tall, smartly dressed guy, never without his old school black Stetson on his head. He wore square glasses and had this skinny moustache and a fucked up goatee. Needless to say, Lester's eyes were always red. He was forty-three and stuck in the old ways, this was all clear 'cos he didn't own a single CD and he played his ancient reggae on a turntable and homemade speakers. I guess Cara linked up with him 'cos he had a ready supply of skunk, mersh and high grade weed... Red Eyes also done a line in rocks but even if we wanted to, me and Noel didn't have the budget for that shit.

Red Eyes' front room had a heavy plasma TV and a pile of pirate DVD copies laying around everywhere. Lester had films that were not even released to the cinemas... My guess was that he got them from those Chinee brothers who always hang out in bookies and the local markets with their rucksacks full of illegal shit. Looking at these Chinee hustlers I guess they needed the P's so they could buy a decent meal. Skinny as spliffs they were.

Lester also had various pictures of his twelve kids about the place. Five different baby-mothers Red Eyes had. You would think after the baggage of three, the fourth or fifth one would have said, 'Wait a minute, this constant breeder ain't gonna wok me without protection.' Dumb-ass bitches.

'So you wanna buy an ounce of weed,' smiled Red Eyes to Noel and me, his two gold teeth glinting. He was sitting in this cream-coloured armchair with a fat-head in one hand and a Bacardi Breezer in the other. He was wearing his hat indoors. Maybe this old school shotta was bald as that black brother in *The Matrix*, I thought.

'Yeah, man,' replied an excited Noel. 'But we call it an oz. And if we sell that, we'll be back for more.'

'What do you want?' asked Red Eyes. 'Skunk, mersh or high grade?'

We had reasoned before the meeting that we'd go for skunk 'cos you get more for your pound. Also, it's mostly old school people like my paps who smoked high grade. Kids at school all smoked skunk; it hit the spot quicker.

'We'll go for the skunk,' answered Noel. 'But I don't want no contaminated skunk. I hear some shottas are lacing the shit with crack just to get us addicted so we'll come back begging for stones fatting up your wallet…'

I shot Noel a querying glance 'cos I've never heard of this lacing shit. Noel should know though, he lives in Tulse Hill estate… Red Eyes laughed. 'You should think about the crack thing, man,' he said. 'Easy money. All you have to do is find yourselves three or four addicts. You sell them a hit in the morning and they'll be back by lunchtime for another. And then another for their evening hit. They can't help it. They always find the money from somewhere, even if they have to jack their own granny. A nice steady flow of money. Just don't give them no freeness 'cos they will always expect it, always begging for it.'

As Noel worked his brain on what crack addicts he knew, I said, 'Burn that shit, man. Not into it. We ain't on that, man.'

Red Eyes laughed again, then went to go and get the skunk for us.

'Why did you burn the idea of selling crack, bruv?' Noel asked in a whisper. 'We could be driving convertibles by this time next year, riding with fit-batty chicks.'

'Maybe,' I said. 'But do you wanna crack addict banging down your gates at some bitch time in the morning wanting his hit? My parents would go nuts. Let's not even go into what Cara will do to your black ass if she found out you were dealing in crack.'

Noel thought about it. 'Alright then,' he said. 'We'll put the crack thing on hold 'til I get my own place and if the weed game does alright then I won't have to wait too long.'

We weren't too sure where to get those little polythene bags but Noel's cousin, Shemera, who worked in the rag trade, helped us out… She gave us hundreds of those little bags for buttons. We had no weighing or scales thing so we just cut up the skunk with my mum's scissors and guessed the amount to place in the bags. Ten pound a bag.

Now we were ready to start shotting but we had another problem to deal with. Skunk gives out a strong smell, more powerful than high grade, so we had to sprinkle aftershave all over our school rucksacks to merk the stench. That morning Mum gave me a funny look as I came down the stairs ready to leave for school. 'A young girl take your fancy, Dennis?' she smiled.

'No, Mum,' I replied nervously. 'I just wanna smell sweet. Don't you always tell me that I must fling away my BO in a proper way and smell all fresh?'

We met outside school and nodded to each other, the difficult part of the day over. Now we had to drum up sales. First lesson was maths and I sat next to Ronnie Taylor, a spotty-faced white boy. Ronnie had been smoking weed since he was eleven and his paps was a plumber. So Ronnie always had money on him 'cos those plumbers charge nuff notes just to get out of bed and Ronnie received a sweet budget for his pocket money. His school bag was always full of those Japanese Manga comics.

'Ronnie, I have some skunk to sell,' I whispered.

'Stop your lying, man. Why try it?'

Ronnie was going through a phase of talking black. Even the Asian kids at school tried to talk black. They all sounded so fucking stupid trying to pimp off black culture…

'I ain't lying, Ronnie. Trust me. Ten pound a bag… Would you rather buy off me or one of them older brothers who always rip you off? It's all legit, I even got this weighing thing at home so it's all bonafide. I know what I'm doing, man. My paps was a famous shotta back in the day.'

'I'll have to see it, man. I ain't buying no broccoli or shit like that.'

'It's the proper skunk, man. You'll burn half a fat-head and be buzzing. I promise you. And the skunk I'm shotting can make a man so relaxed it can delay a virgin man's explosion… Trust!'

After a while, Ronnie offered me a nod. We agreed to make the deal at lunchtime.

Courtney Thompson always sat behind me in maths. He was a salt addict, forever eating Kentucky chicken, McDonald's and the rest. He was also paps-less and ugly. His mum worked late shifts in some call centre and always gave five pound for Courtney to buy his dinner in the evening. He stank of salty breath and 'cos that shit was in his system from the day dot, he was always hyper, unable to keep still and pay attention in classes. I hadn't seen him burn a fat-head before but I thought he was ideal customer material.

'Hey, Courts!'

'What's up, Dennis?' Courtney replied while tapping a pencil on his desk. 'Have you seen that new Asian girl in the school today? She's buff, man! Did you see *Big Brother* last night? A black man will never win that shit. What you doing after school? Come to think of it a black brother will never win a reality game show. They all hate us, you know. Simple as. It's proper out of order.'

Courtney could go on all day like this, you had to break into his lyrics. 'Yeah, yeah, Courts. Listen up. I have some light green to shot.'

'What? You? Shotting? A piece of Brockwell Park turf? Ha

ha! You must think you're a proper Al Pacino. Have you seen *Scarface*? In a survey of West Coast rappers they voted *Scarface* their favourite film of all time. You haven't seen that new Asian girl? Trust me, I would wok that all day. How comes the Asians get their fucking programmes on TV and we don't? If you're shotting I wanna discount!'

'Courtney, man. I ain't joking. Ten pound a bag and the skunk comes all the way from Amsterdam. Proper skunk, not your DIY shit that's grown by cowboys under nuff lights and they're worrying about putting a pound in the meter. *Proper* skunk.'

'I'll have to sample it first. Did you know that in the film *For A Few Dollars More*, the bad guy is smoking *real* weed in his roll-ups! Trust me, man. I ain't lying. I read it in a book. I'm getting some serious munchies. Do you have any sweets, Dennis?'

By lunchtime there was an assembly of thirteen guys in the toilets, all of them sampling the skunk from two fat-heads that Noel rolled; he was always a better roller than me… We sold eight bags that very day with the promise of more sales by the end of the week. Things went very well apart from a couple of brothers like Courtney who after tasting, blasphemed our weed saying it's not bonafide and it had a parsley thing going on. Burn Courtney. Then there was one or two brothers who offered to pay in a week or two. Burn that idea, I thought, recalling Red Eyes' advice.

'No freeness,' shouted Noel. 'If you haven't got the dollars then don't even think about asking credit. Just raid your mum's purse when she ain't looking.'

Everyone laughed at Noel's remark but a few days later we learned that three brothers *did* raid their mum's purses to buy our skunk. It was all good.

My parents had opened up a post office account for me when I started secondary school, so any profits I made I put it in there.

Once a week we would step to Red Eyes' flat and buy our skunk. It was easy money, always shotting to people we knew. I had to resist Red Eyes' sales chat about the rocks but even Noel, proper happy that he was making P's, dropped the idea.

Chapter Four

PAPS

Three weeks after Noel and myself went into business, I had placed a hundred and sixty notes into my post office account. I was well content. It was a Saturday morning and I was whistling some hip hop tune on road when I got a call from Mum. 'Come home, quick.'

Paps had fallen off a chair while trying to drill a hole in a front room wall. He wanted to hang a new photograph of Granny overlooking the TV. Stubborn bastard. I had offered to do it for him before I went out but oh no, he started to give that 'I ain't no useless cripple' lecture.

Mum put a cushion under Paps' head. She was quiet, just stroking his forehead. He was just laying there, still, staring at the ceiling. For a long moment I wondered if he would ever walk again. I had grown used to taking the piss out of him limping along. Hop-along-daddy I used to call him. And he didn't mind. I had this sudden image of pushing Paps around in his wheelchair while I was shotting.

Davinia had already called an ambulance and she stood over Paps with a look that a mother might have for her injured son rather than a daughter has for her father. She then looked at me. I wanted to be all big brother-like and take control of the situation.

'Shall we move Paps onto the sofa?' I suggested.

'No!' shouted Davinia. 'Are you an idiot or what? You're not supposed to move somebody who's injured.'

I felt useless. I just stared at Paps as he continued to gaze at the ceiling. It was obvious that some of the pain he was feeling wasn't just his legs. It was as if his independence and manliness was being fucked up at that very moment, never to be regained. As the tears began to roll slowly down Mum's face, she closed her eyes and kissed him on the forehead. When I was younger I used to sneak outside my parents bedroom door and listen to them having sex, but this was so much more intimate, much more telling of their love for each other. It almost felt like Davinia and I were in the way. I remember thinking that I hoped I'd find a girl who would love me like that.

Coming back from the hospital after six days, I could see Mum's doubts as she carried the walking frame into the house. She left it in the hallway as Davinia pushed Paps' wheelchair into the front room. I helped Davinia roll him onto the sofa and I noticed that his grip on my wrist was strong, too strong, as if he was telling me that all strength in his body had not gone yet.

That evening was the first that I can recall when my family didn't eat dinner on the table in the kitchen. We ate in the front room, surrounding Paps with our plates of food on trays. It was his favourite – lamb, rice and peas. Propped up by three cushions, he looked a little embarrassed as Davinia and I, pausing our usual cussing and fussing, offered to pour him his glass of Guinness or pass the hot curry sauce that he loved.

After Paps had drained his drink, he turned to me and said, 'Dennis, if you're not too busy I want to chat with you.'

'Yeah, Paps, of course. Whenever.'

Mum and Davinia went to do the washing up. I thought I was gonna hear one of Paps' lectures but instead he laughed and turned to me. 'I've been a damn fool.'

I sat down opposite him and I found it difficult to meet his eyes. 'Yeah,' I replied. 'I told you I was gonna do the drilling, but you always wanna do everything yourself.'

Paps nodded… 'It's been hard all these years accepting my condition. I still don't think I have managed it.'

'You're right there,' I agreed.

He looked down at the carpet and I wondered if I had been too frank with him. I remembered him taking me out to the park when I was a boy to play football. I must have been six or seven at the time. He had a walking stick back then and he simply couldn't keep up with me. I know now he went through great pain just to play ball with me so respect was due.

'I know I am always one for talking and lecturing,' he continued. 'Even your mother moans about it. But Dennis, in this life we never know what tomorrow brings. So my most important lesson for you is to enjoy life, enjoy being young and able-bodied. 'Cos if you can't enjoy it then what's the damn point!'

There was a hint of anger in his last words, as if he was addressing them to God. He scrunched up his forehead and angled his eyebrows and I thought he was gonna start cursing.

'Do you enjoy life, Paps?'

He thought about it for a few minutes. 'Despite everything, I have been blessed with your mother,' he finally answered. 'And you and your sister.'

For the next nine months Paps had to go through some bitch intense physiotherapy. In all that time he never used his walking frame. Instead, he would walk along the hallway with his hands pressed on the walls, grimacing as he did so. A fucked-up sight… Now and again, Granny would turn up to see Paps. In fact, Granny used Paps' condition to kinda take over in the house. She was writing shopping lists, interrupting in Paps' physiotherapy sessions, hoovering the front room after Mum had already done it the evening before. Mum and Granny had one of those what I call polite relationships, always sweet to each other and full of compliments when they met face to face. But behind each other's backs they would bitch about each other… Not blatantly. Like Gran would open a window in the front room saying, 'It's a bit stuffy and dusty in here,' knowing that Mum had cleaned and dusted.

The weeks following Paps' accident drama, I kinda withdrew a bit from the weed business. Not totally but just a little. I just felt guilty shotting while some physiotherapist was ordering Paps to stretch and bend his legs. It was agony for him. Noel would complain and shit. 'No, man. My ratings for you have gone down, bruv,' he would say. 'Whether you shot or not ain't gonna make no difference to your paps' legs situation. His legs are fucked, always will be. Deal with it! I thought he said to you to enjoy life when you can?'

I thought about it. Yeah, Paps did give me a licence to enjoy life. And shotting was exciting… It gave me more of a buzz than smoking the skunk itself. Kids at school looked on me different, girls no longer ignored me. I was no longer the black brother who got decent pocket money and wore the best Nike trainers. No longer the spoilt little rich kid. I was one of the cool people now.

Chapter Five

THE ENDS OF SOUTH LONDON

Late summer, year 2000. Paps had been back at work for over a year. His limp was now worse but he refused to even use the aid of a walking stick. I couldn't see why 'cos he used one before. Stubborn old man. Since his accident his old friends came around more often. On Saturday nights they would play old school reggae on the stereo, burn fat-heads, drink their Guinness and chat about Brixton in the '80s. All this deprived me of watching Sky TV on a Saturday night. They would watch old school DVDs with titles like *Burning An Illusion* and *Babylon,* dramas about young brothers living in London in the late 1970s and early 1980s... I thought it was all so wanna-remember-when-I-was-a-young-buck kinda thing. They're lucky to have had that kinda shit though. I can't remember any television dramas about brothers like Noel and me. Black people in programmes like *EastEnders* might as well be white. They don't chat like me, look like me, walk like me or dress like me. The so-called brothers go into pubs and chirps fat white chicks, something that a ghetto brother with any kind of rep would never do. Burn them and the motherfucking BBC...

Anyway, Mum was now working even longer hours. She got some kinda promotion but it didn't seem to make her more happy. She was always bitching about how tired she was and her reaction to dirty plates and cutlery left in the kitchen sink was bordering on the mad side of nagging. I even saw Mum sharing a fat-head with Paps after dinner, a new development. In the front room they would sit, watching some shit about the seals of the Falklands or something with Mum bitching about her day at work. Mum and myself don't talk as much as we used to and I don't have to suffer all those kisses and hugs that I received from her whenever I returned from school or wherever. Maybe it's easier for mums to show nuff love to their little boys and spoil them... But once we reach seventeen we turn out to be selfish, lazy bums who leave dirty plates in the sink and piss on their see-through toilet seats. Anyway, at this stage of my life, my parents were proper boring.

Meanwhile, Davinia was getting untold pats on the back and ratings from teachers. She also noticed that boys were taking an interest in her and I told her straight that young bruvs were only interested in a wok. Simple as. Davinia would say I was overreacting or ignore me so I started to call her a ho. She'd always run off complaining to Paps. Burn Davinia. At times though I had to be nice to her... She had learned to plait corn-row style really neatly and most of the brothers were showing off that style. So when I hadn't called Davinia a ho for about a week, I'd knock on her door, tell her I was proud of what she's doing at school and ask her to do my hair. The stupid girl would oblige me. Davinia's bright with her studies but sometimes she lacks common sense.

Granny was brewing at her own flat in Cowley estate, no longer needed as much as she once was. She came around sometimes for Sunday dinner and Mum was forced to cook rice and peas and lay on a serious salad with peeled cucumber and shit. If she didn't Granny would chat about that even when she hardly had any money she always cooked rice and peas for her family on a Sunday with all the trimmings... Mum would always politely refuse Granny's help in the kitchen... Granny would then sit on the couch in the front room, sipping endless glasses of rum punch that she made at home. She would call for Davinia and me and then she would tell us stories about Jamaica from when she was a little girl. I heard tales about great uncle David's travels in America, mad bushmen, pit toilets, donkeys, three-mile walks to school, outside dances, the maroon wars, pervy preachermen, more mad bushmen and a tobacco-chewing old man with one tooth… Sometimes, Granny would tell her tales by doing this strange dance. Fascinating shit. Davinia even did an English essay about Granny's stories for school and she got more ratings and pats on the back for that shit too! By the evening, Granny was a little tipsy and Mum had to drop her home and walk her to her gates; Paps always had trouble climbing the steps in Granny's block.

As for me I was working part-time at a garage owned by my auntie Denise's husband Everton; my Paps' best friend. Auntie Denise and Everton had eight-year-old girl twins, Natasha and Natalie. Auntie Denise was cool. She never lectured me. Everton and Auntie Denise shared my tastes and they dressed in all the latest garms. Auntie Denise always dyed her hair in a world of different colours and she still stepped to the latest bashment dances and performed her shit on the dance floor. She liked Tupac and watched films like *Boyz in the Hood*. The last DVD my mum bought was *Shaft*, some film where every black brother had a mad afro… Only the Lord knows when my parents will finally make it into today's world.

Everton always had a zoot dangling from his mouth and when one morning break I rolled my own fat-head he didn't say shit. He just looked over with a kind of half smile. Why couldn't Paps be like Everton?

The job I had was a kinda compromise after Paps and myself had a serious row about me not going to college to study history or something. He had this dream of me being a university professor. Burn that dream 'cos I've never heard of a black university professor. We had a beef once about how many black men are in neat jobs like Managing Director of a name-brand company and shit like that. Paps couldn't answer me when I said I bet there weren't more than ten black professors in the country. Even if I did have the qualifications and shit they'd make it harder for me. They always make it more difficult for black people. Black sportsmen, singers, rappers and the odd token black on reality TV shows were the only fucked up role models in my world but even if there was some black history professor out there I couldn't see the likes of me getting that goal and nor did any teachers at my school.

Anyway Everton needed an extra pair of hands to help him out. I learned quite a few things; how to change and gap spark plugs, how to replace break pads, how to time an engine... You know, shit like that. The only problem was, I didn't like the grime and the grease and I was always paranoid about that garage smell when I chilled in the evenings and chirpsed chicks. But the seven notes an hour did sweet up that shit.

To further nice up my wallet on what Everton was paying me I was also shotting at youth clubs, colleges and basically anywhere else where skunk was craved. Even fifteen doors away on my very road, where this white woman lived who worked at the town hall. Her name was June Haver and she wanted her fix every Friday night. She looked so innocent in her trouser suits, pulled up hair and glasses but I reckon I even could've woked her if I wanted to. Anyway, Noel and myself made most of our profit at Stockwell ends. Or to be more specific, Stockwell Youth Club which was right in the middle of Stockwell Park estate.

Most of our deals at Stockwell happened outside the youth club 'cos the white woman who ran the place was no pussy. She was different to the few white women of that age who I knew. She wasn't afraid of black brothers... The way it went was white girls at school who had money felt at ease in black brothers' company, laughing, joking and burning fat-heads with us and allowing us to touch their tits. It's only after they left school for a couple of years when they started to grab their handbags more tightly when you passed them on road. White trash girls never blanked you on the road and they carried on like they were black anyway with their Croydon facelift hairstyles and their cheap gold. Anyway, Julie was the name of the woman who ran Stockwell Youth club. She ran Noel and me out of her club a few times with her cursing and shit...

When we weren't shotting Noel and me would play table tennis, shoot pool, log onto the internet where we entered chat sites and communicated with chicks... All the time we would check out any newcomers and kinda force them to buy our skunk. We spent a lot of our time watching the chicks, who formed the dancing group *Scarman's Children*, performing their dance steps. Nuff bootys and breasts were shaking in tight-fitting leotards and brothers were proper glued to the drama of it all, dreaming of untold woks.

It was while I was ogling *Scarman's Children* when this buff girl proper-catwalked right in front of me. Fit she was with a neat tidy booty and cat-like eyes. She was a lighter skin tone to me, a browning, and she was wearing this proper-tight tracksuit and untold rings on her fingers. She had a confidence about her that I liked. She wasn't as pretty as Akeisha Parris but I guess no-one ever will be. I'd never seen this chick before but I just had to chirps her and get her digits. She was chilling with two of her friends by a pool table. So I made steps towards her, putting on my strut. I heard Noel giggling behind me. He whispered to a bredren that she's out of my league and Dennis doesn't have the game to chirps them kinda chicks.

'What's gwarnin',' I introduced myself. 'I haven't seen you at these ends before. Is it 'cos all the men at your ends are butt ugly?'

She chuckled and offered me one of those glances when you know a wok is a possibility. I knew I was better looking than most brothers. That might sound arrogant but timid brothers don't get to wok fit chicks. Simple as. 'I'm from Peckham ends,' she replied. 'Just chilling here with friends who live Camberwell ends.'

'I don't step to Peckham ends that much but if I knew that buff chicks like you were there I would step there more regular. You know it.'

She laughed again and my confidence grew. 'So what?' I said. 'You're not gonna tell me your name? That's kinda rude seeing as we're having a proper conversation.'

'You tell me your name first,' she smiled.

'Dennis.'

'Ann. Ann Sheridan.'

'Well, Ann,' I said. 'Man would like to see you again and link up so what are you saying? I need your digits kinda urgently.'

Ann thought about it as her two friends looked me up and

down. They were brute ugly. I felt a sweat coming on from my armpits and my face was warming. Finally, Ann smiled and took out her mobile phone from her tracksuit pocket. It was a brand new model… I liked that 'cos it told me she had some P's behind her and I was tired of chirpsing ghetto chicks who couldn't even afford to buy me a Kentucky chicken nugget and a single fry. 'You give me your number as well,' she asked.

Relief…

Not wanting to appear desperate, I called Ann a week after our first meeting. 'So when are we gonna link up?' I asked. 'When are you gonna show me some love?'

'How comes it's only now that you call me?' she said. 'It's been a week!'

'Man is busy, innit.'

'Even in the evenings?'

'Yeah. Man has a little business to attend to.'

'I know,' Ann replied. 'You're a shotta.'

'Where you learn that from?'

'Word gets around on road.'

I paused, wondering who told her. 'Anyway, like I said, this man needs some loving. When are we gonna link up?'

'Next Friday night. My parents are out that night and I have the flat to myself.'

I closed my eyes and imagined running my hands over her bumper but I still wanted to appear calm. 'I'm not sure about your programme,' I said. 'I don't like to be taken advantage of and on first dates I like to get to know the girl first if you know what I'm saying. I'm a respectable brother!'

Ann giggled in contempt. 'What fuckery!'

'So Friday night for real,' I said. 'But I don't know where your gates is.'

'My flat is difficult to find so just make you way to Peckham estate. You know the big one that is near the new library and I'll link you at the main forecourt.'

'OK, that's all good. And make sure you have some nibbles and something to drink. Man needs food and liquor while he's showing some love. Oh, one more thing. Make sure you have some bump and grind music on the go. *For real.*'

'OK,' she laughed and ended the call.

I was proper content 'cos I didn't have to do that dating shit like take her to a wine bar or something and waste my dollars. Burn that shit and the idiot brothers who do it. When I link with a girl I just wanna give her a wok. Simple as.

Next Friday evening I slapped on my deodorant big time and put on my name-brand vest and garms... I usually don't step out with my gold rings and gold chains but what's the point of buying that shit if you don't wear them for occasions like this? I wanted to impress Ann to the max. I finished up dressing by pulling on my new Nikes after checking that they were spotless. Before I left I made sure I placed two condoms in my wallet; I didn't get too much sex education at home but Mum always said to me not to trust no girl and wear a 'jacket' at all times. 'I'm too young to be a grandmother and so much loose girls get themselves pregnant just to get a flat,' she would bark as Paps would try to conceal a grin. It was embarrassing but her message struck home.

I took a 37 bus to Peckham. There ain't nothing looking sweet in Peckham. The place is a proper dump, well grimed, with dodgy people selling phone cards and dodgy people chilling around cheap chicken takeaways and shottas doing their shit in cab stations.

As I made my way to Ann's estate, I said to myself that if she wanted a regular wok she'd have to step down to my ends. The estate reminded me of Stockwell Park with its dirty yellow, brownish brickwork and its long walkways and little squares. I gave Ann a ring when I arrived at a forecourt where nuff cars were parked.

'Ann! Yeah, I just reach. I'm just standing near this big car park next to a kind of square.'

'OK, babes. I know where you are. I'll just be a couple of minutes.'

I had a half-smoked fat-head in my inside jacket pocket so I took it out and lit it. I had taken three tokes when this African brother appeared on a balcony in front of me. He was about sixteen so I didn't really pay him any mind. Then this other brother got out of a car. He was walking slowly with his hands in his pockets and he was watching me, following my every move. He looked African too. One of the rules of the ghetto is that if a brother starts to stare you out you must return his gaze until *he* looks away.

Maintaining my own stare at this brother who was walking towards me, I heard footsteps coming from my left. There were now three of them. I spat out my spliff. Footsteps were now coming from behind me. I spun around and saw the shit was up to my neck… A guy running towards me with serious intent. For a short second it all seemed so comical 'cos this brother was rushing towards me with his baggy jeans falling below his hips showing his Calvin Klein boxer shorts. It was after that when a cold fear struck me. It's a horrible feeling… It starts with a cramping sensation in the stomach, then it spreads throughout your body until it gets to your brain. Your brain is trying to force you to make a choice. Run or fight. I didn't do either. I still don't know why to this day. So I just stood there, fucked up with fear. Rooted to the spot. The brothers rushing me seemed to get bigger and bigger. Their faces had a hungry look about them. Desperate. I couldn't move.

Reality hit me when I felt a punch behind my right ear. It dazed me because I didn't see it coming. I was surrounded by four of them. I only had time to notice that they were all Africans before the kicks and punches pounded my black ass. I felt jolts of pain all over my body and it took me a couple of moments to realize I was on the ground. I opened my eyes and saw a Nike-covered foot aimed for my face. It struck me on the right side of my mouth and I felt the crunching of a few teeth and a splitting sensation. I spat out blood before I choked and then I remember one of the Africans yelling, 'Peel him!'

My rings were wrenched off my fingers and they took my wallet. My Nikes were pulled off as well. Then they took off my gold chains and thieved my mobile. They had found my little bag of skunk in my inside jacket pocket and they even took my ultra-thin Rizla papers and my lighter. The only other thing I remember is that one of them said, 'Who's he think he is? A Brixton shotta coming down our ends and he wasn't even packed. Man, that was a proper easy jack.'

For one bitch of a long time I laid fucked up on my back looking up to this bright sky. The sun was hurting my eyes but I didn't have the strength to lift my hands up to shield them. I felt the warm blood dripping over my jawbone and I remember thinking it was surprising how quickly it cools. With a big effort I managed to roll on to my side and I spat out more blood that was clogging up my throat. Half a tooth came out as well. Everywhere was hurting but the thing that pained me the most was knowing that Ann must have set me up. That motherfucking bitch.

A crying baby stopped me from falling into unconsciousness. I opened my eyes and saw a white trash girl, no older than seventeen, standing beside me with her baby buggy. She had a Croydon facelift, earrings too big for her head and a market bargain denim skirt. I remember her taking out her mobile and making a call. For the next ten minutes or so she stood beside me, saying, 'Don't try to move.' Then an ambulance turned up. I managed to tell the medics my name and address and I also told them that the pussies had nicked my Nike One Tens. My precious Nike One Tens! I don't remember much after that.

Chapter Six

MUM

I was in hospital for three days, spending most of my time staring at the ceiling and trying to make sense of what happened. How could I allow some bitch honey-trap me? Even though I was on some serious painkillers my whole jaw just pounded in agony. And I was hungry. At this point I would've eaten pilchards and rice and felt no shame. I just wanted to eat a meal, any meal.

Confined to drinking soup from a straw, I wasn't a good patient and when Mum drove me home from the hospital the first seeds of revenge planted itself in my mind. I still had visits to the dentist to look forward to. Bitch! I thought, it's 'cos of Ann why I can't eat a Kentucky Zinger Tower. Then some part of my brain blamed me. You dumb pussy, it said. This is all because of your shotting. Simple as. It was your decision to get involved in it, you alone. You're intelligent enough to make good choices and you made a wrong one. Deal with it!

Stepping out of the car all groggy-like and feeling confused, I was led to my bedroom by Mum. While I'd been away she had cleaned up my room a bit. My carpet had been hoovered, my games for my PlayStation all put in a neat pile, my CDs no longer littered the floor and had found a new home on a new shelf. Even my computer desk and stereo had been wiped clean. It was nice to see my life-size poster of Aaliyah still pouting over my bed and under the bed my hidden dirty plates, mugs and takeaway drink cartons had been cleared away. I felt a little humiliated by all this but Mum said nothing. She was in a strange, subdued mood.

As I sat on the bed, Mum closed the door. She then sat beside me and gently cradled my jaw with her palms. Compassion was in her eyes and although I hate to admit it, her motherly touch felt good. She had taken the week off to look after me so I was feeling a little guilty. I know how she is about missing days from work. She then patted my pillow and said, 'Lie down.'

I did as I was told and I tried not to reveal how helpless I was. When my head hit the pillow Mum asked, 'Dennis, are you dealing?'

The question took me by surprise and it took me a few seconds to prepare my response. I didn't meet her eyes. 'What do you mean dealing, Mum?' Every word I spoke was uncomfortable.

'Dennis, look at me. Are you selling weed, Dennis?'

'Selling weed! Course not. I'm not on that.'

'Are you sure, Dennis?'

'I ain't lying, Mum. No.'

'If I find out you're lying to me don't think that you ain't too damn big for me to box you! I'll ask you again. Look at me, Dennis. Are you dealing?'

'No, Mum.'

I feigned tiredness by half closing my eyes. Maybe she would go away if she could see how sleepy I was. I didn't wanna talk. My fucking mouth!

'I'm just trying to think why these bad-breed boys attacked you,' she reasoned. 'You're not a member of the gang, are you?'

'No, Mum!' Raising my voice pained my jaw. 'I was just unlucky enough to be in the wrong place at the wrong time… Simple as. It was a jack, Mum. Simple as. It happens. That's life on road nowadays. We live in South London, not south Berkshire.'

Mum stood up, folded her arms, took a couple of paces and looked out of the window. At that moment she might have questioned why she didn't move away from South London when she had the chance. 'You know, Dennis, back in my day it was violent enough. But badmen would generally harm other badmen. People who weren't involved in drugs and crime were more or less left alone. If you minded your business no trouble would come to your door and you were free to enjoy being young.'

She now had her back to me and I sensed some kinda deep messed-up memory or something that was fucking up her head for many years. Maybe she was thinking about Paps. Obviously she doesn't know that I know how Paps became a cripple: that he was a shotta. Maybe I shoulda told her.

She finally turned around and forced a half smile. 'You just concentrate on getting better. Everyone's been asking for you, Uncle Royston, Grandma, Auntie Denise, Everton and even your great aunt Jenny called from Jamaica last night. I guess Grandma must have told her about your bad news.'

It was kinda nice that the family were thinking about my black ass but that ho Ann was in my head. Burn her! Mum sat back down on my bed. 'You know,' she opened with, 'in many ways things are more difficult with your generation. So many distractions. So many things that demand your attention.'

'What do you mean, Mum?'

'Everything is in your face. You can't watch the damn TV without some friggin' advert trying to hustle their crap. Remember those trainers you wanted, Dennis? You was about seven. Screamed the friggin' house down 'cos I refused to buy them.'

This was weird. Mum was turning into Paps. I've never heard her talk like this before.

'But I spoiled your black behind anyway,' she went on. 'Buying you name-brand crap that you didn't need and in some cases you grew out of the friggin' clothes in a few months. Your paps was always cussing about it but no, my children had to looked neat and sweet on the road. I spoiled your black behind. Maybe it's because of that you want things so quick. Maybe you didn't have the money for what you wanted. So you decided to deal. Is that how it went, Dennis? Because you wanted to look better than the other ghetto kids? I've heard the way you chat with your friends. I ain't stupid,

Dennis. Is that how it go? You better tell me the *bloodclaat* truth, Dennis.'

Mum could cuss with the best of them, including Grandma but she's never sworn in front of me. I looked at her in disbelief wondering how long she had been angry and why. She had a good job, strong marriage, nice house, fat wardrobe and at least one of her children had great potential. She wants to try and be Cara, Noel's Mum, for a day. Then she's got a right to be vexed. 'I ain't lying, Mum! Brothers I went to school with are on that but not me.'

'You better not be lying, Dennis. Selling weed can lead you to all kinds of crap you'd never believe. I still don't understand why these boys attacked you. Were you teasing them, Dennis? You know I never liked you teasing other kids at school. I taught you to appreciate good clothes if you have them but *not* to go on like a puppy show in a sufferer's face. Didn't I tell you that, Dennis?'

'Yeah you did tell me. I don't do them things anymore, Mum.'

She then caught me in a fierce gaze, searching my eyes for any clues of insincerity. The intensity of her stare forced the back of my head deeper into my pillow. 'I'll ask you again, Dennis. Are you dealing?'

'No, Mum. It's like I said, I'm not on that.'

Suddenly she got up and went towards the door. 'I'll check on you in about an hour. Try to get some rest.'

I let out a long sigh. Then I worked my mind over to see if I had left any incriminating evidence in my room. Rizla papers, half cigarettes and little bags of skunk weed for my private use. I'm sure I had been careful. I didn't even dare smoke fat-heads in my room when everybody was in bed. Maybe Davinia said something. She once caught me smoking a zoot in the park when I was with Noel. No, she wouldn't say anything. She knows what's good for her.

For the next few days I was expecting Mum to burst into my room with an oz of weed in her hand and my fingerprints all over it. She never did but my suspicion of her knowing something deepened because she was being extra-nice to me. She even bought me a new mobile! It was much better than the old one. It was slim and cool and didn't look like a brick. I wasted no time in showing Davinia my new toy and she went off in a sulk chatting something about I didn't deserve it. I couldn't wait to show it off to the poor-assed ghetto kids in youth clubs.

That same day, Noel came around in the evening. As Mum showed him in she was being over-polite to him, asking how Cara was and the rest of the family and all that shit. Mum was always extra-polite when she didn't like someone. As for Noel he looked like someone had just farted in his face. Brooding was an understatement... I took him upstairs to the privacy of my room 'cos it was obvious he had some shit on his mind.

As I closed the door behind me, Noel took two hundred and fifty pounds out of his back jeans pocket and threw it on my bed. It was wrapped neatly in an elastic band. 'Your share,' he said. 'While you've been honey-trapped I've still been on road making dollars.'

'Thanks for that, bruv,' I said. 'Appreciate it.'

Refusing to sit down as he usually did in the chair by my bed, Noel kinda fidgeted on the spot, looking uneasy. 'Spill it out, bruv,' I urged. 'What's on your mind?'

He pointed a finger at me, stopped shuffling his feet and said, 'You!'

'What do you mean, me?'

'People been chatting,' he explained. 'How you got honey-trapped by some bitch from Peckham ends. It's not good for our rep, bruv. Some brothers been laughing about it, saying that you and me are pussies. I ain't tolerating that.'

'Let them chat, bruv,' I said. 'What do they know?'

'Is that all you can say? Let them chat? Do you think we're gonna have any mileage in the skunk game if man on road thinks we're pussies? Every Tom, Dick and Jezebel are gonna test us, gonna try and jack us. And I ain't stepping on road with that shit over us. I want my rep back.'

'I've been thinking, bruv,' I said. 'Maybe it's time for me to get out of this business. We've had a good run.'

I looked up at Noel and I could see frustration brewing in his face. 'What do you mean, get out of the business!'

'Keep your voice down, bruv. My mum might hear you.'

'And if we stop our so-called business,' Noel went on, dropping his tone, 'what am I supposed to do? I'm never gonna get a good job. I ain't got shit qualifications. What are people on road gonna respect me for? How am I gonna get a decent ride to drive? I ain't gonna be like my mum, working in some shit supermarket and getting brushed by some pussy white man 'cos I'm five minutes late. You know she was passed over for promotion by this white lady who had only been working at Mum's store for a few months. Mum's racist boss told her the reason she didn't get the promotion was 'cos she needs to improve her customer relations. Burn that! If I see this pussy on road I'm gonna pound him… I'm not gonna struggle like that. I'm not gonna be a good nigger boy only for some white pussy to tell me I can't get promotion. All for an extra fifty fucking p an hour! Fuck that! You know what my mum does? She counts two pences and five pences to see if she's got enough money for the electric key. Burn that! No way I'm gonna do that shit. And I ain't gonna shop in no deadbeat stack-them-high supermarket looking for bargains. Burn that shit too. I'm gonna hustle for what I can get in this fucked up racist world and *fuck* anybody who don't like it! Including *you*. Do you know how it feels to walk with your mum when she's carrying Lidl bags?'

I didn't know how to answer so I switched the attention back on myself. 'Them African brothers wanted to kill me,' I muttered.

'Wanted to kill you? They just slapped you around a little bit. You're walking and talking now, right? My mum used to beat me much worse than the shit you got. But then you was always a spoilt little rich kid.'

'Fuck you!'

'You know I'm right,' Noel added… 'Look at you bitching about a little beating you got. Wow! You lost one tooth! I see your mum tucked you up in bed alright when I knocked on your gates yesterday. She didn't want you disturbed. She's making your soup in an hour's time. I'm surprised you haven't got no bell to ding her. Always a mummy's boy. What do you know about a hard knock life? It's always been easy for you. You're a pretend badman,

Dennis. Everyone knows it. A motherfucking wannabe. You ain't too different from those white and Asian people who try to talk black. You're a motherfucking pimp! Pimping from street culture.'

'You're lucky my mouth is all mash up 'cos for what you just said I would bang you up for that. Who do you think you are, coming to my gates and cussing about my mum? Take your ugly self from my eyesight and go back to your ghetto flat and eat your ghetto pilchards with the rest of your shit-poor family. And tell your mum to stop coming around our gates and begging for money.'

'Can't take the truth, can you?' Noel went on ranting. 'Man is crying about a little slap he got from some African brothers at Peckham ends... Well, hear this, Dennis. To keep my rep I'm gonna personally look for any of those brothers who jacked you and I'm gonna show them what it means to fuck with a Brixtonian. I can't afford for our business to fail.'

'What you gonna do?' I asked, leaning in closer to my friend. 'Don't resort to arms, Noel.'

Noel smiled an ugly smile, like he was thinking of some old school, bitch torture that he had seen in some old Samurai film. 'I have a ride now,' he said. 'A little Fiesta. Bought it at an auction for three hundred notes. And now I've got my ride, I'm going in for a little stakeout, to see if I can find that bitch who honey-trapped you. It would be good if you could come with me. You could identify any of the African brothers who jacked you. It was probably a Nigerian. I hate them motherfuckers with their scarred up faces and ugly mothers... They're all over Peckham these days with their crater-legged women and mad-coloured clothes. And then we could deal with them in medieval style. There's something I've got, two piece of long shanks. And I will use them. But if you're gonna go on like a pussy then I'll do this shit on my own. And I can remember what the bitch looks like. Man won't find her too buff by the time I'm done with her. And when I am done the phantom of the motherfucking opera will turn his back on her nigger honey-trapping ass.'

'Give me time to think,' I said.

'OK,' Noel replied, all casual like. 'I will allow two weeks for your mouth to heal, then I will come for you. If you're ready or not, I'm gonna deal with those African pussies. Believe it.'

Then he was gone. Without a goodbye.

Mum came up forty-five minutes later with a bowl of chicken soup. She didn't say nothing as she placed the tray on my lap. Instead, she just put her right palm on my forehead the way mothers do and smiled. She then sat on the bed, waiting for me to give her the verdict on the soup. Noel was right. I was spoiled.

'Is it too hot?' she asked.

'No, Mum. It's fine.'

'Drink it all up, it'll do you good.'

The guilt I had returned but an idea came to me. 'Mum, take me to Granny tonight… I'll stay there for a few days and you could go back to work. Granny is always complaining that no-one stays with her these days.'

'You sure, Dennis?'

'Yes, I'm sure, Mum. You go back to work.'

Chapter Seven

GRANNY

Running parallel to the Brixton Road, between Kennington and Myatt Fields, is the grimy Cowley council estate. Legend has it that in the past, way back in the '70s, this sound system operator who went by the name of King Tubby, used to test his eighteen-inch bass speakers on one of the greens within the estate. I think Paps was exaggerating when he said you could hear hardcore reggae music from the top of Brixton Hill. Anyway, Granny has lived in Cowley for over thirty-five years and obviously it was where my paps, Auntie Denise and Uncle Royston were grown. There aren't so many Jamaican and Irish families living there now as in the past and their places have been filled by skinny Eastern Africans with long foreheads and Eastern Europeans who have no garms sense and beg a lot.

Mum walked me to Granny's third floor flat and as usual, when Granny opened her door they were polite and sweet to each other as could be. But Mum never entered Granny's flat. Instead she performed an over-the-top farewell, kissing Granny on both cheeks before her name-brand heels echoed off the concrete along the balcony... 'Hortense, if you need any money for extra shopping for Dennis then just give me a call,' Mum said casually, not looking back.

'That's OK, Carol, me dear. Me know how to look after me grandson and me *not* broke. No worry yourself about nothing.'

Granny's home was like a time capsule. There were old black-and-white family photographs hanging up in the hallway but all this was overshadowed by a 1950s film poster that Paps had bought and framed for Granny one Christmas. It was of the film *An American in Paris* and the female lead, Leslie Caron, was looking well buff in her pose. For a white girl she had a seriously round, firm butt. I have to admit that over a time of coming to Granny's flat I kinda fell in love with that pose of Leslie Caron's and at home I had looked her up on the internet and downloaded untold images of her. It's something I told no-one about, especially Noel. He would only laugh if he found out I had a crush on an old white Hollywood musical star.

Granny still had flock wallpaper in her lounge and neat little white doilies upon the arm-rests of her furniture. The multicoloured carpet mirrored the flower shit from the walls and the television was seriously small; I suddenly remembered that Granny didn't have cable or Sky TV so it was a good job I had a couple of books and a hip hop magazine with me. The mantelpiece was crammed with photos of Paps, Auntie Denise and Uncle Royston and the mahogany coffee table, the only thing of class in the room, was reserved for framed photographs of Granny and her long dead husband Cilbert. Granny always said I looked like Granpa Cilbert and I didn't argue 'cos he looked very cool in his single-breasted suits, skinny ties and angled hats. He looked really hench and must have been a proper player. Maybe I came from a long line of shottas? Granny was quite a looker herself and she seemed full of energy and attitude in the photos she had taken when she was young. She was always talking about that she used to dance a lot back in the day and I could believe it looking at her photos.

That evening, as I flicked through Granny's photo album, I asked her, 'What advice would you give to a hench-looking young brother today, Gran?'

She smiled as if reliving some sweet memory and then she replied, 'Enjoy every day if you can. Life is precious and it must be lived. Because when you get to my age all you have left is pleasant memories. So get busy living and store those memories up. Tomorrow isn't promised to anyone.' She then looked at the framed photo of her husband Cilbert on her wedding day. She smiled at him as if she was greeting him after a long absence. 'Yes, Dennis. Live hard, play hard and most of all, love hard.'

'I will try, Gran.'

She then turned to me and stroked my left cheek with the back of her fingers. They were unusually broad for a woman, like fat, creased sausages. She must have got them from that tough, hard knock childhood in the Jamaican bush. 'When me go me will miss you, Dennis.'

'What are you talking about, Gran? There is nuff life in you.'

'No, no,' she laughed. 'Me don't mean passing away. Lord have mercy! Me mean going home.'

'Home to Jamaica?'

'Yes, Dennis. Where you think home is? Greenland? Me thought me would never say it out aloud but me miss my cantankerous, argumentive, know-it-all sister. And the hot sun on my cheeks. And a nice ripe mango!'

'I could never understand you and Great Auntie Jenny. You two were always arguing…'

'Nor do I understand!' Granny laughed. 'But me miss her same way… I have been fortunate, Dennis. I have seen me children and me grandchildren grow. It'll be soon time to let go. Time to let your mother care for your father without me interfering. It's another reason why you must try to enjoy every day the Most High gives you. No-one knows what tomorrow brings. Your father never knew that from running one day the next he would be a cripple.'

I went to my bed that night thinking on Granny's words. I guess she meant follow my heart's desire. And my heart's desire wasn't to be known as some fake wanksta or a spoilt little rich kid. Live hard, Granny said… I'm gonna have to if I'm gonna change my image.

The following Sunday morning, along with my sister Davinia, Uncle Royston, Auntie Denise and her twins, Natalie and Natasha, I escorted Granny to church. Mum had pussied out saying she had too much work at home to do and Paps was never a regular church goer; Paps once told me why should he praise God when all he got from Him was twisted legs? No-one save Granny and Davinia looked too keen about the service and I guess that once Granny is feeling the Jamaican sun on her cheeks, the tradition of the Huggins family attending church will die. Well, perhaps not 'cos Davinia will probably continue when she has a family. She even gets ratings in church for her singing! Can't she be shit for at least one thing in her perfect life?

As for myself I didn't have to attend church and my family didn't expect me to. But I guess I was looking for a counter argument to my messed up path to revenge and violence. And all throughout the service, Noel's words echoed in my head. 'Everyone knows you're a spoilt little rich kid.' I looked around the church to see if there was any nice chicks around... Perhaps after the service I could chirps a chick or two to take my mind off this revenge thing. But there were only three wokable chicks in the house and they were with their men. Burn them. In fact there weren't many young faces in the place at all. A disappointment I know Granny felt 'cos Great Auntie Jenny's husband, Jacob, set up the very first black church in South London... For the life of me I cannot remember what the preacher was preaching about on that Sunday morning.

Performing all the duties that a good grandson is supposed to do, like listening to Granny's tales and not looking bored, massaging her shoulders after she finished the washing-up and taking out the rubbish, I felt a proper sadness for her. The modern world doesn't cater for someone like her. Auntie Denise had bought Granny a computer two years ago, mainly to keep in touch with the family in Jamaica via e-mail, especially Great Aunt Jenny and save on phone bills. But she just couldn't get the hang of it. So the computer just gathered dust in Granny's bedroom. A waste. She was happiest when she was shopping in Brixton market for groceries. It's the only time she came alive, apart from when she watched her old school Hollywood musicals with Leslie Caron, Eleanor Powell, Vera Ellen, Rita Moreno, Cyd Charisse, Ginger Rogers, Bojangles and the Nicholas brothers. And she even loved films that starred that little brat of American goodness, cuteness and whiteness, Shirley Temple. Burn her!

I can't believe I can remember all those names but that's what you get spending most of your Sunday afternoons as a child with Granny.

In the market Granny would inspect fruits with her eyes and fingers and if the food didn't come up to her ratings she wasn't afraid of saying so in her raw patois and that exaggerated Jamaican body language. It was so cool to watch...

I wish I could have been as blatant with Noel as Granny was with the market traders. I wanted to tell him, 'Burn you with your shotting! I'm not on it no more. Find a new partner.' That would have been the right thing to say. But my ego and vanity got in the way. I knew going down the vengeance route was wrong and it could lead to all kinda bad shit. But I just couldn't stand the fact that some brothers were calling me a pussy and a spoilt little rich kid behind my back. So when Noel arrived outside my gates in his Fiesta tooting his horn, two weeks after he gave me that ultimatum, I filled the passenger seat... It was a cool Friday night in late September. Noel looked at me hard and then broke out in a half smile. 'Shizzle me nizzle,' he said, another way of saying everything is cool with the world. He started the car and as he shifted through the gears I closed my eyes and I could feel my heartbeat.

'Are you ready?' Noel asked, keeping his eyes on the road. 'Ready like a Wu Tang rap?'

'Would I be sitting in your ride if I wasn't?'

'Then it's all good,' Noel replied. 'Anyway, we might not see any of them African brothers who jacked you. It might be a patience thing we have to deal with.'

That remark relaxed me a bit and as we drove along Camberwell New Road, I inspected the inside of the car. 'You could have least taken out the Kentucky boxes from the back seat, Noel. And the fat-head butts. And is that what I think it is on the floor in the corner? Your ride stinks!'

'Yeah. My mother's always telling me that I better not catch no dose from no ho so I'd better wear protection. Anyway, the car gets me from A to B and I have already woked a girl in here; a slim portable bitch but too loud. I just haven't tidied up after it yet.'

'What girl?'

'Some junz called Nisha. She didn't care the ride wasn't clean… She's got a buff body but the face ain't saying too much. It's only good for a BJ, not a kiss. And unlike you, I go for local chicks… She lives in those flats off Upper Tulse Hill. She's got this best friend that I wanna wok too. She's prettier.'

'Is your ride insured?' I asked, purposefully changing the subject 'cos I didn't want to get involved with the morals of Noel's love life.

'Nope, you know I haven't passed my test yet.'

'Then how did you get the tax disc?'

'Hassan. He's gonna deal with my insurance thing too.'

'Who the fuck is Hassan?'

'Hassan. This Asian brother. You've seen him. He's got bandy legs and a Gonzo-like nose. You know him, Dennis, from playing football in the park. He's shit at football like all Asians but his older brother's got an *ill* ride. A Mercedes sports! He goes out with that Spanish-looking chick Ida Lupino and he lives in those flats off Denmark Road, near Flaxman sports centre. His mum wears them garments that only let you see the eyes. You know, she probably wears that shit 'cos Hassan's paps doesn't want other brothers to know how buff she is. His family, or I should say his brothers, are in dodgy passports, fake documents and shit. They even do positive HIV test results. That shit is really popular with the Africans. Anyway, I just had to give him four pinkies and he just dealt with everything. Insurance, car tax, MOT. The deal was sweet so I gave him an eighth of skunk to show my appreciation… I'm telling you that Hassan is an artist. It was all good and Dennis when you find yourself a ride Hassan will deal with you too.'

Four pinkies was four fifty pound notes and Noel loved the look of them. He would go into a post office or a bank with a wad of tens just so he could change them to pinkies… It made him feel good having them inside his wallet. But this car scam seemed too good to be true. 'Yeah, Noel. When I get a ride I'll deal with this Asian brother.'

Mary J. Blige was singing one of her heartfelt songs on Noel's slide-out audio system. He was humming along with the lyrics. How could he be so laid-back about everything?

'So you're packed?' I asked.

'Well, not packed with a gun but I've got two metal bars under my seat. At first I put a couple of my mother's kitchen shanks under the seat but the Feds could pull you up on that shit.'

'Your mother could pull you up on that shit,' I replied. I swear I saw Noel wince.

We pulled up outside the main entrance to the estate where I was jacked. Noel switched off the engine but kept the stereo system still playing. He looked at me hard again and I nodded. 'Shizzle me nizzle,' he laughed once again. He then torched half a big-head and passed it on to me after three tokes. 'We'll deal with those pussies,' he added.

Half an hour later, the sun was now hidden by the tower blocks and I was getting some terrible munchies. 'There's a chicken takeaway place just around the corner, do you want anything?'

'I'll go,' Noel replied.

'Why can't I go?'

''Cos you can recognise who jacked you and I can't. Say I'm in the ride now and one of your jackers went by, how the fuck would I know? The pussy would get away. Can't allow that, man. Burn that. Any of your jackers *has* to be shanked. Simple as.'

'Yeah, yeah, I get your point. Get me two pieces of breast and fries.'

Noel seemed to be gone for ages. My eyes were checking out the entrance of the estate and I wondered what I would do if I saw all of my jackers come out from the gloom. Maybe I would just sink lower into my seat and let them pass without them noticing me. Then again, if they did spot me they might want to jack me again. I picked up one of the black metal bars that was under Noel's seat and placed it on my lap. For some reason I pictured a scene in the film *For A Few Dollars More*. Clint Eastwood and Lee Van Cleef were loading their guns and waiting for the moment to settle the shit with the Mexican gang. They both had this impatient look on their faces and now I felt the same. Whatever happens I want to get it over with and go home.

By the time Noel returned it was dark. The chicken and chips was a sweet relief 'cos I was well hungry and by the time I was licking my fingers, a sister and a brother walked out of the estate. They were both wearing hoodies and tracksuit bottoms.

'Dennis! Dennis!' Noel called. 'Ain't that the bitch Ann?'

It was her. I recognised her walk instantly. She was laughing and joking with this guy... He looked like one of my attackers, the oldest one of the crew. He had those wide-faced Nigerian features. He was the one who said, 'Peel him!' I'll never forget those two little words. *Burn him!*

'Is it the bitch yes or no?' Noel raised his voice.

'Yeah, that's her, bruv.'

Before I had time to compose myself, Noel had leaped out of the car. I quickly followed him. Ann and this guy looked behind. I soon caught up with Noel 'cos I was always the quickest runner. Ann and the Nigerian ran back into the estate but we was only ten yards behind them. Ann couldn't run too good in her thick-soled trainers. She was frantic. Desperate. I went by her, wanting to get to the Nigerian. He glanced over his left shoulder in panic. Then he looked over his right shoulder. I was closing on him. My adrenaline was pumping. I heard a scream behind me. *'No! Please, no no!'*

I didn't look behind. I knew Noel would beat the shit out of her 'cos he didn't give a shit whether she was a girl or not. Noel's like that. The Nigerian made the mistake of looking behind to see what was happening to Ann. I latched onto him with my left hand and I clubbed him on the back of the head with the black metal bar with my right. He fell down face first into the concrete, scraping his cheeks. With a rush of excitement I hit him again on the head and heard this muffled whimper. 'Fuck with a Brixtonian, would you? You piece of African shit!'

I rolled him onto his back and his nose was pouring out blood. He had cuts and grazes in his face and his eyes were rolling in his head. He didn't know where the fuck he was. His mouth stank of some spicy African food he had just ate. Before I went through his pockets I banged him in the crotch. His knees went up in a reflex reaction and caught me in the jaw. I blammed him again upon the forehead with the metal bar. When he was still I claimed his mobile and his wallet. I even took his weekly Travelcard. I then booted him in the head. Satisfied, I then backed away. 'Come on!' screamed Noel. 'Come on!'

Walking slowly backwards, I looked at my victim writhing in agony. I wondered if he went shopping with his granny and if he massaged his granny's shoulders after she completed the washing-up. Would he be the kind of grandson to take out the rubbish for her? No, burn that notion. I couldn't picture it and that made me feel better. I bet he won't try and honey-trap a Brixtonian in a hurry. I stepped by Ann and she was out cold laying in a curled-up position on the concrete. Blood was spilling from the top of her head. I paused, just to check if she was breathing. She was. Fuck knows what Noel done to her but I'll bet Ann Sheridan won't fuck with Brixtonian shottas again.

'Get your motherfucking black ass in the car!' Noel screamed again.

The ride home was quiet with both Noel and myself trying to get our breath back. We looked at each other, well satisfied. I couldn't help but grin. It's only when we reached Tulse Hill when Noel said something. 'Shizzle me nizzle, Dennis! You proper dealt with that African. Banged him up neatly. To be honest, I didn't know you had it in you, but shit! You're up in my ratings!'

The words were sweet music to my ears but I didn't enjoy the moment for too long 'cos I was playing in my mind what had just happened. 'We were kinda reckless,' I said. 'Next time we do shit like that we're both gonna be wearing gloves. Did she scratch you or anything, Noel?'

'No,' he answered. 'She just begged me for mercy but I just booted the bitch in her head.'

'Did you notice anybody looking down from the balconies?'

'I dunno. I wasn't really looking up.'

'Next time,' I said. 'If we do a banging again then we'll pull on balaclavas. I don't want no pussy to identify us.'

Noel nodded.

When Noel dropped me off outside my home that night he stepped out of the car and hugged me tight. He'd never done that before. 'Look after yourself, bruv,' he said.

'Yeah, and you look after your mad self too.'

I went to my bed that night feeling as content with myself as I could remember. I had proved myself in front of Noel and he wouldn't dare call me a spoilt little rich kid again. In a corner of my mind there was this little picture of Paps, Mum and Granny wagging their fingers saying we didn't grow you like that... But it couldn't spoil the feeling I had, the feeling of being a *badman*.

Chapter Eight

A NEW DEAL

It was a week after Ann and the African brother got a banging. I was still vibing in the glow of my badman success as Noel drove me and his latest chick, Priscilla Lane, to Red Eyes' place. Biggie was rapping on the car stereo and Priscilla was in the back seat bopping her head and chewing gum. She was a typical ghetto chick, mobile phone stuck to her ear, greasy kiss curls running down her cheeks, some piece of jewellery stuck in her nose and a council estate full of attitude…

'Got the dollars, Dennis?' Noel asked.

'Of course, bruv,' I replied. 'What do you take me for?'

'We're buying four oz you know, bruv. Not the usual two.'

'Yeah, I'm on that. Drive on, James.'

Noel couldn't drive on because as he was just about to turn into Myatts Fields North estate, we found the familiar sight of blue and white tape all over the place and the area was polluted with Feds with their yellow Day-Glo tops.

'Must have been a shooting,' said Priscilla. 'There's bare shootings in this estate. I wonder who got merked this time?'

'Tell us something we don't know,' said Noel. 'Man! You're a stupid bitch sometimes. Always saying the obvious.'

'Who you talking to like that, you ugly mother?'

'You're calling me ugly?' Noel challenged. Him and Priscilla were always like this. 'Why do you think that when you're sitting in my ride it's the back seat for you?' Noel went on. 'And you didn't have to come. I already done said Friday night is a business night.'

'I wanted to come for the drive, innit,' returned Priscilla. 'And can we stop over for a Kentucky when you done your business.'

'I might do if you're paying. I ain't your fucking boops!'

'What? You can't even buy your girl a chicken and chips? You're proper mean like them Asian shopkeeper who refuse to give you a free cigarette so you can build a fat-head!'

'You're my girl?' snapped Noel, now getting vex. 'You better rephrase that before I make you get out of the ride and step. And don't think I wouldn't do it, bitch! I hope your trainers are fitting neatly.'

Noel wasn't joking and Priscilla did shut the fuck up. Sociologists or better minds than mine should research how the fuck them two ever got to have sex.

I was looking out of the car window and I noticed that the Feds had sealed off a large area. Some families were booted out from their flats and there were forensic officers in their white jumpsuits crawling on the ground. It was a sure sign that this was a murder scene. Even more worrying was the fact that they were searching right next to Red Eyes' flat.

'Noel, don't park the ride in the estate,' I advised. 'Park it near the church and we'll walk up. This don't look good...'

'No, it don't,' Noel agreed. 'It must be Red Eyes. Who else in that little block of flats is a shotta or a gunman?'

'Little Louis, Maaga Benz,' replied Priscilla. 'And there's Ponytail Ranger, Jamaicy Jim, Lambs Bread Larry and Chemical Collie. Then again, Chemical Collie's doing bird in the Mount. But they all at one time or other lived in these ends.'

Noel and myself looked at Priscilla with wonder. 'How comes you know so much badman?' Noel said. 'You better not have been woking them brothers.'

'No! Fuck you! I have not been woking them brothers!' Priscilla shrieked in that head-moving-but-the-neck-keeps-still way of hers.

How the fuck do ghetto chicks do that shit? 'What do you take me for?' she went on. 'I know them shottas and badmen through my older brother, innit. He's always walking with man he shouldn't walk with.'

'Her brother's doing bird in Glen Purva,' Noel remarked.

We climbed out of the car and after Noel had taken out his car audio set, we made steps to where the Feds were. A tonk looking brother was approaching us and Noel recognised him. This guy had He-Man muscles on his neck and probably owned an eight-pack of Madonna-like size. You see a lot of guys like that in Bricky. Tyrese wannabes… As if Coca-Cola are gonna come down to Bricky and cast a tonk Brixtonian in a fucking drinks advert. It ain't gonna happen.

'Doosh,' Noel greeted. 'Doosh, what's gwarnin? Untold Feds are all over the place. Something happen to Red Eyes? Has he been duppied? Did he decide to go out all *Butch Cassidy and Sundance Kid*-like?'

'Who the fuck is Butch Cassidy and the Sundance Kid? Chi chi men?' Doosh asked.

'No, they're not gay,' laughed Noel. 'Don't you watch westerns? What I mean is did Red Eyes go out blazing? Was it a shoot-out?'

'Haven't you heard? Red Eyes has been burst. Stabbed over forty times. The man's got more perforations than Tetley motherfucking teabags. Word on road say it was a crack addict looking for a hit but he didn't have any P's. He's been dead for two days but no-one knew shit 'til the gas man came to read the meter this morning. It didn't smell too good… The door was open and apparently the blood was dripping everywhere. It's proper Christopher Lee Hammer movie shit. Word on road says the Feds have found untold drugs in Red Eyes' flat and they have taken away his plasma. There's gonna be a skunk and crack party at Feds HQ tonight and they're gonna be watching *The Bill* on one big bitch plasma TV. Some people get all the luck.'

I was listening to all this with my mouth wide open. Red Eyes dead! Merked. And what the fuck is Doosh on? Some East German steroid shit? This guy has pecs in his jawbone!

I know Red Eyes was in a dangerous business but it was still very hard to imagine that someone that you used to sit with and watch kung fu films and have a laugh with is dead. Murdered in his own flat. His life taken in the very place where every week Noel and myself scored our skunk. Even Priscilla and Noel shut the fuck up for a second trying to take it all in.

'We better find a new dealer,' said Noel after a while. 'Anyway, I was thinking of getting our skunk from someone else for a number of weeks now… Red Eyes' inflation's as bad as London Transport. *Burn* London Transport and the price of their motherfucking Travelcards!'

'You don't have to worry yourself about Travelcards, Noel,' I said. 'You've got a ride now. Anyway, wasn't Red Eyes an ex of your mum?'

'Yeah, he was. But that was a long time ago. Mum was only interested in getting her ten pound of high grade off him every week. Let's face it, he was reckless. I would never do shots from my own gates.'

We went back to the car and once Noel had started it up he didn't bother playing any music. For twenty minutes we just sat there in silence before Priscilla said something. 'So what are we gonna do now? I'm bored.'

'I dunno what Dennis and me are doing but you're going back to your gates now,' Noel replied.

'But I don't wanna go home yet.'

'If you don't stop bitching in my ear you can step it to home from here. Are your trainers comfortable, *bitch!*'

After dropping off Priscilla we sat in silence again for a while. I wondered if what happened to Red Eyes could be a reality check for Noel. Recently he had been thinking of moving onto the crack game. Think about the P's we could make from that shit, Noel said. I had talked him out of it by telling him that crack shottas get at least five years bird. Noel reckoned he could do two years bird but five years? He couldn't put his mum through that stress.

With Red Eyes now dead I even wondered if Noel would want to carry on with the skunk game… He knew Red Eyes well. He saw him all the time when he was a kid and like me, he would try to sneak into his mother's bedroom and watch them have sex... Sometimes I wondered if all young boys did this or was it a ghetto thing?

'Dryneck,' Noel said after a long pause.

'What? Who?'

'Dryneck,' Noel repeated. 'A relative, cousin of cousin or some shit like that. Or he could be an uncle, not sure. He used to come around to my gates when I was young. He used to go to our school. He's about ten years older than us. He's got eczema or dry skin or something but it's all cool 'cos he said you can't catch it from him. It ain't like other contagious shit like old school plague.'

'Noel, you can't catch eczema or acne off anybody.'

'Anyway, he deals in ozes and shit and we could set up things with him neatly...'

'Can you trust him?'

'Yeah. I don't think he'll spill to my mum. He's a Jehovah's Witness and he was even there at all of his kids' christenings. That makes him a decent brother in my ratings. He don't deal on Sundays though... He lives on Lansdowne Green estate, you know, Stockwell ends, behind the tube station.'

'What? You wanna check him now?'

'Why not? He stays up late all night watching Dick Dastardly and *ThunderCats* cartoons so he'll be awake.'

'Ain't we gonna have a period of mourning for our former dead dealer? He was *stabbed* over forty times. I'm still trying to get my head around it.'

'Dennis, stop being a fucking pussy. Red Eyes would have wanted us to carry on. Trust me, he would have carried on the same way if someone shanked your black ass forty times.'

It was close to 2 a.m. when we was climbing the steps to Dryneck's fourth floor flat. The lift didn't work. I was proper screwing 'cos I wanted to stay in the car and listen to some music but Noel insisted that I meet Dryneck.

Noel pressed the buzzer and after a while some chick came to the door and asked, 'Who is it?'

As she looked at us through the spy-hole, Noel answered, 'It's me, bruv... Noel, Noel Gordon from Tulse Hill ends. Your nephew. Or cousin. Remember me? You know my mum Cara. Man coming on business. Open the fucking door, bruv. Tell the bitch to open the door.'

We could hear the chick walking away. 'Can't you ever have manners?' I cussed in a strong whisper.

'Dryneck should know my voice,' Noel said, irritation all over his face.

Then the door opened to the sound of clicks and rattling keys. This white chick with Lana Turner-like hair stood there in a pink dressing-gown with fluffy white cuffs and the reddest lipstick I have ever seen. She stood aside with a bunch of keys in her left hand and only let us in after offering Noel one bitch of a stare. She then led us along this short hallway which had framed photographs of Daffy Duck, Donald Duck, Bugs Bunny, Barney Rubble, Betty Rubble, Cheetara from the ThunderCats, Jessica Rabbit, Pepe the skunk and a painting of an aroused Wily Coyote hanging from the walls. I offered Noel a quick glance and he read my mind instantly. This was fucked-up childhood, strange crazy, public enquiry, social worker issues shit. I didn't want to stay in that place for too long.

We came to a halt in the lounge that had a fake polar-bear rug on the wooden-tiled floor and almost covering one wall was a cinema-like screen. It was showing a *Top Cat* cartoon with the volume turned down. This black leather sofa was in the middle of the room like in American sitcoms and I could see smoke that came from its direction. Some Japanese cartoon Manga shit was hanging from the walls in wooden frames. I glanced behind me and opposite the gigantic TV screen was a life-size picture of Michelangelo's *David*.

Just as I was thinking of making a run for it, Dryneck raised his head from his laying-down position upon the sofa. He was one ugly mother. He was wearing a yellow silk dressing-gown like the one Sylvester Stallone wore in *Rocky* and he was smoking a big-head with one of those Marlene Dietrich cigarette holders. He didn't look cool, he looked like a fucking idiot, as is always the case when a ghetto brother tries to look classy. He was burning high grade if my senses wasn't fucked up by the surreal environment of that place. I had to close my eyes for a couple of seconds and open them again to see if all this shit was real. Unfortunately it was and I still felt like running to the exit screaming... Noel didn't seem to flinch but I guess being ignorant in certain things is sometimes a blessing.

'Noel, Noel Gordon from Tulse Hill ends,' Dryneck said. 'Yes, I remember you well. From when you was a child. We're second cousins.'

The chick joined Dryneck on the sofa and she laid her head upon his chest. She took a generous toke from his zoot and formed her mouth into an O to blow the smoke. I had an immediate erection. Dryneck's neck wasn't as bad as I imagined it to be. It was just, well, a little dry. But Lord Jesus was he ugly!

'Nasser,' greeted Noel, choosing not to use the nickname. 'What's gwarnin?'

'Well, Noel,' Dryneck said. 'Trying to be successful. And the definition of a successful man is that he can always earn more than what his girl spends.'

'And the definition of a successful woman is to find *that* man,' the chick added.

This was getting more weird by the moment. I nudged Noel. Hopefully he would have got the message that we had to finish the deal so we could get out of this crazy place and away from these crazy people.

'Yeah, Nasser,' Noel began. 'We're looking to do a bit of business.'

'I don't usually do business at this time of night,' replied Dryneck. 'And especially if I am entertaining.'

At this point the chick kissed Dryneck on the cheek and ran her fingers over his bald head... I swear I heard a happy sigh. My erection was still tenting my jeans. 'But I know you are in need,' Dryneck continued. 'I have heard of the misfortune that has befallen Red Eyes and during the course of the last day and a half many people in our business have made enquiries to find out if I will take up the slack.'

Alex Wheatle

'So what you saying?' Noel asked. 'You gonna deal with us?'

'I suppose your money is as good as everybody else's,' Dryneck nodded. 'Gloria, can you go and get my merchandise and the scales please… How much are we talking about, gentlemen?'

'Four oz of skunk,' answered Noel.

'I think I can accommodate you.'

The chick got up and went to a room that led off the hallway. I tried hard not to look at her legs as she walked by. She was wearing Lisa Simpson slippers. I closed my eyes yet again. She returned a couple of minutes later with the scales and the skunk wrapped in kitchen foil and went to the coffee table, pushing aside cartoon video and DVD cases to make a space for herself. It was then when I spotted the lines of cocaine and a credit card all neatly placed upon a smaller, matching coffee table. Gloria worked quickly and neatly, soon balancing four oz of skunk on the scales.

'I'm forgetting myself,' said Dryneck. 'This is Gloria… Miss Gloria Grahame. Obviously it is not her real name but that is the name you will address her by. As you can see she is quite efficient. When you leave she will give a mobile number to you and for any future transactions that we might have I urge you to dial that number first. The number will change every month but you will be notified a day beforehand what the new number is. You will *not* come here again. Is that clear? You will be met by Gloria or myself in a designated meeting spot. Any orders over four ounces please give me two days' notice. Is that clear?'

'Yeah, loud and clear,' said Noel.

Dryneck then looked at me for longer than what was comfortable. 'I know your father,' he said. 'He had quite a rep when I was a kid. I haven't seen him for many a year.'

'Yeah, er, a lot of people know my paps,' I managed.

As Dryneck turned his attention back to *Top Cat*, I fished for my wad of P's inside my jeans and found that my erection was still rampant. Gloria got to her feet, made her way over to me and took the money. She counted it carefully, licking her right index finger and her thumb. When she finished counting she offered me a wink and by then my dick was hurting me. She then gave Noel her mobile

64

number and walked us to the exit. 'Don't call during working hours,' she said. 'Call from seven to eleven in the evening.'

Dryneck didn't even say goodbye.

When we got back to the car, I asked Noel, 'Where did he get *her* from?'

'Gloria?' Noel replied. 'She works in some bank up in the city and she shots for Dryneck up those ends as well. When he's entertaining, Dryneck likes her to look like those old-time movie stars. He's got a thing about blondes and cartoons. Did you notice?'

Chapter Nine

REVELATIONS

Red Eyes was buried six days later in Streatham cemetery. All five of his baby mothers were there, all wondering if he had left anything valuable behind. It was kinda freaky to see all those little versions of Red Eyes running around the place and getting cuss by all these different women. I wondered if any of the boys would be a shotta like their paps was.

The allegation that said the Feds had taken Red Eyes' plasma TV was the living bullshit. In a place like Bricky, people will believe that the Feds are capable of shit like that… Even Paps sucked in the hype, saying that almost twenty years after the Brixton riots, blah blah blah, the Feds can never be trusted blah blah blah. Margaret Thatcher and the Feds were all racists blah blah blah. Back in my day they wanted to purge young black males off the streets, blah blah fucking blah. Will he ever stop going on about it? Paps still has issues with the Feds that needs serious closure but I guess he's a man of his generation. I wondered how do young brothers of my age feel when they join the Feds with all that bad vibes coming from the ancients.

Red Eyes' mum actually claimed the huge TV set and she was planning on sending it to her home in Jamaica. Meanwhile the Feds were doing flat-to-flat enquiries in Myatts Fields and that meant a sizable majority of the Bricky underworld had to put all their drugs, contraband, arms and dodgy foreign people in lock-ups and garages. There won't be no evidence on CCTV about the murder 'cos every time Lambeth Council and the Feds set the cameras up on lamp-posts, walls and shit, the kids in the estate nick all of it. They even dig up the wires with pick axes. The little hustlers sell all the hi-tech shit to the criminal minded and they get electricians to rewire the cameras and shit to keep a serious watch outside their own gates. Only in Bricky.

If Red Eyes' killer was a white man then someone might have said something but if he was black then the Feds would get more words out of a dumb-ass ghetto brother answering a question in chemistry class. Word on road said the killer *was* a crack addict who was desperate for a hit. But you couldn't be sure. Anyway, I don't think Reds Eyes' merking will be played out on *Crimewatch*. That programme's about bad shit happening to white people in nice little Surrey suburbs. Burn *Crimewatch*.

I was a little nervous at the graveside 'cos not only was Noel's mum Cara there but my paps as well. How did he know Red Eyes? Cara and Paps were standing side by side in some deep reflection. Of course I said to Paps that I was only at the funeral to support Noel who had lost a close family friend. I'm not sure if he bought my excuse for attending a known shotta's funeral but he was trying to hide something too. Many guys of his generation were going up to him saying hello and shit and I could see Paps getting more uncomfortable by the minute. It was like watching that scene in *The Godfather* when everyone was going up to Michael at the funeral of Marlon Brando. Judging by my pap's body language my guess was that most of those brothers were ex-shottas, hustlers, whatever. Some of them looked proper dodgy with their facial scars and those 'I've seen a lot of shit in my life' eyes.

After Red Eyes was laid to rest we all went to the house of Red Eyes' sister, Glenice, and she made a speech about how Red Eyes was the best brother she could have hoped for 'cos he helped her put on a deposit for her house in Thornton Heath. He was a 'community' man, Glenice continued and always helped those less fortunate than himself. I have never heard so much blatant fuckery in my life! For a second my mind brought up an image of Red Eyes wearing a red cape with the 'community man' shit emblazoned on it and his Calvin Kleins worn over tracksuit bottoms. And if Red Eyes could help to buy a house in Thornton Heath, why the fuck was he living in Myatts Fields?

I had to give credit to Glenice 'cos she did provide nuff drinks, Jamaican beef patties, rice and untold roasted chicken legs. And she invited Akeisha Parris! She was there and I couldn't believe it. I had to go to the bathroom and make sure that my short trim was looking sweet and neat. I returned and there she was right in front of me dressed in a black trouser suit. I forgot to blink... She was still slim but she now owned a cute booty and nice little cute breasts... Her buffness was so fine it was hard to look away. She didn't move and walk like an every-day ghetto chick and that was a plus. She still had elegance... So I made my move when she was alone nibbling peanuts and sipping red wine out of a glass. This was another plus. Most of the ghetto chicks present were downing Barcardi Breezer and beer bottles as if someone was gonna call *time* any second... I went over to her, my heart beating like the bassline of one of them garage tunes and I could feel the sweat developing on my temples. Don't fuck it up, Dennis, *don't* fuck it up! Should I tell her about the bracelet? *No!* Try and be cool, laid-back. Think of Thierry Henry after he's scored an ill goal.

'Are you a member of Red Eyes' family?' I asked.

'Well, kind of,' she replied. 'My older cousin has got a son from him.'

She had some sort of black Croydon accent, kinda half suburban, half BBC. I couldn't quite nail it. It certainly wasn't Bricky. I remember thinking I could take this chick home to see Mum and wouldn't have to worry about her manners or what comes out of her mouth. 'Red Eyes was alright,' I said. 'He never done me any wrong anyway.'

'He was a low-down bum,' Akeisha whispered. 'He never gave my cousin a penny.'

I just had to chuckle and Akeisha had to cover her mouth to stop herself from giggling… My nerves eased up a bit.

'I usually wouldn't do shit like this at a funeral but I'm kinda fretting I won't see you again,' I chanced my luck, remembering how it pained me so bad when she went missing from the track. I maintained eye contact all the time and hoped she'd realise I was seriously on her case… Obviously the perfect end-game would be a wok. Maybe I could get her to wear that skin-tight Lycra shit? My heartbeat gathered pace again.

'I can't believe you're moving on me at a funeral!' Akeisha laughed.

'Look, some people are staring at us, man. Is it so bad to chirps a girl at a funeral if she's the most buff girl there? Just give me your digits and I'll step. To save you the embarrassment.'

It was to save my embarrassment. The sweat was now pouring down both sides of my face and my heart was about to pump through my chest. I also felt Paps' and Cara's eyes burning into my back. Noel was probably saying under his breath, 'Go on, dog!' Akeisha looked at me hard for two seconds and if I say so myself I was looking proper neat in my black suit, tie and shit. I had a handkerchief in my jacket pocket but would it look cool to wipe the sweat from my face. Better to do it out of her sight I decided. She discreetly took out her mobile and we exchanged numbers. *YES!*

'Hold on,' I said. 'Before you go. What ends do you live?'

'Excuse me?'

'Where do you live?'

'Oh, Angel Town.'

Angel Town? Central Bricky? With a voice like that? That place was so bad the Feds were only admitted if they had ghetto passports. Residents there owed years of rent but bailiffs refused to go there to boot them out. Anyway, that was all good… It ain't too far and I know nuff brothers who live in Angel Town so there was a pretty remote chance that I would get jacked if I stepped there to see her. Besides, she could have lived in deepest Deptford or white trash central and I would have still checked her out. 'I'll call you yeah.'

I left Akeisha munching her peanuts and rejoined my paps, Noel and Cara. There was a bounce in my step and a fucked-up grin on my face. Until she left I followed her every move, every sip and every bite of a chicken piece or a sandwich. God! Was it good to see her.

'So that's the girl you always thought was perfect,' remarked Noel... 'Bit on the maaga side for me. She could do with a good dinner. Nice little round booty though and prettier than most.'

'Prettier than most!' I replied. 'Are you kidding me? She's easily the most buff girl in Bricky.'

'Maybe,' said Noel. 'But I bet you won't get to wok it... She looks too stush.'

When the drink and food were done, everyone drifted away. Even those who were burning big-heads in the garden departed; the big garden thing was quite an experience for many ghetto people there. A couple of teenage chicks decided to see who could go highest on the swings and it all ended up with one of them fucking up their ankle. I dunno, ghetto people can't go anywhere without embarrassing themselves.

As people were heading out of the front door I saw one of Red Eyes' baby-mothers swiping a bottle of Jamaican rum. I guess it was a typical Jamaican funeral affair...

I decided to follow Noel to his flat 'cos Cara didn't seem to be holding up that well. I'm not sure if she had too much Jamaican rum but she was in a right state. I helped her into the back of Noel's ride. She was cussing all the way home about how Red Eyes was worthless, useless in bed, refused to wipe his dick after he had sex, couldn't fry an egg, didn't clean his toenails and didn't know how to commit to women. Trying to calm her down, I said to her, 'It's understandable that you're upset, Cara. You knew him well. But it's not good to cuss badword about the dead.'

'Understandable?' she said. 'You don't know fuck all! And don't fucking talk to me like I'm your daughter! And as for cussing badword about the dead, do you think that just because someone is dead it changes their character? Red Eyes was a dogheart and he always will be whether he's in heaven or hell!'

'Dennis was only trying to help, Mum,' Noel said.

'Who asked you to speak, you dumb fuck!' Cara yelled.

This was embarrassing. I could see the anger in Noel's face rise as he pulled up outside his block.

'Do you think I'm a fucking idiot, Noel?' Cara yelled as we helped her towards the lift. She slapped him on the back of his head. 'I know you went to Red Eyes for your herb! Yes, I know! I know you sell weed on the streets. You think you can fool your mother? I ain't as stupid as I look…' She cuffed him again.

'Mum!'

Cara's sister was babysitting Noel's younger brother and sisters and that was all good because I didn't want them to see her like this. I've seen her high on high grade and a little tipsy but nothing like this.

'Baby, sorry for swearing at you,' Cara apologised to Noel, suddenly sounding all motherly. 'You know I love you, don't you, baby? Come here and give your mother a kiss. You know I really love you. I'm feeling very emotional right now and you know I hate funerals. Why can't they just get on with the business of burying people without all the shit that goes on beforehand?'

'I love you too, Mum,' Noel said, kissing his mother on the forehead. 'Just remember that the next time you're thinking of flinging a plate at me.'

With a family like Noel's it's very rare that you see acts of affection but this was one of those moments. Cara was almost strangling Noel as we carried her into the house, pressing her left cheek against his right cheek. We managed to lay her on the sofa in the lounge but instead of trying to sleep off her drunkenness she sat up and started crying. No sound came out, just tears rolling down her cheeks.

'What's a matter now, Mum? Can't you just go to sleep?'

'I've got something to tell you, baby.'

'What's that, Mum?'

'Before I do, baby, go to the kitchen cupboard where I keep my drinks. Gimme a whisky with ginger ale on the side and don't be stingy, baby.'

Noel went to do as he was told.

'Pour one for yourself, baby. And one for Dennis.'

Cara then turned to me. She smiled at me but the eyes remained sad. 'Dennis, your family has always been good to me. Your mother Carol is a diamond. She or Noel would never say how much she has helped us in the past. That's because of pride. Yes, I'm a proud bitch, Dennis. Too fucking proud. I didn't want you to know how desperate we have been, Dennis. And trust me, we've had *many* desperate times. Sometimes your mother helped us when my own family wouldn't. When you and Noel was little she would come to help me in the early hours of the morning if I called her.'

'Yes,' I said, feeling very uncomfortable. 'I respect my parents to the max.'

'And so you should,' said Cara. 'You know, I don't know no other black couple living on these sides who have been together for so long.'

'They've had their ups and downs,' I remarked. 'You know, with Paps' legs and everything. It hasn't been easy for them.'

'But they're *still* together. You know, Dennis, my family hate the way I have lived. Having children for different daddys and all that. My dad kicked me out when I was seventeen 'cos I was screwing a man in my room. But your dad and mum? They have never looked down at me. Yes, they have cussed me, told me to sort myself out, thrown my drinks in the trash and everything, but *never* looked down on me.'

Cara paused as she looked towards the kitchen. 'You find the whisky, baby? Don't be mean with it.'

'Just getting the ice out, Mum,' Noel called out.

Cara turned back to me. 'None of my so-called men could ever commit. None of them even wanted to commit. Is it too much to fucking ask? For a black man to commit to his black girl? That's the story of the black man. Maybe your daddy is the exception to the rule but most black men are dogs. Fucking doghearts! But sometimes I do wonder if your daddy would have stayed around with your mum if his legs weren't fucked. You know what I mean, Dennis? No offence to you, Dennis, 'cos you're obviously a black man. But even if I had crippled my men's legs with a sledgehammer they would have crawled away on their knees when I wasn't looking, and found some way to fuck another bitch. I should've castrated the doghearts when I had the chance.'

Cara's fingers were twitching and she couldn't keep still. She looked in the direction of the kitchen again. 'Such is my luck with men,' she went on. 'No, fuck that. They are not men. They are dogs! Not interested in raising families and only interested in raising their dicks and then they piss all over you and bitch about giving you money to live on.'

Carrying a tray of drinks, Noel returned to the lounge. He sat beside his mother and Cara caressed the left side of his face. She looked at him sweetly. Then she picked up her drink, downed half of it and then poured ginger ale in it to top it up again… 'Take a drink, baby.'

After passing me a glass of whisky and coke, Noel sipped his own drink with his mother watching him intensely. She placed her glass on a small coffee table and took in a big breath. 'Now, baby,' she began. 'I should have told you this a long time ago. There's no good way of saying this so I'm gonna come right out with it. The worthless, nasty dog and sad excuse for a man you saw buried today was your daddy.'

For a couple of seconds time seemed to stand still. Cara was waiting for Noel to respond but he just sat there looking vacantly into his whisky and coke.

'He never knew he was your daddy,' Cara added. 'I never told him, although if he had the intelligence he would've worked it out. But with your daddy, his brains were inside his dick. We saw each other on and off for a few years. If it's any comfort to you when we first start seeing one another, we was together for eight months. He bought my kitchen table in the January sales years back and he once helped me cut the carpet for the toilet. He even took me out ice skating and bowling a couple of times but your daddy always had his floozies on the side. Most of them were white but they had the good sense not to get pregnant. I could get my head around him having the odd affair with a black girl, but a white girl? No way was he gonna invade my crotches after he dipped his dick in a white pussy. NO FUCKING WAY!'

'Why tell me now?' Noel finally said, all calm like. 'Why now?'

'I know I should have told you before, baby. I just couldn't. What was I gonna say? Hey, baby! There's your daddy and he sells weed and crack and you're a big brother to all those little bastards running around his feet.'

Noel seemed to be taking this all well but then he stood up. He started to breathe hard. 'I'll tell you why you told me now. Because it eases your guilt... Feel a bit better do you, Mum? Eased your conscience a little? As for me, Mum, I FEEL LIKE SHIT! YOU FUCKING HO! YOU'RE NOTHING BUT A JUNZ!'

I had to react quick because Noel went to hit her. I leaped upon him and took him to the ground. 'YOU FUCKING HO! YOU FUCKING HO!'

The ginger ale was knocked off the coffee table and was spilling on the carpet. A tumbler hit me on the head as I wrestled with Noel. He was much stronger than me and if he wanted to he could have easily beaten me off him to get his revenge. But he allowed me to pin him down. Allowed is the only word for it. Tears were in his eyes and I just gripped my hands around his body, holding on for dear life. Cara grabbed her drink, done a funny walk to her bedroom and slammed the door.

For two minutes I held him to the ground and I felt the accelerated breathing from his chest. 'Get your hands off me, bruv.'

'You ain't gonna do anything stupid?' I asked.

'No! What do you take me for? You think I would actually lick her? My own mum?'

I released my grip. Noel picked up the tumbler and ginger ale bottle from the floor, placed them on a table and then took out his Rizla papers. He was calm again. 'It's kinda funny,' he said after a while. 'I was always scared of asking Mum who my paps was. I always wanted to know. Now I do... In a fucked-up way I even got to know him. If my shit was on *Jerry Springer* people wouldn't believe it.'

He was right. I was finding it hard to believe and I had witnessed it. I took a generous gulp from my whisky and coke. 'Pass me the Rizlas, bruv, I think I'm gonna join you.'

Both of us built two big-heads and for some reason smoking it felt better than it had for a long time. It proper relaxed me and although we had never burned in Cara's house before, I don't think she would have cussed our behinds if she had walked in.

'It's true what Mum says about your parents though,' Noel confirmed. 'I remember once when Mum had to lock herself in her bedroom 'cos her boyfriend at the time was beating her. I was only about six or seven at the time. Anyway, Mum managed to call your mum and ten minutes later I let your mum and paps in as well as your uncle Everton and this guy called Brenton Brown... Mum's boyfriend was proper shocked but not as shocked as me when Mum came out of the bedroom. Her face was proper banged up. I could hardly recognise her. Blood was all over her face.'

'What happened after that?' I wanted to know.

'Everton and Brenton dragged this guy out and proper banged him up. He seemed to have heard of this Brenton guy and he was begging for mercy. I'll never forget that night. They booted him down six flights of stairs and into the forecourt of the estate. People were watching. Someone called the Feds but no-one said shit 'cos he was a known woman beater. Mum always picked the wrong men...'

'Mum told me that she was tight with your mum at school,' I said. 'They used to go raves together.'

'They are tighter than you would ever know, bruv. If there is one thing about the old school people, they look out for each other. When I was young I used to see your mum and you around my gates all the time with her friend Sharon. Don't you remember those days, Dennis? We was about three or four. And sometimes even your auntie Denise would come over. They helped decorate the place. Your mum hasn't been here for a while now, though.'

Noel must have had a good memory 'cos I couldn't remember any of that shit...

'Work,' I explained. 'Takes up all her time. Even on weekends...

But since my mum started to earn good money she's gone a little stush…'

'I would *never* call your mum stush,' Noel raised his voice. 'From the chats I have heard from your mum, my mum, Sharon and your auntie Denise, they all lived a grime life, bruv. Trust me, they had it tough. They were all *sufferers.*'

When Noel spoke the word *chats* I leaned forward towards Noel. 'What else did you hear from these chats?' I wanted to know. 'What were they talking about? Anything about my paps?'

Noel poured himself another drink and took a generous toke from his big-head. He looked at me for two seconds and then tipped his ash into an ashtray. 'I'm not supposed to talk about that. Mum's orders.'

I was about to raise my voice but I checked myself. I didn't want to wake up Cara. 'Don't fuck with me, Noel,' I said. 'I'd never keep shit from you.'

The stain on the carpet caused by the ginger ale was now a magnet to Noel's eyes… He took another two tokes from his big-head before I heard his voice again. 'Your paps, Everton, Brenton Brown, they were all serious thugs, bruv. Proper gangsters.'

'Yeah,' I nodded. 'I know something about that. Go on.'

Before he did go on Noel checked to see if his mother was still sparked out upon her bed… He returned with this weird excited expression on his face, as if he was about to say Al Pacino had came to visit. 'They duppied an old school Brixton don.'

'They what?'

'They merked a proper G. This G was well famous back in the day and he ruled these ends like a proper Al Capone.'

'How did they duppy him?'

'Shot him,' Noel replied. 'Right between his eyeballs. Like how Lee Van Cleef shot that ugly man at the start of *A Few Dollars More.*'

'Who shot him?'

'That's what I don't know. It was the night your paps got his legs fucked. On that night, along with your paps there were three of your paps' brethrens, Brenton Brown, Everton and this white guy called Frank. This big-time G had kidnapped your auntie Denise and made himself her pimp. It was a fucked-up, grimy situation, bruv. Your paps and his brethrens went after him.'

'What!' was all I could manage. 'Auntie Denise was a ho? You're lying! What else you know?'

'I *ain't* lying. I wouldn't make this shit up. But that's it, bruv. That's all I know. *Never* tell your paps or mum that I talked about this. Otherwise my mum would get blanked 'cos she wasn't supposed to tell me.'

My mind was spinning with different scenarios. Did Paps kill this badman? Was it uncle Everton? I couldn't see the white guy Frank killing an old time Brixton don. Frank? That name rings a bell. Could it be the Irishman who was friends with Granny? Anyway, he was probably the look-out. Did it happen on the street? Was there a massive Feds investigation? Did Mum have to put up an alibi? How did Auntie Denise became a ho? Fuck me. Auntie Denise a ho! I had to get to my feet and have another drink.

Noel went to look in on his mother. I followed him into her bedroom and Cara was fast asleep, snoring loudly. Noel pulled the duvet over her and then bent down to kiss her on the forehead while placing his hands tenderly upon her cheeks. He closed his eyes and tears appeared on his face. He soon wiped them away and then he looked at her once more, his face breaking out into a sad smile. I don't think I will ever see a sweeter show of love until the day they bury my black ass.

Noel and I were tighter than a church lady's crotch after that night. I'm not sure how to explain it but after that night of Jerry Springer shit, beefs and respect, I felt I would do anything for my best bredren, Noel Gordon. I guess there must be something deep, something so sweet between Jamaican mothers and their first-born sons. Maybe it's because of all the Jamaican sons I know, hardly any of them are close to their dads. I respected Paps to the max but wasn't close to him the way I was with Mum.

I reached home just after 3 a.m. in the morning. I was well tired and was gonna go to my bed but there was a light on in the front room. I went to see and found Paps sitting down on the leather sofa draining a drink. It seemed like he had been thinking things through for hours. He was wearing a blue dressing-gown over a Crystal Palace football shirt and pyjama bottoms. He took a sip of his rum and coke and asked, 'Cara told Noel about his daddy?'

'Yes,' I nodded.

'How did he take it?'

'All considered, quite well.'

'We've been telling Cara for years to tell him,' said Paps.

I sat down in an armchair facing Paps. I so much wanted to ask him about the night he and his bredrens killed a man. But I just couldn't bring myself to do it. I would betray Noel's confidence and Cara's. 'Paps,' I started. 'I know you was a shotta back in the day, selling weed on the front line. My guess is that you knew Red Eyes in that line of business back in the day?'

It took a few seconds for paps to look at me but when he did, he simply nodded. 'Yes,' he said. 'Your guess is right. I reckoned it would have to come out sooner or later.'

'Why didn't you tell me before?'

'How could I try and discipline you and bring you up right if you knew what I did to survive in the past?'

'I would have understood.'

'Maybe you would have, maybe you wouldn't have. But I didn't want the risk. You see, Dennis, if you knew everything about my past you would always have ammunition to fling back in my face if we had a bone of contention.'

Paps swirled the drink around in his glass a little and then took a sip. Every time we had our chats he always maintained full eye contact. I always found it a little unnerving... It's probably why that night I decided against asking him about the guy who my paps and his bredrens duppied.

'I knew Red Eyes back in the day,' Paps revealed. 'Before he was known as Red Eyes his nickname was Sceptic. He was one of our crew. He was doing the same thing as me, as you put it selling weed on the front line. He was a hustler, no worse, no better than I was. I think at the funeral today we all realised, well, my age group realised that it could have been one of us lowered into that grave.

It could have been one of us who had lived the way he did in the past twenty years or so. He was alright. A friend. It was just that he could never see any other life for him than the one he led.'

As Paps spoke that last sentence, I noticed he was looking down at the floor. Sadness was in his eyes and I guessed that Red Eyes was more than just another friend.

'I'm tired and I'm going to my bed,' I said. 'You better come up soon if you don't want Mum coming down here looking for you. Goodnight, Paps.'

'Goodnight, Dennis.'

I left Paps sitting there with his rum and coke and his grief and as my head hit the pillow I promised myself that I must encourage Noel to try something else to earn P's than just shotting.

Chapter Ten

AKEISHA PARRIS

Three weeks after the funeral I kinda felt I was going through the motions. Well, maybe not going through the motions but just doing all the shit that Noel expected me to do. The fallout of Red Eyes' death was still messing up my head and I couldn't work out how Noel just adapted to his situation and got on with his life. He and his mum were closer than ever. He even started to pick her up from her workplace and we would burn big-heads together at their flat. I had to admit I was kinda jealous 'cos I didn't have any chill-out time with my mum. I couldn't ever imagine burning a big-head with her. But always at the back of my head was the merking of Red Eyes.

All this stressing led me to think how I would react if there was a death in my family and for the first time in my life, I realised that my parents might not always be there… I kinda got obsessed about Paps' near death shit. I wanted to know how Paps felt when he had his near fatal incident, what was going through his head? But I couldn't find a way of asking. He might think of me as being morbid or shit like that. I hung around him at home, hoping for the courage to come to me so I could ask him about *that* night. But courage never came. We ended up talking about third-world debt and boring shit like that. Paps thought that I was taking an interest in world affairs. Little did he know. While all this discussion was going on I did find out one thing though and that's if you get too much knowledge it can make you too grumpy and vexed to enjoy the life you have. That was Paps.

It was one of those chill-out Sunday afternoons when I was trying to work out a way of confronting Paps about the night his legs got fucked. I considered waiting until we were alone in the house and after striking up a conversation about the World Trade Organisation, a topic he always ranted about, hit him with his own gangster shit and demand answers. As I made these plans in my head, Paps was reading a book. I was also trying to summon up the nerve to call Akeisha. I had nearly called her every day for three weeks but at the last minute I had pussied out. It was driving me nuts.

Meanwhile, Mum and Davinia were leafing through an Argos catalogue and when I wasn't observing Paps, I was watching MTV Base. Mya was performing a sexy dance routine with Beenie Man on screen and that's when I said to myself that if I don't call Akeisha now I never will. Tackling Paps was no longer my first priority.

So I prepared my game, slapped on my confidence, took in some deep breaths and I made my call sitting on the stairs. 'Hello. What's gwarnin, Akeisha?'

'Who is this?' came back the reply.

'Dennis.'

'Dennis?'

'Yeah, the bruv you met at Red Eyes' funeral.'

'There were quite a few young guys there at the funeral.'

'None as good looking as me though,' I laughed nervously.

Silence… I felt my pulse gathering pace. 'So when are we gonna link up, Akeisha? You see, I remembered your name and your buff self. When are you gonna show me some love? You know, take me on a tour around your proper buff body.'

'Excuse me!'

'When are we gonna connect, man, in the plug, wall socket sense. You know, to do what young people do. Aren't you feeling me? I'm not feeling any love from you right now. Why you so quiet? Akeisha?'

She cut me off. I couldn't believe it. No chick had done that to me before. My head spun. Oh my God! I fucked it up. Me and my Brixtonian macho self! I'm not Noel, I'm not Noel! Why didn't you be yourself? You dumb fucking prick!

I returned to the front room. Paps was still reading. Mum and Davinia were looking at designer handbags in another catalogue. 'What girl is it this time, Dennis?' Davinia asked, big grin on her face.

'How do you know it's a girl?'

'Because every time you sit on the stairs and make a call, it's usually a girl you're talking to. Am I right or am I right?'

She was right. Burn Davinia. 'Davinia, zip your beak, take off your Halloween mask, deal with your acne and mind your business.'

'Don't talk to your sister like that, Dennis,' Paps reprimanded, his eyes looking over his book. 'I keep telling you, Dennis, to show an example. *You're* the oldest.'

Burn, Paps... I gave Davinia an evil stare. She just grinned with that know-it-all face of hers. I'll deal with her when Mum and Paps have gone out.

I decided to try call Akeisha again, this time showing some politeness. I returned to the stairs to make my call and pulled the lounge door closed. 'Hi, why did you—'

Akeisha interrupted. 'If you wanna talk to me you talk to me with respect! You understand? I ain't no junz so don't chat to me like I am one!'

'Yeah, that's cool,' I managed. 'Sorry about that.'

'Alright,' said Akeisha. Her voice was still sounding stern. 'What can I do for you?'

'Er, I was wondering if I could see you again.'

'Why?'

Why? Damn, she was making it difficult. I had to think hard. ''Cos you're the kinda chick I could talk to. You seem intelligent and know what's what. I'm sick and tired of them ghetto chicks without any manners and they don't know how to behave when you're with them.'

'Any other reason?' Akeisha asked.

'And because you look better in black than Will Smith, Tommy Lee whassisname and Halle Berry in *Catwoman*.' It was all I could think of. Sweat was now appearing on my temples but she couldn't see that, nor the panic in my brain.

She laughed… Yes! I've got her now. I could see her wearing a skin-tight Lycra in my bedroom. I could see that wok coming my way, my hands pulling her booty towards my crotch. I'm slowly woking her and R. Kelly is providing the soundtrack… She's moaning with serious pleasure. 'So you wanna meet me, like in a date?' she asked.

I opened my eyes and my hands had become suddenly clammy. A date? I didn't do dates. No self-respecting *road* brother did dates. I had to burn that shit… Akeisha's incredibly buff an' all but fuck if I'm gonna spend P's on her in a cinema, nightclub or restaurant like I'm a pussy or a boops. What am I thinking about? I'm not Noel! Be yourself! Of course I can take her on a date, I've got the P's. I ain't no grimed ghetto brother. I've got the game.

'I was thinking more of you come to see me around my gates or I go around to see you at your gates?' I offered. It came out all wrong. *Damn!*

'No,' she said. 'I don't work like that. You really *expect* me to come around to your place and I don't know you that good? You could be a rapist! A psycho. You might be one of those people who gets their freak on in a weird way. And you cannot seriously expect me to invite you to my place. It ain't gonna happen until I know a lot more about you.'

'Er, OK,' I managed. 'Maybe we can link up for a coffee or something and slowly get to know one another?'

'That's better, Dennis. That's how we should do things. You're getting with the programme.'

'So where are we gonna have this coffee?' I asked. 'Then when we have that we could forward on to your place and have *Basic Instinct*-like sex.' That last line just came out accidentally too. I just couldn't help myself. In my mind she was now naked. I was also hanging loose, my limbs tied to the four posts of a kingsize bed.

She walked around the bed and stopped behind the headrest. Then she purred this delicious purr. Fuck my days! I'm a proper perv.

'Nice try, Dennis,' Akeisha laughed. 'But trust me, it ain't gonna happen like that. As for where we're gonna have this coffee, forget Bricky. Streatham is good. There's a few places on the High Street there.'

I opened my eyes once again and tried to 'clean' my mind. 'When?'

'Next Saturday, say about two in the afternoon. Weekends are easier for me because Mum looks after my baby.'

'You have a baby?'

'Yes. Curtis is his name. He's ten months old. Everyone loves him because he has cute little dimples. Is this a problem for you?'

I thought about it for a few seconds. She didn't look old enough to have a baby but then again she lives in Angel Town. All kinds of fucked-up, American south, Jerry Springer shit goes on there. Noel once introduced me to a twenty-nine-year-old grandmother who he sold skunk to. He woked her 'cos she couldn't pay for her eighth of skunk one day and he could have woked her fifteen-year-old daughter too. Jealous on seeing her mother get some action, the teenager outrageously flirted with Noel but even Noel has his limits. So he didn't wok her but he still allowed the teenager to give him a BJ. At the time, the grandmother and her daughter were studying together for their mock exams. Only in Bricky.

Akeisha seemed so confident, intelligent. How did she get herself pregnant at such a young age? Let me check this. The baby's ten months old, I think Akeisha is about two years older than me so that means she gave birth at eighteen. Not too bad. Not like those ghetto bitches who get pregnant at fifteen. But maybe the pregnancy fucked up her running career. Damn! She looked good in black.

'No, it's not a problem, Akeisha,' I finally answered. 'Can I ask how old are you?'

'Nineteen,' she answered. 'Twenty in January. I'm an Aquarian. Remember to buy me a present for my birthday.'

This was all good. She expected me to be around by January. She's twenty in January? One and a half years older than me.

Damn! When we finally have sex it's gonna be the bomb because of her experience and shit. Noel woked this woman who was thirty-three once. She was one of our white trash clients. I wouldn't go for someone as ancient as thirty-three but Noel still talks about that wok with a pleasure overload and a stupid-looking grin. I couldn't wait to have sex with Akeisha. Now, God, here's the time for you to prove yourself. Make this wok happen!

'Only if you buy something for me for Christmas,' I finally replied.

When she finished the call I fretted on whether I should return her bracelet and tell her I watched her for two years running around Tooting Bec track. At least it would be honest. But I didn't know if I could do that. She might think I'm nothing more than a petty thief. No, burn that. I can't have her thinking of me like that.

Akeisha and I met at one of them coffee places where it costs more than a pound fifty for a hot chocolate. No way I would've paid that if I was with the brothers so I had to grin and bear the pain. Burn name-brand coffee places. I reckoned Akeisha had a job 'cos she bought a couple of croissants and a cappuccino and didn't see much change out of a ten pound note. She didn't even flinch. Best of all she didn't see the nervous twitch that my left knee developed. This wasn't no normal ghetto chick.

'So when is Curtis's birthday?' I asked.

'In two months time. Didn't I tell you he was ten months?'

'Oh yeah you did. Who's his paps?'

'Don't mean to be rude but you don't have to know. It's my business.'

'So do you find time to work or go college?'

'Yes, I want to be an accountant. I was always good at maths at school. Mum helps me out looking after Curtis while I'm at college and I work part-time at Marks and Spencer on Fridays and Sundays. The one in Clapham Junction. No-one should use an excuse that they lived a grime life in the ghetto to stop them progressing... So many of my school friends use that excuse and it's weak.'

While Akeisha was speaking I allowed myself to look her over. She had this pink beret over her pitch-black straightened hair and although she wasn't wearing any lipstick she had this lip thing on that made them shiny. She was sporting a denim jacket and knee-length denim skirt and all this was underlined by a pair of black leather boots. The only bling she wore was a small gold ring that decorated the baby finger of her left hand. As for me I had an erection.

She was one of those very few black people of my age who still lived with both parents. Her paps worked nightshift in some factory and he was saving up to buy some property in the Caribbean where him and his wife could spend their retirement. The family had lived in Angel Town for over twenty years so they must have seen all that Feds shooting black men who were armed with water pistols and high on crack shit.

Akeisha had two older sisters and no brothers. I was glad 'cos sometimes in Bricky you might have some hardcore brother coming up to you and saying, 'Fuck with my sister and I'm gonna fuck with your breathing.'

When Akeisha asked me if I smoked weed I did say yes but I didn't tell her I was a shotta. I intended to keep that shit quiet. I still remembered my pounding at the hands of the Nigerian crew in Peckham. Akeisha had smoked the occasional spliff too but she claimed she never 'inhaled'.

For the rest of our date I impressed Akeisha with my knowledge of Jamaican history. I spoke about the maroon wars, slave uprisings, how Christopher Columbus's ass was saved by the native peoples after his ship was fucked and I explained that the first mass migration to leave Jamaica wasn't to journey to England but to work in Panama to construct the famous canal. She really enjoyed the story of Caribs going from island to island throughout the Caribbean hunting for human flesh. All that listening to Granny paid off. I did stress in my tale that I was descended from the Maroons and we hated the taste of human liver. But Bajans wouldn't say no, I joked. I couldn't believe I said that but luckily Akeisha was third generation Jamaican just like me so she let the bad taste joke pass. By this time my knee had stopped twitching.

'When you see the way some brothers eating Kentucky chicken

I can believe that story about the Caribs being cannibals,' she chuckled.

Finally, I thought to myself, she's warming to me. I might have to wait a serious time for my wok though. Akeisha ain't no junz.

Akeisha allowed me to escort her back to Angel Town. As usual the brothers there eyed me as I walked through the estate. If they didn't know your face then there was a ninety per cent chance of getting jacked and stepping home in just your boxers. In these kind of situations you have to acknowledge them with your eyes and not go on like a pussy. Show any sign of weakness and it's running like Linford Christie time. Most of them knew me so it was cool and Akeisha just ignored them… There is an off-licence in the estate and judging by the thick metal grilles that covered that place you would think they were looking after the Crown Jewels… Rumour had it that the shopkeeper kept a Uzi behind the counter and brothers believed it 'cos the shop hadn't been raided for two years. Quite a miracle in Bricky.

Akeisha lived in a second-floor flat that overlooked a courtyard and as we neared her front door I asked, 'So when can I see you again?'

She thought about it, her keys poised an inch away from the lock. 'Have you ever been to a poetry jam, Dennis?'

'A what?'

'A poetry jam. Where conscious people let off steam and chant inspiring words.'

'Oh yeah,' I said. 'I've heard of raves like that. Haven't been to one but I heard it's all good.'

'It's not exactly a rave, Dennis. It's more of a spiritual vibe thing. A lot of consciousness. A sit-down affair.'

'Yeah, yeah, I know. I'm all up for that.'

Akeisha smiled. 'Good! You can take me to the Arches behind Morleys in Bricky High Street. They have a jam every last Friday of the month and this coming Friday there is a special Black History Month event. Come for me about nine. See ya.'

'Hold up a minute. My throat is kinda dry-like. Can't I come in for a drink or something?' I also wanted to spill the shit about the wristlet… It was bothering my conscience and I really wanted to tell her about the whole Tooting Bec thing.

'If you go down to the courtyard and turn right there is a sweetshop that does an excellent line in throat lozenges.'

'And I need to use the toilet,' I lied, desperate to get into her flat.

'Then you'd better get on home then. Bye, Dennis and thanks for a nice afternoon.'

She closed the door. I couldn't believe it. Akeisha closed the door. I still hadn't told her about the bracelet and those Friday afternoon games lessons… It'll have to wait but I better step carefully. I don't want her thinking of me as some sort of obsessive perv and a thief to boot.

Being with Akeisha for the afternoon had roasted my crotches and I had to get that seen to. So after I reached level ground I made a call to Tania Blake. I knew Tania from Stockwell Youth Club and I knew she was always on me. She was a bit of a junz. When I was playing pool or something she would come over and pinch my butt or pose in a way to put me off my shot. She was fit and curvy in the right places but her face was not saying a lot. It was just about good enough for a BJ. Unfortunately Tania had this bitch of a nose that almost covered her face. Another minus was her hair that was full of extensions. Usually when a ghetto chick goes to the trouble of having so many extensions put in, it means they haven't got too much of their own real hair. I didn't like the idea of woking a bald chick but hey, when your crotches are roasting then you can't be too picky…

'Hi, is this Tania?'

'Dennis? Is that you?'

'Yeah, what's gwarnin?'

'You know how it goes. This and that. Same shit, different toilets.'

'Yeah, I feel that too.'

'So how comes you calling me, Dennis?'

'Well, I've come around to my senses. This bruv thinks you're buff, Tania, you know what I'm saying? This bruv reckons it's time to feel a sample of your buffness.'

I heard a noise to my left and I looked up.

'Hold up, Tania. Something's gwarnin in Angel Town.'

A number of brothers had surrounded this delivery van and at gunpoint they were ordering the driver to open up the shutters at the back. I thought I'd better ignore that shit and I walked off in a different direction.

'What's gwarnin?' Tania asked.

'Oh, some sufferers are jacking a van. I'm alright though, they know my face. I think they're using a fake gun.'

'Well that's alright then.'

I looked up again and the sufferers were removing a washing machine and a fridge from the van. The driver, a gun pointed to his head, was giving away his wallet, his mobile phone and his trainers. Only in Angel Town.

'I *knew* you was feeling me,' said Tania, resuming the call. 'I knew you wanted some of this booty. You were just fronting. All the time you were pretending that you didn't like me. Maybe 'cos your bredrens were around.'

'Yeah, you're right, Tania. I was just fronting. I did like you from the start but I didn't know how to tell you. Especially with all them men who surround you at the club. You know what I'm saying? It was proper difficult to walk up to you in the club and reveal my game.'

'You could have called me, Dennis.'

'I didn't know what to say.'

'Dennis Huggins lost for words?'

'Well, it's always harder to chirps a chick you *really* like than just a plain ugly bitch.'

I hoped my game was working. It should do 'cos Tania's dumb as a trailer load of shit. I was only gonna wok it the once though, just to take care of the roasting in my crotches. *Damn!* Did Akeisha look fine today! Maybe for Tania it would be paper bag time. No way can I look at her face while I'm woking it.

'So, Tania, can we link up later on at your gates?'

'I would love to, Dennis but right about now this girl's getting her weave on and you know how long that takes. Girl wanna look her best. There's also another problem.'

'What's that?'

'I've got a man now. He treats me all good. Taking me out and shit. You know him. Courtney Thompson.'

'Courtney Thompson?' I repeated. 'I went school with that brother... We used to call him Billy-No-Bredrens. The takeaway brother. *Burn* him... He's a pussy.'

Silence... I was sure I played my game right. Ghetto chicks like a dominant male telling them to do shit. I was sure this pussy who Tania claimed was her man probably hadn't even woked it yet.

'You can come around on Monday, Dennis,' she finally answered. 'Say after half eight when *EastEnders* finish. I will get my sister to go out for the evening. You know where I live, New Park Road ends. Streatham Hill side.'

Why do dumb-ass ghetto chicks love *EastEnders*? It can't be for the idiot coconut black people in it. Anyway, it was all good. While I'm woking Tania I will close my eyes and think of Akeisha. 'Yeah, I know where your gates is,' I said. 'Oh, before I go, get some protection yeah. In case I forget. But don't get that fruit-flavoured shit, just get the normal dick macs.'

'No problem, Dennis. See ya on Monday!'

I finished the call with a smile on my face. I heard Fed sirens behind me but I ignored that sound and couldn't help feeling it had been a good day. I took a 109 bus to take me up Bricky Hill and home. It was after six o'clock when I turned my key in the latch. I entered the hallway and found Davinia sitting halfway up the stairs looking proper fucked off. Then I heard this arguing from the front room. It was Mum and Paps. The door was slightly open and Davinia and I could hear every word.

'Why you spending so much time at work?' Paps shouted. 'Why's your boss only ask for you to stay behind? If you're screwing him I'll break his head.'

'Why don't you believe me, Lincoln?' Mum yelled. 'It's only work! I've *never* wanted to screw anybody else. Why don't you believe that? I'm with you, aren't I? Been with you for about twenty years!'

Silence... Davinia looked at me all sad-like and whispered, 'They been at each other for half an hour. Can't you stop them, Dennis?'

'They have to sort it out themselves, Davinia. What can I do?'

'Maybe you can explain to Dad that because of his condition, he doesn't see himself as a "full" man no more. Therefore his self-esteem drops with every birthday and he is becoming more paranoid. That's why he's convinced Mum is having an affair. He can't see why Mum stays with him.'

God! This girl was so smart it was frightening. I climbed the stairs to where Davinia was sitting and I could see she was hurt by all the arguing. There were probably more rows that I didn't know about. I knelt down to one knee and touched her left cheek with the four fingers of my right hand. It's something Mum used to do to me. 'Even if it comes from me it will hurt him badly,' I said. 'It has to come from Granny. Paps will listen to her. He always listens to her.'

Davinia held onto my hand, gave it a gentle squeeze and then let go, as if embarrassed by her emotions.

'You always question me!' Mum ranted on. 'Why can't you support me? Like I have done for you. For so many *fucking* years with your fucked-up legs! Was it my fault? WAS IT MY FUCKING FAULT, LINCOLN? And trust me, Lincoln, you was and still are a terrible patient. You know how many times I thought of walking away? Those nights, endless nights of agony. How did you think it was for me? Listening to your pain? BUT NO! I FUCKING STAYED! All I ask from you is a little support for me and my work. Is that too much to ask? All I get from you is accusations. That I'm screwing my boss. That I'm not home enough. Well fuck you, Lincoln, I'm not standing for it no more! *You* can sleep downstairs.'

Mum came rushing out of the front room wiping away her tears. She brushed past Davinia and myself and ran up the stairs. Then we heard her bedroom door slam. Davinia ran after her and I sat on the stairs wondering if I should enter the front room and talk with Paps. I sat there for nearly an hour and although I tried to think what's best for my parents, I couldn't help but concentrate my mind on how I was gonna impress Akeisha on our next date.

Eventually I walked into the lounge. Paps was sitting in his favourite armchair. I parked myself on the sofa and at first Paps failed to acknowledge me. It was only after five minutes that he turned around his head and said to me, 'I've been an idiot, Dennis.'

'Yeah, I know,' I nodded.

'I didn't mean to say the things I did,' he said.

'I know that too. If I was you I'd apologise when Mum calms down.'

'I will, Dennis. I will.'

Silence... We looked at each other for the next twenty minutes without saying a word. He was obviously feeling more uncomfortable than I was.

'Do you know I'm smoking weed, Paps?' I suddenly blurted out.

There was no rapid head movement from Paps. No look of surprise. He just sat there, staring into space. 'Your mother and I had our suspicions,' he said. 'But I can hardly rebuke you about it because I have been smoking since I was thirteen. It would be hypocritical. I just hope that you're intelligent enough not to use harder drugs.'

'No, I'm not on that, Paps.'

'That's good to hear.'

Silence again. I guessed Paps was still kicking himself for talking to Mum the way he did. But before he hobbles upstairs to apologise, he's gonna answer some of my questions. It was the right time.

'Did you kill a man, Paps?'

He looked up and searched for my eyes. It was hard not to be intimidated but I held his gaze. He answered after a long pause. 'I don't wanna lie to you, Dennis. Yes, I did. Along with others. Just don't think that we never think about it. We all do. Them things never leave your head.'

'Who pulled the trigger?' I wanted to know.

'We all pulled the trigger, Dennis. And that's all I'm gonna reveal about it. It was a long time ago.'

'There was Uncle Everton, Brenton Brown, Frank, Auntie Denise and you, Paps. You was all there. Doesn't a son have the right to know if his paps might be a *killer*?'

'DENNIS! That's enough! We all killed Nunchaks and that's the end of it. And you're one short! Sceptic was there that night. Yes! Red Eyes, Noel's dad. So maybe you can go away, play at being Miss Marple and try to work out who pulled the trigger. I know this much, I will never tell you. You don't have to know. It is *we* who have to live with what happened that night. Not you.'

At that point Paps looked down at his legs and I knew that he was doing his best not to weep.

'What did it feel like, Paps? That night? I know you went to rescue Auntie Denise...'

Again Paps stared into space, as if he was mentally rewinding back the years. He closed his eyes for a minute and he spoke when he re-opened them. 'It was the first night of the Brixton uprising. Yes, we went off to try and get Denise back... Crazy fools the lot of us. But with the riot blazing off all around us we could hardly go to the police. I'm not sure where my courage came from that night. It was the scariest feeling I ever had.'

He trailed off and looked at me. 'That's all you need to know, Dennis. Don't bother me with this again. I'd better now make my apologies to your mother.'

As I watched him get up and hobble out of the room, I guessed he was protecting someone. I didn't think it was Paps who pulled the trigger.

Chapter Eleven

SOMETHING ABOUT ROAD RAMPS

The next Monday morning I made sure I spoke to Davinia before she left for school. I joined her at the breakfast table and as I was spreading marmalade on my toast, she was eating Ready Brek with cinnamon and nutmeg in it. Davinia was always particular like that.

'Davinia, what goes on in a poetry jam?'

'You don't know?'

'If I did know I wouldn't be asking, would I!'

'No need to bark,' she said. 'Why do you want to know?'

'Why? That's my business. Are you gonna tell me or what?'

She grinned that know-it-all grin of hers. Then she fed herself two spoonfuls of her morning starter, enjoying the moment of me having to come to her for help.

'Well!' I said, beginning to get frustrated.

'Usually you get a few headline performers who are well known on the poetry jam circuit,' she finally explained. 'They usually rant about the government, poverty, racism, you know, that sort of thing. In the audience people cheer and clap, everyone is respectful to each other and in the breaks you sip herbal teas and mineral water and make friends; it's not cool to drink alcohol. Then when the headliners have done their performances it's the time of the open mic session. Basically, anyone who has the nerve can go up to the mic and have about five minutes in front of the audience. Everyone is given encouragement…'

'And that's it?'

'Yep, that's it.'

'The audience, they are not ancient-like, are they? Mum's generation?'

Davinia laughed and nearly choked on her breakfast. 'No, audience is youngish… You get a decent crowd.'

'What? Does that mean there's lesbos and chi chi men doing their shit in the back rows?'

'No, Dennis. Just a mixture of black, white, brown, whatever. Lord knows why you want to go to a poetry jam, Dennis? You're not exactly cultural.'

'Burn you, Davinia. You don't know shit. I can be cultural when I put my mind to it. Fuck!'

Just as I said that Paps walked into the kitchen. 'Dennis! Stop using bad word to your sister! *Set* an example. How many times do I have to tell you?'

Paps went to make himself some toast; he always spreads this honey that he gets from some herbal shop on his toast. That's where Davinia gets her fussiness from…

'Are you taking some girl?' Davinia asked with her know-it-all smile; it was bigger than ever now Paps had told me off. 'To a poetry jam? It must be love!'

I offered Davinia an evil stare as I put two Weetabix in a cereal bowl and covered them with Corn Flakes. There was brown sugar in the sugar bowl. Why did my family have to be different and have brown sugar instead of white in the fucking sugar bowl? Anyway, I poured too much over my cereal. 'If you have to know, I'm going to a poetry jam on Friday night to see a bredren. He's proper good with his lyrics.'

'Yeah, right,' laughed Davinia.

Pissed off with smart-ass Davinia, I ate my breakfast in my

room. Mum didn't like us eating meals in our rooms but she wasn't here. She had left for work an hour ago.

In my room I wondered what I should wear when I go to see Tania Blake for my wok. Name-brand tracksuit or garms made by Tommy Hilfiger? Mum told me that although brothers of my age wear nuff Hilfiger clothes, the man himself is a racist. But he doesn't mind black people buying his garms 'cos then they become cool and everyone else buys them too. Mum went on to say that I shouldn't really be fatting up no white man's wallet who don't like black people but if I did that I would walk on road naked. I didn't really give a shit as long as he makes nice garms. So I decided on my Hilfiger jeans and jacket and my Timberland boots. I would just have to step out when Mum ain't looking.

New Park Road council estate is one of them places where politicians like to go before elections so idiot people think they really care about the Nike-less and the ghetto folk. It stretched either side of Brixton Hill and Streatham Hill and basically the place is proper grimed. You can always tell how a council cares about their estates by the state of their road ramps. In New Park Road, it looked like they just dropped loads of cement all over the place and ran for it. As an after-thought they called the mess they left behind road ramps. This shotta I know who lives there is forever complaining about how the so-called road humps fucked up the suspension on his Benz and now he parks his ride outside one of his girlfriends' gates in Streatham...

New Park Road ends was just a ten minute walk from my gates. I reached Tania's gates just after 9 p.m. I didn't want to arrive on time 'cos that would have looked like I was proper desperate. I didn't want her thinking that.

Tania opened the front door wearing only a silk-looking burgundy nightgown. She had a smile of expectation on her face but she went a bit over the top with the brown lipstick and the blue eye make-up. She also had this gold stud in her nose that only brought attention to its enormity. She grabbed my arm and ushered me to sit in the lounge. The lights were dimmed and Jodeci was playing on this cheap stereo that the family probably got from a car boot sale. The room was cramped and the sofa I was sitting on had lost all its bounce and colour. At this point I remembered that I hated visiting shit-poor ghetto people, save Noel...

'You got any drink?' I asked.

'Er, yeah. My sister's man left a couple of Stella bottles in the fridge last night.'

'Bring one for me then.'

I needed a bit of liquor to help me forget my surroundings. As she went to get me a drink I started to build two fat-heads. One for her and one for me. Mine would be bigger... By the time she came back I had already finished wrapping her one; I was proper mean with the skunk. She sat beside me, put an arm around my neck and torched the fat-head. I started to build my own spliff and drained a third of my bottle in one go. 'So what about Courtney?' I asked.

'He's been going on weird lately,' she answered. 'He's started to read the Koran and hanging out with brothers who have fucked-up beards and shit.'

'Is that right? Courtney now has bredrens?'

'Yeah. He's been telling me that I must not eat bacon and not to wear my revealing garms. I told him to fuck himself. *No* man gonna tell me what I should and shouldn't wear. I'm not into that woman must pay homage to her man's religion. Burn that shit. If you ask me it's just a way for weak-heart men to control the sisters. And that's the way of most religions. Burn the fucking lot of them I say.'

Tania's reasoning proper surprised me. This ghetto chick wasn't as stupid as she dressed.

'Courtney was always an idiot from schooldays,' I remarked. 'And his mum goes to the same church as my granny. So why the fuck is he turning Muslim?'

'So they can order their girlfriends around,' reasoned Tania. 'Haven't you been listening to me, Dennis? And I'm proper fucked off with it. I'm gonna sack him after Christmas.'

'Why after Christmas?' I asked.

''Cos he's promised to buy me a gold chain and name-brand

shoes from this store in Bond Street. We was up West the other day and I pointed them out to him.'

I laughed out loud. 'So Courtney is nothing but a sad boops! I'm gonna tell you blatantly, Tania, if me and you ever have something going on I ain't buying you shit! I ain't no boops.'

Taking a mighty toke Tania blew the smoke over my head. She looked a bit pissed off at my last remark but it's better that she knew where she stood with me. 'I don't need no man to buy me shit!' she said, performing her head moving sideway thing. How the fuck do ghetto chicks do that? 'But if a man's offering I ain't saying no,' she went on. 'Man take what they want from you so I'm gonna take what I want from them. Besides, you didn't come here to chat about Courtney, did you?'

'No,' I answered. 'I'm just kinda wondering why you linked him in the first place. He's a pussy-hole.'

'When his bredrens are not around him, he's cool, you know, on a level. But when he's with them he changes. Acts like a hardback man on road. You get me?'

'Courtney ain't no hardback,' I stated. 'At school this maaga little African brother broke him up, punched out two of his teeth and ran off with his sandwiches and crisps.'

I looked around for an ashtray but couldn't find one. 'Where shall I tip my ash?'

'In the bedroom. Follow me.'

I knew what was coming next but I didn't have an erection. Tania led me to her box-room and the walls were covered in posters of LL Cool J, Usher, Will Smith and Tupac. At least they covered up the cheap wallpaper. The bedroom was so small that if you wasn't careful you might broke the window with the mortise key when entering. She closed the door behind me and she invited me to sit down on her single bed. The duvet had no cover on it and I reckoned it had never been washed. There was an ashtray on her dressing table and I placed my fat-head in it and my half bottle of beer beside it. She did likewise and seconds later we were rolling about on her bed, taking off each other's clothes. Underneath her dressing-gown she was wearing a black bra and a black thong. It didn't take me long to get her naked and she had the most buff body I had ever seen in the flesh. But I so much wanted to see Akeisha's face in front of me. I tried to imagine it was Akeisha's face but that didn't work. Closing my eyes only made me imagine how big Tania's nose was.

I rolled her onto her belly and started to kiss her neck, caress her back and feel up her bottom. Her face was pressing into the bed. But Tania moved onto her back and stuck her tongue down my throat. As she circled my tongue with hers, her big nose was bumping into my face like a dodgem car driven by a fucked off bully at the funfair. I just couldn't carry on. I pulled myself off her and sat up… For a moment I thought that I should have just let her give me a BJ. At least that would have kept her nose away from me.

'I'm not in the vibe to do this,' I explained. 'It don't feel right. Courtney was a proper bredren at school and I don't want to do him any disrespect…'

'What!'

I shook my head.

'Are you a fucking chi chi man or something?' Tania yelled. 'You don't want none of this?'

She raised her bottom in the air, gyrated her hips and all her business was revealed. *Damn!* She was fit! Her bottom was proper peach-like but I couldn't wok her with *that* nose. And she wasn't Akeisha. It was then when I noticed the condom packets on her dressing table. She even got the plain ones that I asked for, no fruit flavoured shit.

'Come out of my fucking house, man! Wasting my fucking time with a someone who prefers a man's bottom. I can't believe you diss me like that. Fuck off and remove your chi chi self from my gates. It's a good thing you stopped when you did 'cos I ain't catching no Aids from a chi chi man. You thought you could cure your chi chi self on me? Fucking liberty! *Remove* from my gates, man!'

All I could do was pull my clothes on and step. I didn't even bother collecting my fat-head and drink. As I left the insults still kept flying.

'Invite man to my gates and find out he's a chi chi man! You secretly wanna rinse man's bottom but you wanted to front it out with me to try and prove you're straight. That's a *diss*, man. *Real* men love this.' She cupped her breasts and then squeezed her buttocks and performed that gyrating thing again. I reckoned if I was Noel I would have rode her like a sex-starved rhino. He didn't mind too much if the face was lacking.

'Fuck off from my gates and take your nasty, shit-caked dick with you!' she ranted.

As I quickly hot stepped from Tania's block, I couldn't help but think of Akeisha and how I wished it was her I was seeing for a Monday evening wok.

I was reluctant to go to Stockwell Youth Club two nights later. Tania had a big mouth when she was vexed and I was proper shitting myself that because of our little incident she might have spread some fucked-up rumour all over Bricky that I'm a chi chi man. Some shit like that could really fuck up my shotting career... But duty called. Noel and myself were shotting outside the club and chirpsing the chicks. I was kinda relaxed 'cos we were making nuff brown sheets and there was no sign of Tania.

But then Courtney Thompson appeared. He was dressed in some weird white garms that looked too big for him. He was wearing the same stubble and walking all slow-like as if he was in some Sergio Leone western. He looked straight at me. I never really looked too hard at men's features but Courtney was my God ugly. His eyes were close together, his ears stuck out and his face had this lopsided kinda look to it. Tania was with him. She was wearing a mini-denim skirt, black fishnet stockings, a white clingy T-shirt and a loose-fitting tracksuit top. She was chewing gum the way ghetto chicks chewed gum and she had a trailer load of attitude. On a normal day I would have cracked up laughing at the sight of this weird couple but this wasn't a normal day. Courtney had come with a crew. Most of them were wearing skull caps, white garms and messed-up beards. It was like watching a fucked-up TV series about Jesus and those Jewish baddies in the temple.

Noel noticed the cranking up of the tension. 'What's gwarnin, bruv?'

'I ain't too sure, Noel,' I answered as Courtney and his crew walked up to ten yards away from me and stopped. Courtney was still bad-eyeing me so I just returned his glare with interest. Others who had been in and out of the club had now stopped what they were doing and watched to see if any violence would be happening. Courtney and myself were still having our staring contest until finally he took two paces forward. I noticed Noel slipped his right hand into his inside jacket pocket and there it remained.

'My girl says you've been hitting on her,' Courtney accused.

I remembered my paps saying to me once that when you're in a dangerous situation, never let your foe become aware of how frightened you are. *Always* look them in the eye and don't look away. It's one of those ghetto rules.

I took three paces forward and I sensed that Noel had moved in close behind me. He had my back and I'm sure he was ready with his shank. Noel owned one long bitch piece of a shank. Now there was only a couple of yards between Courtney and myself. I could feel the tension cranking. I kept telling myself, Dennis, *don't* blink. Stare out this motherfucker.

'Yeah,' I admitted. 'I did hit on her. But you know what? I didn't wok it 'cos I realised she was too fucking ugly to wok... A man doesn't wanna have a reputation that he woks any junz on two legs... *Deal* with it!'

Courtney looked at me as if his eyes were gonna fire off lasers. I held his gaze and I even stepped a further pace forward. My heart was thumping but this time I was ready. I wasn't about to freeze like I did with the Peckham crew. My limbs were alive, ready for action. Why should I be scared of a brother who got jacked at school for his sandwiches? Why should I be scared of a brother who didn't have no bredrens at school?

'I ain't gonna waste my energy on pussy non-believers,' Courtney said. 'But if you diss me again then me and you are gonna kick off.'

I sensed a hatred in Courtney's eyes that went beyond me

hitting on his girl. Since we left school I dunno what or who had influenced him but it was obvious to me some serious shit happened to Courtney.

'So what?' Tania yelled. 'You're gonna let the man walk away? After he hit on me and dissed me? Are you a fucking pussy, Courtney? Proper hardback brothers I know would have shanked a man for that shit. And you're gonna let him just walk away? Don't you care when men hit on me and show me disrespect? Anyone from these ends who is watching this gonna call you a *pussy!* Are you gonna stand for that shit, Courtney?'

The tension I was feeling was now unbearable. If anything was gonna kick off then that would be better than all this stand-off shit. Courtney's eyes were drilling into me. I knew now that he had to save face somehow. Everybody had heard what Tania had said. I could feel their eyes switching from me to Courtney. There was no way he could just walk away and leave it or give an excuse that I wasn't worth it to deal with. Mentally I prepared myself to fight. Mentally I prepared myself for pain. For me to have an edge I knew that I had to convince myself that the man standing in front of me was just as scared as I was. Maybe even more so... It was something Paps taught me. There would be no freezing today. I felt the breath of Noel upon the back of my neck and I knew he was probably more ready than I was. My shank felt cold to the skin inside my jacket and I wondered if I would christen it today.

'If you didn't dress like a ho then men wouldn't hit on you!' Courtney suddenly turned on Tania. 'If you wanna walk with me go home and change your garms!'

Tania looked at Courtney with an open mouth. She kissed her teeth and then stormed off... I relaxed just a little bit.

'Don't think this is over,' said Courtney. 'Cross my path again and it's gonna be jihad on your backside. You fucking *kaffur...*'

I went to step forward but Noel's hand on my shoulder stopped me. 'Leave it,' he said. 'He's stepping. You won. He's the one who came with a crew looking for war. Now he's stepping.'

As Courtney and his crew turned and walked up the road, I wondered where Courtney learned words like *jihad* and *kaffur* from. He was dumb as shit at school so someone must have been influencing him, telling him shit.

'Noel.'

'Yeah, bruv.'

'Any other brothers from school turned into Muslims?'

'Yeah. Two I know. Milton Davis and Adrian Callan.'

'Why you think them brothers are turning into Muslims?' I asked.

'Fuck knows,' answered Noel. 'The only thing that Courtney, Milton and Adrian have in common is that they are all fuck-ugly. And if you're a Muslim don't their girls have to obey anything what their men say? I think they do. So I reckon that if any other non-Muslim girls was thinking about linking with the three beasts, would they obey Courtney, Milton and Adrian? Like fuck they would! They're too fuck-ugly to be obeyed, bruv. So what do they do? They turn Muslim so they can find a girl to obey them. Simple as.'

There was a strange logic to Noel's fucked-up reasoning but I had a different theory. In my paps' day it was all rebellious and shit to be a rasta with locks. I know that from my paps' lectures about rastas getting it in the neck from the Feds back in the day. It was all Public Enemy Number One shit. Now, if you locks your hair you can still be a doctor, lawyer, teacher or whatever you want to be. Having dreadlocks is acceptable. Fuck! On some mornings, I see white people with dreads in ponytails wearing suits and making their way to their offices. They look fucking ridiculous but that's not the point... So if you're a wannabe rebel from the street you ain't gonna wear dreadlocks. That's too lame. If you're a wannabe rebel you wanna do something that really fucks off your parents, your grandparents, the Feds and those Tory voters who listen to the *Today* programme on Radio 4. You become a Muslim. Simple as.

Chapter Twelve

THE POETRY JAM

Next Friday night. It was 8 30 p.m. and I was half an hour early standing outside Akeisha's gates. Hip hop music was blaring out from the floor above and in the forecourt below three brothers were trying to start a car. All this was backdropped by the sound of faraway Fed sirens. My heartbeat raced as I knocked the door. I shifted uneasily on my feet and wiped my clammy hands on the back of my jeans. Remembering that Akeisha was wearing denim garms the last time we met, I decided to wear a name-brand denim shirt and denim jacket. I hoped it was gonna impress to the max...

The door opened and Akeisha was wearing black leather trousers, black leather jacket and a pair of brown cowboy boots. She was topped off by this cream-coloured Panama-style hat that she tilted at an angle to make it almost cover her left eye. She looked better than any R&B chick on MTV Base, Crystal Palace winning the cup final, and me driving through Palm Beach in a top of the range Mercedes sports.

'You're early, Dennis,' she smiled. 'You'd better come in.'

I followed Akeisha into her home and it was one of those flats where you walk down a flight of stairs to get to the front room. The place was well decorated, smelt good and there were images of leopards and tigers hanging from the walls. Where Tania's place was cramped, Akeisha's home was cosy. A black leather three-piece suite dominated the room and there were cream-coloured cushions placed in its corners. The mahogany coffee table looked as if it might take three people to carry it and the flooring was pine wooden tiles. There was a bookshelf that included novels by Toni Morrison and Richard Wright. A rubber plant was in one corner and propped up upon a mini-stereo was a framed picture of Billie Holiday... She was posing beside an advertisement for 'Strange Fruit'. Davinia would have called the place proper cultured.

'Mum,' Akeisha called. 'We have a guest.'

I know it's polite to say that your potential girlfriend's mother doesn't look old enough to have a nineteen, twenty-year-old daughter but Akeisha's mum *really* looked as if she had yet to see thirty. With her make-up neatly applied and her hair all straightened and shit she reminded me of one of those thirty-something chicks who appear in black American sitcoms. For some reason I imagined Noel making embarrassing attempts to chirps her.

'This is Dennis, Mum,' Akeisha introduced. 'He's taking me to the poetry jam at the Arches tonight.'

'Good evening,' I greeted in my best English.

'Good to meet you, Dennis,' she said. 'But you can call me Myrna... I hate all that Mrs and Miss thing. My husband would have been glad to meet you but he's in Jamaica for a while.'

'OK, Myrna,' I said.

'You don't find too many young black men who are interested in the arts and performance poetry so it's reassuring to meet a fine young black man who does,' Myrna smiled.

God! I felt such a fake. Myrna spoke very well. Even better than my mum when she puts on her proper English voice when she's chatting business on the phone or talking to white people. It'll be cool to see Myrna and Mum trying to out-English each other if they ever meet.

'Yes,' I finally replied. 'Rhymes and stuff has always given me a neat vibe.'

'Would you like a drink while you are waiting?' Akeisha offered.

'No, I'm alright.'

My nervous tension had left me thirsty as a celeb on a chat show but in these situations I didn't want to be any bother to anybody.

'OK, Dennis. I'm just gonna look in on Curtis and then we'll be away.'

'He's still sleeping,' Myrna said.

'I'll kiss him goodnight then,' Akeisha insisted. 'Dennis, you're standing to attention like a Coldstream Guard. Sit down and relax, man.'

Those minutes when I was parking my butt on that black leather sofa are probably the most nervous of my life. There I was sitting opposite Myrna who was occasionally glancing and smiling at me. Any bad remark or wrong word here and my promising romance with Akeisha would be fucked like a chav orphan girl on a casting couch. I thought Myrna was expecting me to start a conversation but I couldn't think of anything to say. She seemed too sophisticated for me to deal with and I wondered what she did for a living. After ten minutes of me feeling this strange heat in my head, Akeisha appeared. No-one had looked so wokable since Lisa 'Left Eye' Lopes did her sexy thing in the 'Unpretty' video.

I'm gonna try it tonight, I said to myself. Later on. He who dares gets between the crotches. I'll try it when we come back to her gates and Myrna and Curtis will hopefully be sleeping. It was a duty to mankind to try it. Damn! Did she look good in her leathers. I wondered how many woks the black couch had witnessed. I glanced at Myrna and guessed none.

'Ready, Dennis?'

I shot out of my chair like a Yardie hearing the customs and immigration people were approaching…

'I'll be back after midnight, Mum,' Akeisha said. 'Don't wait up.'

The feeling was good walking alongside Akeisha through Angel Town. There was an extra boing in my step and as brothers shot me envious glances I said under my breath, 'Look and shed tears, motherfuckers!'

'So how long you've been going to poetry jams?' I said after a while.

'About three years,' Akeisha answered. 'It was at a poetry jam where I met Curtis's father.'

'What? Your eyes kinda met when you were both checking out the performances and the audience?'

Akeisha laughed. Every time she done that her big eyes just sparkled and it brought her cheeks to life and made her mouth look kinda filthy. I liked that. 'No, it wasn't like that,' she explained. 'Curtis's father was a performer.'

'What was his name?' I asked. 'I might have heard of the brother...'

I faked maturity talking about Akeisha's ex. I was proper jealous of him because he woked Akeisha and I hadn't. He even had a child to prove it even though he don't seem to be around. Burn him.

'You don't need to know that, Dennis. Sorry for being so evasive but Curtis's father has no place in my life now. He could preach a good game but when it came to being a father he didn't want to know.'

That made me feel better. 'OK, let's burn his memory.'

Akeisha giggled but just for a fleeting moment her eyes revealed some kind of pain and despair. Burn her baby-father like Guy Fawkes.

The Arches venue was beneath a railway line very close to Bricky High Street. Whoever had taken over the building had done the best they could with little money. The brown brickwork was mostly covered in banners and fabrics that had been painted and graffitied upon; the Egyptian ankh seemed to be the artists' choice of design. The wooden seats looked like they had been borrowed from a local school and there was only a single light bulb that hung from a long stretch of wire above a black painted wooden box that acted as a stage; to me it just looked like a soapbox big enough for three people and a skinny sister to stand on.

Upon the stone floor in front of the stage rested beanbags, large cushions and two multicoloured armchairs that had been rebuilt untold times. On the ground along the walls, candles placed in cup saucers provided another source of light. For me it was all a bit New Age, dying celebrity icon shit gone over the top but the candles did make Akeisha's big eyes look even more sexy. Akeisha herself was in her element, nodding and smiling to people she knew on our way to our seats. I just glared at the brothers, making sure with my body language that they knew Akeisha was mine so don't even think about chirpsing her.

The chairs were quickly filled by confused hippies, disillusioned rastas, strange brothers with mad afros and fucked-up sideburns, single ugly brothers who came with no brethrens and sat alone, French students who were showing off their anti-war badges and big boots, other foreign students who didn't appear to have come for the show but came to score drugs, black women decked out in African robes, beads and all the bangles their wrists could carry, rich white people who had dressed down for the occasion and had a cocaine-zonked-out look about them. I guessed they were rich 'cos what kind of people would try and pay their entrance tax at a venue like the Arches with a Visa card? There were chi chi men who were wearing baggy jeans, baggy sweaters and fucked-up hats and a couple of white goth chicks who sat in the corner with all their black make-up shit and black-netted hand accessories… Sitting to my right was this white couple and judging by their gossip they were members of the Liberal Democrats. It was then I realised, as I watched Akeisha standing up and waving to a friend of hers, that I was in a fucking nightmare.

I said to myself, keep cool. You are doing this for a good cause. To wok the seriously wokable Akeisha. *Don't* fuck it up. *Don't* flop. Act like you actually get on with chi chi men. Pretend that you like brothers with fucked-up sideburns. Try not to think about the P's I could have made if I was shotting my skunk in this place. Ignore and don't get turned on by the lesbos behind me who are making out and pay no mind to the bewildered brother who was wearing a Ku Klux Klan kind of robe thing and yellow striped sandals…

'How long does the show go on for?' I asked Akeisha.

'Just enjoy the vibe,' she replied.

The white woman beside me, who was now building a skinny

roll-up with hash sprinkled in it, answered the question for me. 'About two hours, maybe three or four if the vibes are really hot tonight. This place is *sooo* cool, don't you think?' I wanted to give her a hard slap.

Four hours! There was no way I could spend four hours with this crowd without going insane... 'I have to get us something to eat at some point, Akeisha,' I said. 'Maybe we can go to that new chicken place in about an hour? I hear that they do some serious hot wings.'

'Maybe,' is all Akeisha managed.

Ten minutes later this fat black woman appeared on the stage. She was the mother of all salad dodgers. Suddenly the stage looked tiny. She was wearing the obligatory African robes, beads, bangles, Nefertiti head-wrap and a giant pair of silver earrings that could have fitted around a tractor's wheels. 'Greetings to everyone,' she welcomed. 'My name is Queen Manashmanek from the golden and prosperous lands of Nubia and I am your hostess and priestess for the night.'

'Greetings,' the audience echoed, including Akeisha.

I couldn't believe this shit. Was it for real? A wind-up? From the golden prosperous lands of Nubia? Is she taking the fucking piss? From what my paps taught me those lands are modern-day northern Sudan and Ethiopia. Now, they're not exactly oil-rich and the ghetto brothers over there don't wear Nike One Tens. Queen Manash-her-face must have visited there recently and ate all the food. I looked at Akeisha and she was taking it all in, everyone was taking it all in. I half-expected Queen what's-her-face to morph into Oprah Winfrey and to start talking about the *inner you* and all that meditation shit. Queen Salad Dodger then waddled about the stage and for a minute I thought the thing was gonna collapse and her weight would force her underground and she would end up roasted in the core of the earth. Unfortunately it didn't happen.

'We really have an excellent show for you tonight,' she continued. 'So without any more delay, first on the Arches stage tonight, all the way from Forest Hill in south east London, is Soulful Sonia!'

The crowd stood up, clapped and cheered as if Muhammad Ali,

Nelson Mandela and Bob Marley was in the house. Meanwhile, I wondered if I knew anyone who lived in Forest Hill... Nope, I didn't. Forest Hill is *the* most boring place in the whole of South London and if any cool people did live there they would never admit it... As the bird shit drops, Forest Hill is only about six or seven miles away from Bricky but I've never heard in my entire life of anybody going to a party, a rave, a drink up, a wine bar, to wok a girl, to shot some skunk or to buy some garms in Forest Hill.

Anyway, this tall black chick climbed onto the stage. She looked like Eryka Badu after a very generous dinner. You guessed it. She was wearing a Nefertiti head-wrap, robes, bangles and cheapo necklaces with crosses and ankhs hanging from them.

She gazed at the crowd and then she sort of hugged herself before closing her eyes... I had the vibe that something seriously fucked up was about to happen. Then Soulful Sonia started to go on like one of them black women who are receiving the spirit in one of them fucked-up churches. Her head started shaking and I half expected her to froth at the mouth and give birth like John Hurt in *Alien*. Trust me, it was hard not to fall off my chair in hysterics. Everyone around me was taking this shit serious, including the few Muslim brothers at the back and that was surprising 'cos usually they have no time for women doing their shit.

'I want you all to embrace your Africanness,' Soulful Sonia urged, her eyes still closed, her head still rocking.

Then the audience proceeded to hug itself. I was amazed. Even Akeisha was doing this shit... I nudged her. 'Akeisha, that tall chick is crazy, man. The sister needs some serious counselling. I ain't doing her shit, man. I'm not on it. I ain't feeling this at all. She's probably got issues about her mother not rocking her to sleep when she was a baby. Are all the acts psychologically fucked up?'

Akeisha chuckled. 'No, Dennis, and you don't have to do what she says... Just relax, I'm sure there will be an act that you might like later on.'

'Is this crane-legged chick gonna tell us all to start playing with ourselves next?'

'*Don't* be flippant, Dennis.'

'I'm kinda peckish, Akeisha. Do you mind if I step out and get something to eat?'

'No, course not. Feel free.'

'I'm gonna get some hot brutal chicken wings, do you want any?'

'No thanks. Dennis, keep your voice down.'

I started to resent paying the brother at the gate five notes for this show. I looked up to the stage and Soulful Sonia now had her eyes open and she was glaring at me. Burn Soulful Sonia! As I left I heard Akeisha giggling and I walked to the exit with a zip and a boing in my step. Maybe sex *was* a possibility after the show.

Deciding to eat my hot wings and fries outside the Arches I made sure I cleaned my fingers and mouth with the tissue provided. I then sprayed a little aftershave on my hands and dabbed my face before re-entering the poetry jam. To my relief Soulful Sonia had finished her fucked-up routine. As I returned to my seat I couldn't resist a laugh to myself as I wondered what would Tupac think of it all. The wafer-bread-dodging hostess returned to the stage as I took my seat. Akeisha smiled at me and asked, 'You alright? You might like the next act.'

'Yeah, sorry I had to go out but I just had to fill that hole. You know how it goes… What's the next act?'

'The next act? Oh, just the reason why I brought you here.'

'And now for your spiritual nourishment,' the fat chick announced. 'All the way from the Notre Dame estate in Clapham, we have the legendary Yardman Irie in the house tonight! Yardman Irie was the mic man for sound systems like Soferno B, Neville King, King Tubby and Crucial Rocker. But he's gonna chant for us tonight!'

I've heard of that name! He looked familiar. This Yardman guy had been inside my gates when Paps has his people around on boring Saturday nights.

Dressed in green army fatigues and black army boots, Yardman Irie took to the stage as the crowd whooped and hollered. His dreadlocks were tickling his backside and in his right hand he was carrying this trophy thing. It looked like a golden microphone…

He was followed onto the stage by this dread who was carrying a nyabinghi drum under his right arm. He looked like the kind of man who would eat you if you booed him. Yardman scanned the crowd and as he saw the Muslims at the back, he scowled... This might be interesting, I thought.

'I know the brother,' I nudged Akeisha. 'I know the brother! My paps is his brethren. He comes to my gates. He killed out the fried dumplings last time he came.'

'But have you heard him perform?' asked Akeisha.

'No, but I served him mango juice and snapper fish nuff times.'

To be honest when I used to see Yardman inside my gates I thought he was a brother down on his luck. His wardrobe was always well sad. He didn't wear Nikes, Adidas or even Reeboks.

'Greetings to each and everyone,' Yardman bellowed. 'May the Most High be with you.'

'And He with you,' the crowd responded, save the Muslims.

The dread started to lightly tap on his drum as Yardman held up his golden microphone thing for the crowd to see.

'I won this so-called award a couple of weeks ago in a poetry slam,' Yardman revealed. 'This slam was organised by a poetry performance agency that call themselves Sour Pears and Maggots. They're all white, nobody black on their fucking committee. They told me they would get me into the *right* places where I've never been. The *right* people will get to see me perform and they'll say I'm good. I'll be featured in the *right* magazines and be interviewed on the *right* radio stations... They thought I was stupid. I replaced *right* with *white*.'

Yardman paused and looked into the crowd with his fiery eyes. I reckoned he smoked a massive head before he bounded onto the stage. The tension cranked up and I wondered how the white people in the audience were feeling. It was getting interesting.

'But you know what?' Yardman continued. 'My mother thinks I'm good. My brothers think I'm good and my sisters think I'm good. I DON'T *NEED* NO RAAS VALIDATION FROM ANY WHITE MAN. SO *BURN* THEM AND *BURN* MY TEMPORARY VANITY!'

From his trouser pocket, Yardman took out a lighter, clicked it and showed the flame to the crowd. To loud cheers he placed the lighter under the golden microphone. The thing refused to catch alight but now everyone was on their feet with their arms aloft in a clenched fist salute, even some obviously confused white people did this. I began to feel the vibe as the drummer increased the tempo. Akeisha started to nod her head as Yardman prepared to deliver his sermon. Before he began chanting, he threw the microphone thing over his shoulder. He then stood with his arms spread wide apart, imitating a cross. I've seen Michael Jackson do this shit but it seemed more real with Yardman doing it. He then burst into song, well, more like a chant. His voice easily filled the room.

'Purify your heart clean
I beg you give it up
Give up your heart to Jah Kingdom
Don't you know that you are the children of the Negus.

Too many youths simmering in the ghetto
They don't know which way to turn
As the government puts them on go-slow
Programmed by dumb programmes.

By the age of thirteen
They start selling the grammes.
Nobody to teach them how to be a man
How macho they can be is their only plan.

As I look across the Brixton skyline
Once there were schools
Now expensive flats are designed.

Many victories have been fought and won
But the racists out there are still not done
Too many glass ceilings for my black people
They are put in place by the high officials.

Too many black brothers opting out of the system
For they only see blatant discrimination.

Not too many will pass their examinations in June
They don't even have the attention span to watch a cartoon
So many young brothers on the quick-march to their ruin
Wearing big Nike trainers and their gunshot wounds.

Too many black brothers in institutions
Forgetting who they are and where they come from.
Now we have the black politicians
But all them worry about is their rich pension plans.

Too many brothers refuse to have Jah in their lives
Others fill the gap and they're telling pure lies.
The crescent moon is getting dangerous and stronger
But resist the hype you Lion of Judah follower.

So purify your heart clean
I beg you give it up
Give up your heart to Jah Kingdom
Don't you know that you are the children of the Negus.'

The crowd was in a frenzy as Yardman punched the air and kept the pose of a clenched fist... At the back the few Muslims who were there were incensed but their shouts of *'Kaffur! Kaffur!'* were drowned out by the cheering and applause... I nudged Akeisha, 'You know what them Muslims are saying?' I asked.

'No,' Akeisha admitted. 'What does kaffur mean?'

'Unbeliever,' I revealed.

As we swivelled around to look behind us we spotted a number of Muslims cursing as they departed the poetry jam.

'Yardman is not exactly PC, is he, Akeisha,' I remarked. 'All that crescent moon is getting dangerous shit. He certainly fucked off the messy beard crew.'

'He's taking a stand,' explained Akeisha. 'Haven't you heard that black Christian kids are being threatened by Muslim kids in schools?'

'What? No, I don't believe that. That's what them scaremongers say. The Muslim thing is just a tiny thing in Bricky. There are a few black brothers who wanna play the rebel 'cos they can't get no girl and shit… That's all. It will never take hold and it will soon blow over.'

'I wish it was that simple,' said Akeisha. 'Six months ago you would never see a Muslim brother at a poetry jam but we've just seen about five of them step from here tonight. Have you seen all those brothers trying to get into that mosque in Gresham Road? I'm telling you, Dennis, it's no fashion thing. It's here to stay. Some black girls I went school with are now wearing long garms and covering their faces. Now they bitch to me about how their new men treat them. They're too scared to confront them themselves. In my opinion for women Islam's a subservient religion. Christianity and Rastafari will no longer be the dominant faith in Bricky, Dennis…'

Because the rest of the show was so bad, Akeisha and myself argued the Muslim issue until we left the place. It felt good to talk about serious issues with an intelligent sister. We even discussed the crusades and how Saladin kicked the butts of the Christians.

'It's worrying, Dennis,' Akeisha continued the religious theme. 'So few young people go to my church. And my mum, who's always had a thing for rasta, says you don't see the red, gold and green of Rastafari all that often these days. Brothers and sisters of our age don't wear them colours proudly like our parents did.'

'What do you expect, Akeisha? Bricky used to be controlled by West Indian people, they had it under a serious lock. And with them they brought their beliefs and the church. And in that community in my paps' time you had that generational conflict with Rastafari and the church. But at least that conflict was with basically the same religion. Now, Bricky is slowly turning African. And most of Africa is Muslim… So you're gonna see your Mosques and these things rise up. They're gonna fill the vacuum.'

'But I don't like it,' said Akeisha. 'I can accept most of it but some of it is bad-mind. Look how Christian kids are being bullied at school.'

'People are just making elephant shit out of rat piss, exaggerating all the while... Maybe those kids weren't even Muslim at all but pretending.'

'That's my point, Dennis. That's why it's so worrying... Why would black kids with West Indian grandparents go around pretending they're Muslims and threaten other kids?'

I couldn't answer that one.

We walked along Bricky High Street talking about some aspect of Caribbean history. I can't really recall what aspect of history we were discussing but what I do remember is how good I felt walking with Akeisha. *Look and shed tears, motherfuckers...*

Reaching her gates at 11 30 p.m. I was relieved that there was no sign of Myrna. I parked myself on the black couch in the lounge as Akeisha went to a bedroom to check on her son, Curtis. In those moments when I was waiting for Akeisha to return, I was looking forward to wild sex like that Tommy Lee guy and Pamela Anderson on their bling boat. I closed my eyes and visualised Akeisha naked. She had toned thighs, generous breasts and her eyes were begging with me.

She returned and she had taken her hat and leather jacket off to reveal a tight-fitting white crew-neck pullover and her hair pulled back in a ponytail. It improved the look of her perfect cheekbones. 'Would you like a drink, Dennis? We haven't got much alcohol but there is still some of Paps' Jamaican rum, but I can't imagine you drinking that, Dennis?'

Jamaican rum? If I was with the brothers I would have gladly drained the fire-water but I was with Akeisha. 'Jamaican rum?' I said. 'That drink messes up your kidneys, man. No, I don't drink that. A coffee will be cool. Two sugars, brown sugar if you have it and a little bit of milk.'

I didn't normally take brown sugar with my coffee but I thought it was kinda cultured and classy to ask for it.

Sitting on the couch I couldn't see Akeisha. I heard her tinkering in the kitchen and I just had a sudden urge to go to her. So I got up and made my way to the kitchen. My heartbeat started to sprint and my forehead suddenly felt warm. Lust filled the rest of me. The kitchen was small but everything was neat and fitted... There was a washing machine and the fridge was taller than me. The fitted cupboards were clean and paint-advert white. A Flash kinda cleaning smell got up my nostrils...

Akeisha was filling the kettle with water and she had already placed two mugs on the side... I walked up behind her wanting to kiss her. She turned around. 'Dennis, you scared me. What is it? You want something to eat as well?'

Instead of answering her I lunged forward and kissed her hard on the mouth. At the same time I squeezed her left breast with my right hand and I placed my left hand over her crotch. Akeisha pulled away her face, backed off and with a mighty swing of her right fist, punched me slap bang on the nose. 'WHAT DO YOU THINK?' She checked herself and lowered her voice. 'What do you think you're fucking doing, Dennis?'

Dazed, I reeled back, covering my face with my hands. My eyes began to water but as I re-focused I saw Akeisha looking at me with disgust. I think she busted my nose...

'I'm proper sorry, Akeisha,' I apologised. 'Shit. I didn't mean to do that. I got caught up in the vibe of the night. Proper sorry, for real. *Believe* me, man. Trust! It won't happen again...'

'You're fucking right there!'

'I didn't know what I was thinking, Akeisha. *Damn!* I just thought... I fucked things up, haven't I? I just thought. Proper sorry, man.'

Shit! Was I in pain! Couldn't let her know though.

'That you could taste some pussy tonight,' Akeisha finished the sentence for me. 'All because I have one child it doesn't mean I'm some kind of skettel or ho on road. You understand, Dennis?'

'Yeah, yeah, I understand. I'm so sorry I disrespected you.'

'I just didn't expect you to be like that, Dennis. I was just thinking that you know so much about things and life and history. You've just spent the last half an hour giving me a lesson in Jamaican history. And now *this*! I thought you was different from the rest, Dennis. But you're just like the other brothers in Angel Town and Bricky, just looking for a wok and don't care how you get it or about the consequences.'

'I am different, Akeisha. Trust me, I am different.'

'I think you'd better leave.'

'Can I make it up to you next week? Let me take you out for a proper dinner.'

'Just leave, Dennis. I'm tired and I want to go to my bed.'

'I'll call you. You will pick up, won't you?'

'Dennis! Go home.'

'Akeisha, I am proper sorry. You must believe that. You will pick up when I call you?'

'I have to think about that.'

'Don't kill me for one mistake, Akeisha.'

'This conversation is *over.*'

'*Akeisha!*'

'Remove yourself from my house, man!'

She then marched to the front door and opened it for me. Did I feel like shit. Slowly I walked out of her flat and I heard the door slam behind me. I was feeling too ashamed to turn around. I'm not sure how I got home that night but when my head hit the pillow I was still cursing myself. She was right, from an articulate young brother I had turned into a sex fiend. How the fuck am I gonna win her back?

Chapter Thirteen

THE GIFT

It was a long time until I saw Akeisha in the flesh again. Following the night of the poetry jam she didn't pick up or return my calls for five weeks. I sent her a Christmas card and I wrote 'sorry' all over it. I even drew little red hearts all over it… But she still wouldn't agree to see me. At times I felt like going around to her gates and demanding to see her but I knew if I did that then I might fuck everything up. I couldn't bear to think that she might never want to see my black behind again. We did start to have long chats on the phone but this made me even more frustrated in not seeing her. I took to spying on her on a few occasions as she left her flat in the morning. Fuck! Was I obsessed.

I wrote her a long letter, telling her that I behaved like a damn fool and the groping shit would never happen again. I told her that if I had to wait two months or two years for her then so be it. I won't even consider linking with any other girls. I told her that I want us to be like my parents, who still love and care for each other after twenty odd years. I delivered the letter myself at some bitch time in the morning. After that I prayed like the way black people pray in the deep south.

That Christmas Eve Noel took me out to a party to try and cheer up my sad ass. I didn't even look at the bitches there. Didn't even have a drink or eat any roast chicken wings. Noel got himself drunk up so I had to drive home. It was about 4 in the morning when Noel saw Santa Claus staggering up Tulse Hill. Santa Claus was obviously drunk, singing his yo ho ho shit and he was wearing all the right garms that stupid children like. I guessed he was making his way back from a party but Noel had a long hard stare at him and switched.

'Stop the motherfucking ride,' he said.

I did as I was told and suddenly Noel leaped out of the car and started to sprint towards Father Christmas. I got out and followed him but I wasn't quick enough to stop the beating. Noel pounded the fuck out of Father Christmas, shouting, 'My mum always said I had to pray for your fat white ass! Pray to Father Christmas and he'll come in the night to give you shit! Well, I didn't get shit! Never got shit! You know how much I wanted a motherfucking Game Boy one year! Give me your fucking money, you pussyhole!'

Noel jacked Father Christmas's wallet, his black belt and his hat and I was just glad to get him back inside the ride before the Feds come. *Shit!* Only in Bricky...

My bad mood stayed with me all through the Christmas holidays and after that.

I was getting proper depressed and I needed to chat to somebody about this 'cos it was fucking my head up. Paps was out of the question 'cos he would offer his advice while giving me a fucked-up lecture that would last for hours. I was too embarrassed to reveal my chick problems to Mum and she would say shit like 'My little boy's in love! How sweet!' So Mum was out of the question. Davinia would probably know all the answers to my problems and what I should do about it, but she would be too fucking smug with it. And I wasn't feeling that so burn Davinia. So I ended up chatting to Noel about my Akeisha situation. I told him everything, even the groping shit in Akeisha's kitchen. He laughed like a D-list celeb on a chat show.

Noel thought I was crazy to still chase Akeisha and he tried to set me up a few times with ghetto chicks he knew. I was not on that and I told these girls that I wasn't feeling no bitch who's never heard of Marcus Garvey or Angela Davis. That was an excuse though. Basically, they were intellectually and physically light years away from how Akeisha was and in my world nobody else came close and nobody else would do. Simple as.

It was a bitch cold February night in 2001 when I was in the passenger seat of Noel's ride. I was thinking that Akeisha's baby, Curtis, was now a year old. Akeisha herself was gonna be twenty later on in the year and soon I'd be eighteen.

The heater in Noel's ride wasn't working and that just bottomed off my downer neatly 'cos I had asked Akeisha if I could take her out on Valentine's Day and she gave me an automatic *no*. What fucked me off is the way she said no. It was blatantly brutal, the kind of no you would get from a male Jamaican dancehall artist if you asked him if he would consider sleeping with a man. Not even a moment's thought. *No!* She then finished the call with the classic 'I'm really busy so I gotta go' line. What she really was saying is that she's fucked off with my pleading, begging and shit. I tried to blast the rejection out of my mind but it hung around like a dog shit in a hard-to-find corner of Brockwell Park.

Noel and myself were on our way to collect a debt when Noel decided to run his gums on the Akeisha situation and my non-existent sex life. As always, Noel's girlfriend, Priscilla Lane, was in the back seat. She was bopping her head to some Mary J. Blige tune in that ghetto way of hers while burning a cigarette. At least the smoke made the car feel a tiny bit warm.

'What's a matter with you, bruv?' Noel asked. 'All because one bitch doesn't like you grabbing her crotch you're going on like a baby! Akeisha ain't feeling you, man. Get over it. You flopped... You messed it up when you made a peckish grope for her pussy. For some reason the bitch made you into a fucked-up sex fiend. You're the Gary Glitter of Bricky, bruv. You should have neon signs on your motherfucking pervert ass so chicks know not to approach you. Shit happens like that when a man worships a pussy of a classical standard.'

Noel said this all with a straight face. But what else could I expect? This was Noel. He continued. 'And I can imagine you building a motherfucking altar for the pussy Akeisha's got. What's so fucking special about her anyway? Yeah, she's got a decent face but she's a bit on the slim side. Slim girls might be OK for woking in a world of positions 'cos they're proper portable in a telephone box, but a man needs a pair of breasts to sleep on when he's done. He needs to feel some Beyoncé-like curves of heat when it's a bitch cold night. You get me? That Akeisha bitch couldn't keep a dwarf warm in a sauna, bruv. She's too damn skinny. She has to dance like James Brown in the shower to get herself wet... Shit! Weren't James Brown a perv too?'

'Yeah he was, Noel,' Priscilla cut in. 'Or was it Chuck Berry?'

This was so embarrassing with Priscilla in the back, taking all this shit in. I could hardly tell Noel to shut the fuck up. After all, I did tell him everything and this was his way of being a 'best bredren'. He was taking this agony uncle thing seriously.

'It's about time you woked a next bitch and you'd better do it quick 'cos if I go for a long time without woking a bitch then the next one that comes along I shoot my juices too rapid and can't perform proper... That's how men are. We gotta wok regular to perform proper. Trust me on this. Ain't that so, Priscilla?'

'He ain't lying,' nodded Priscilla, looking as serious as a BBC newsreader.

'Course I ain't lying,' said Noel. 'Listen to a man who's woked a world of girls in his time.'

Only Noel could say something like that in front of his present partner. But at the end of the day, I wanted Akeisha. I didn't want no dumb ass ghetto chick who had never heard of Constantinople, Saladin and Paul Bogle.

'And even if you did get to wok Akeisha,' Noel continued, 'she would have you under lock, bruv. You'd do anything for that Akeisha bitch... The way you go on anybody would think her piss is Frog perfume, bruv. It ain't healthy.'

'Not anything,' I argued.

'Stop lying, bruv! If she asked you to buy her period shit at the chemist or somewhere you would go if you was promised a wok. And she would definitely make you buy your own condoms.'

'What's wrong with buying a girl her tampons or getting your own condoms?'

'Everything, bruv. It means she has you under some big bitch piece of medieval lock... You know it! This Akeisha bitch has got you locked down and you ain't even woked it yet! What's a matter with you, bruv? A stush girl has turned you into a pussy. Them kinda black girls always end up with white brothers anyway. Them kinda black bitches like all that wining-and-dining-being-a-gentleman-opening a door shit. *Fuck that!*'

When inspired Noel could go on like this for hours. One of these days I'm gonna tape one of his rants and try and sell it as a radio play. He went on. 'They make you spend nuff dollars on them before you even get to stroke a toe, bruv. And they *don't* even consider linking with a brother if he ain't earning more than her. If you weren't shotting or working with your uncle Everton there won't be too many girls who would want to wok your black ass. Trust me on this. If you wanna get to first base with them bitches you have to chat about what kinda schools will your children go to when you're just dating and shit. Fuck that shit! You might as well go Upper Tulse Hill and pay for one of them east European hos for a wok. I hear that they're so desperate they even take a fiver for a BJ. A brother I know takes some Kentucky clean wipes with him and he says to the hos they gotta clean their lips first before they give him a BJ. I'm feeling that 'cos it's cheaper than taking some bitch out for a double bitch vodka and a Red Bull and all they can talk about is fucking *EastEnders*.'

'I hear what you're saying, Noel, but will you stop calling Akeisha a bitch...'

'Hasn't she got a pussy? That's what she is, ain't she? If it makes you feel better I'll call her a Honey Thumby. In other words she lets you smell the honey but she won't let you dip your thumb in it. She's a cock sore, bruv, a prick tease. Men have choked their bishops so much 'cos of chicks like Akeisha that their dicks fall off. Trust me on this. You'd better drop that bitch before she sends you crazy...'

'I think it's sweet that Dennis really likes this Akeisha girl,' Priscilla remarked. 'At least he ain't like them fuck-a-bush ghetto man who wok anything if it ain't menstruating or crippled. At least he's focusing on just the *one* girl. Not like some *man* I know.'

'Who asked you to speak?' snapped Noel. 'Who even asked you in the ride? You can't see this is a *man's* conversation? And nobody invited you in it. So shut the fuck up and keep your Bricky fish market mouth under lock.'

'Who are you talking to like that? I'm getting fucked off with the way you chat to me, Noel. Carry on and the only pussy you will get tonight is the motherfucking tom looking for scraps in them big council rubbish bins! Talk to me proper with respect, man. I ain't no fucking muppet! I'm your girl.'

'Three things,' Noel said. 'First of all, you are a proper living motherfucking muppet. Secondly, I have never, ever, in any way or form, referred to you as *my* girl and, Priscilla, I ain't like Dennis and go on like a pussy when I have a scent of crotches. I don't give a fuck if you don't spread your pins for me tonight. I will just go to the snooker hall and play some pool with the white brothers. Make some P's while I'm doing it too. Them white brothers love off the hardcore skunk and they always pay over the odds. Then I'll go and wok a white bitch I know. Then I'll sleep 'til afternoon 'cos I don't do shit in the mornings. Simple as. With a white chick a black man don't have to work too hard for the pussy. You just find a white bitch with a Croydon facelift, bring the liquor, bring some skunk, they sample it and they wanna wok your black ass off all night. Simple as.'

'Wok a white bitch and you can chant farewell to my crotches,' Priscilla retaliated, doing her head moving thing as the neck and shoulders kept still. 'In fact, have you been woking any white girls, Noel? Tell me the fuck now! 'Cos if you have I'm stepping out of this ride and your sad fucking Jerry Springer life! Have you woked any white bitches, Noel?'

'Course I haven't, Priscilla,' Noel answered, putting on his soft voice. 'I'm just winding you up. You know how it is. I just want Dennis to get some sex. Any sex. He needs it. The brother's gonna froth like Muttley soon. You know it!'

I still found it hard to believe that Noel and Priscilla had ever knocked the boots.

We pulled up in a council estate somewhere behind Stockwell tube station and close to the Wandsworth Road. A bitching breeze was picking up and I kept my hands in my pockets...

'So, whose money are we collecting?' I asked.

'Nathan,' Noel answered. 'Nathan Taylor. The brother owes me a hundred and seventy pounds. He said he's gonna pay me tonight. He better pay me tonight or I'm gonna give him a pounding.'

'How did he get to owe you a hundred and seventy pounds? That's unlike you, Noel. You're slipping.'

'I felt sorry for the brother 'cos his older brother joined the Feds. It brutally fucked up his road cred. He can't walk on road anywhere without man shouting *Five-O* or *The Bill* after his black ass. Man on road won't take him seriously if he tries to shot his skunk. They just laugh and whistle *The Bill* theme tune. It proper fucks Nathan off. Although his paps never lived with the family I hear he's proper gutted about his oldest son joining the Feds too. The family's going through a shit time so I kept on giving the brother free eighths when he was waiting for his P's at the end of every month. He works on the twilight shift on the bakery section in Sainsbury's... He usually paid me when he said he would but I haven't seen no P's from the brother for six weeks. So, Dennis, get your psycho face on, let go of some of that sentimental shit you always carry with you 'cos we might have to pound a brother tonight.'

'Shouldn't Priscilla stay in the ride?' I suggested.

'I ain't staying in no ride!' Priscilla complained. 'Look how fucking cold it is and this is the estate where the government secretly put bare perverts and paedophiles in! No, man, I'm coming with you. Burn this under-lit car park.'

I looked at Noel, 'I don't really give a fuck whether she comes or not,' Noel said. 'As long as Nathan gives me my P's.'

We went to one of those tower blocks that architects in the 1960s thought was a cool idea... As usual the lift stank of piss and other shit that I couldn't describe... We got out at the thirteenth floor and the wire-meshed windows gave us a neat view of Stockwell and the surrounding ends all the way to the Thames. There were eight flats on each floor and Noel wasted no time in knocking the letter box of one of them. After a while, Nathan appeared. He was a skinny brother with what seemed a permanent look of panic on his face. Seeing Noel, he quickly closed the door behind him, making sure whoever was inside the flat didn't see or hear what was happening.

'Where's my P's?' Noel barked.

'Yeah, where's my man's money,' Priscilla repeated. 'You're messing with *my* man's money and I ain't feeling that.'

Noel turned to face Priscilla and I wondered if I would have to dive in to stop him from pounding her. 'Squeak again and your feet are gonna get their groove on with concrete and pavement,' Noel warned. 'Believe it!'

Returning his attention to Nathan, Noel said, 'I'm gonna ask you one more time. I ain't gonna shout, I'm gonna be calm. Understand these lyrics. You done English at school and by all accounts the subject wasn't as difficult for you as it was for the rest of us. *Where's my P's?*'

Scared as fuck, Nathan stood with his back pressed against his front door. His mouth was open but no words came out. Why did he close the door behind him? I wondered... He glanced to his left and then to his right. Still no reply. Sweat appeared on his forehead. Noel slowly walked up to him, Lee Van Cleef-like. His eyes bored into Nathan's face, never blinking. This shit was even scary for me. Priscilla was proper liking the vibe of it all, shifting her weight from foot to foot, her eyes alive in anticipation like one of them rich white people sitting ringside at a world heavyweight title fight.

'Where's my P's?'

'Just give me two more days, trust me! It's gonna come all good. Don't worry about nothing. You know me, Noel, have I ever let you down? I've always showed you love, bruv. Can't we just reason about this like two proper bredrens? You know how it goes when someone fucks up. Well, someone has fucked up with my money but it's coming in two days. If you can just—'

Noel hit Nathan with a perfect right hook. He went down slowly 'cos his back was kinda supported by the door. Priscilla's eyes grew big. Just as Noel was preparing to boot Nathan's back with his Nike-covered right foot, I stepped in to stop the beating. 'Not outside his gates,' I said. 'His mum might come out.'

'Then tell the brother to get my fucking money!'

I helped Nathan to his feet. 'Can't you give him something?' I asked. 'Just give him a gesture for now 'cos if my man wants to pound someone I can hardly stop him, bruv.'

Nathan, caressing his left cheek, thought about it.

'Yeah,' shouted Noel. 'Give me a gesture. A twenty pound gesture... Just to save your pounding.'

'I dunno if I can ask my mum,' said Nathan, almost in tears.

'NATHAN IS GAY!' Noel suddenly began to yell. 'NATHAN IS GAY! NATHAN IS GAY! NATHAN IS GAY!'

If it wasn't so surreal I would have collapsed in laughter. But Priscilla proper lost her composure and she was on the floor in stitches as Noel's chant echoed around the thirteenth floor.

'To stop him you're gonna have to get that gesture,' I told Nathan.

Nathan ran inside as Noel continued his shouting. 'NATHAN IS GAY! NATHAN IS GAY!'

A brother emerged from another flat, took a look and decided to go back inside. Noel, not giving a shit, kept on chanting.

'NATHAN IS GAY! NATHAN IS GAY!'

Moments later, Nathan appeared holding a twenty pound note. He quickly gave it to Noel... The right side of his face was now swelling. Noel snatched the money and stopped his chanting. He had this fucked-up grin on his face. He then, Michael Corleone-like, walked over to Priscilla, tossed the twenty pound note at her and said, 'Now you can stop asking me to use my mobile. Put some fucking credit on your own motherfucking mobile!'

Priscilla picked up the money from the ground, put it inside her handbag and chose not to reply.

We went back to the ride and I realised why I just had to be around someone like Noel. He was unpredictable, spontaneous and crazy. All the things I wasn't. I could see why Priscilla didn't give a fuck about Noel's floozies... She must have assured herself that at least she's the only one who gets to sit in his ride and as far as

I knew she was. I had yet to see Noel be polite to any girl but they wanted to be with him, wanted to be around. None of these chicks were in Akeisha's class but I guess there wasn't no other bitch in her class.

'Why did you come up with the "Nathan is gay" chanting shit?' I asked Noel.

Keeping his eyes on the road, Noel replied, 'My mum has this saying. *The squeakiest hinge gets the oil.* Capish?'

'Yeah, I comprehend,' I nodded, thinking that despite Noel's ghetto mentality there was something poetic about him.

Noel dropped me off outside my gates when my mobile rang. It was Akeisha. She hardly ever called me, it was always me calling her. I felt my heart thump as I answered my phone.

'Hello, Akeisha. Didn't expect you to call me at this time of night.'

'I was thinking about your proposal,' she said. 'And I re-read your long letter.'

'Oh yeah. Have you changed your mind?'

'Sort of.'

'What you mean, sort of?'

'I think dinner is a good idea. Did you really mean a proper restaurant? No hot chicken takeaway on Bricky High Street?'

Was this happening? Did she just say that?

'Of course I meant a proper restaurant! You sure about this? You're not playing me?'

'I wouldn't do that, Dennis.'

'So Scoffers it is.'

'Where is it?' Akeisha asked.

'Eccles Road that is just off Battersea Rise. A number 35 or 37 drops you right outside. You see, Akeisha, I'm a brother that can take a girl places. So what in the letter changed your mind?'

'That bit about your parents. It was sweet. Also, I kinda got used to chatting to you every night on the phone so chatting over dinner is not too different to that. Besides, I want to see you again. You've learned your lesson.'

'You really want to see me again?'

'As long as you don't get carried away the minute you see me.'

'I won't, Akeisha. Trust me!'

'It's alright, I trust you.'

'Valentine's Day is on the Wednesday, shall we go for our munchies on the Friday?'

'Yeah, a good idea. But, Dennis, I'm paying half.'

'Don't worry about it, I've got it covered. You don't have to do that.'

'No, Dennis, I can pay my way.'

'You sure?'

'Yes, I'm sure. What time you gonna pick me up?'

'About seven.'

'Oh and make sure you shave off your stubble.'

'What's wrong with my stubble?'

'Too prickly. I like a smooth man.'

'But you've never… OK, it's definitely coming off. It'll be smooth like a Harrods chocolate mousse.'

'Your training has started well!'

'You know I'm on you in a big way, Akeisha. I would even do that Jewish shit if you asked me to. You know, the snip thing. They say it's cleaner, all hygienic and shit.'

'That won't be necessary, Dennis.'

'I'm really looking forward to this, Akeisha. I'm gonna show you I can be a gentleman.'

'I'm looking forward to it too, Dennis, but bring yourself, not the gentleman… I'll see you Friday. Don't be late.'

'Bye.'

She ended the call. Was she kidding? Don't be late? I'll probably be two hours early.

I entered my house with a bounce in my step and as I bounded up the stairs I met Davinia on the landing. She had come out of her room and was on the way to the toilet. 'Evening, baby sis. How was your day? Good I hope.'

I then bear-hugged Davinia and wouldn't let her go until I gave her a noisy sort of kiss upon the forehead. She kicked me twice in the leg but I simply didn't care. After I let her go she looked at me like I was crazy and then she said, 'Akeisha agreed to go out with you then? This is all good, it'll cheer you up. Might make you stop moping around the house feeling sorry for yourself. We was getting worried.'

Burn Davinia! Too damn clever for her own good.

My head hit the pillow that night with a satisfied sigh. Then I thought I'll have to get her a present. Something to remember me by. Yeah, a Valentine's Day gift that she'll never forget. There was no way I could return her wooden bracelet to her after all this time but maybe I could buy some kinda replacement... Yeah, something for her wrist. A gold bracelet. Yeah, no High Street, nine carat, white trash black single-mother ghetto shit. The proper bling. Sixteen carat gold from Hatton Garden has to go on Akeisha's wrist. Or maybe even twenty-four. No other shit will do. I'll ask Everton if I can have Friday afternoon off so I can go up West and buy it. Everton was good like that, as long as I put in the hours later on in the week. He was now paying me nearly eight notes an hour and wanted me to go to college. I said I'd think about it. But damn! I can't wait to see the look on Akeisha's face when she sees what I'm gonna get her. She might even kiss me for it.

Chapter Forteen

THE DATE

I was seriously thinking of wearing a suit for my date with Akeisha but Davinia talked me out of it. She reckoned that I would look too desperate to impress. I thought about it and she weren't wrong. So I wore a pair of black shoes, blue slacks, cream-coloured shirt and my black leather jacket. Earlier, I received a neat trim from my barber at his salon in Lavender Hill and when I looked into my bedroom mirror before I left my gates, I reckoned I looked wokable enough even for daughters of BNP members to shout an interest.

Calling for Akeisha at 6 40 p.m., I made sure I had my gift safely tucked away in the inside pocket of my leather jacket. The sixteen carat gold bracelet was inside one of the cutest little velvety boxes I had ever seen. It cost me over nine hundred pounds in a jeweller's off Chancery Lane where you had to have proof of ID before they allowed you inside the shop. All eyes were on me as I browsed around looking for what I wanted and I'm sure they thought I was scouting the place for a possible grab and run. Anyway, the stush assistants behind the counter were happy enough when I finally paid cash. I could easily afford it. I was making two hundred notes, sometimes three hundred notes a week shotting on top of what I was earning from Everton.

Wearing black slacks, a black crew-neck sweater and a light-brown suede jacket, Akeisha looked a dream. As I was checking her out she caught me unawares by kissing me on the cheek. 'Hi, Dennis,' she said. 'Good to see you after so long. You look well! Very smart. And you got rid of your stubble! You don't have to do everything I say.'

I wanted to say that if she asked me to clean a ghetto sewage drain with a fucked-up toothbrush, I would gladly do it. But I checked myself, remembering Davinia's *don't try to impress too much* shit.

Akeisha explained that her mother, Myrna, was out visiting relatives with Curtis so we had the evening and the night to ourselves. I tried not to think about the possibility of sex. For a moment I wished I'd proposed that I'd bring a bottle of champagne around while she cooked something. The black settee looked so like it was ready for rampant sex. It was comfy and long enough to neatly fit us both. Her legs would look so good if they dangled over the armrest. Damn! Can't think about that. Remember, you're a gentleman, not a perv... Focus, Dennis. Concentrate. Rid the image of a naked Akeisha laying on the settee saying, 'Come here, big boy.' I had to shake my head.

As we stepped out I felt like a road-sweeper going to a film premiere with Angelina Jolie... Of course I insisted on a cab. No fucking 37 or 35 bus for my queen.

Mum and Paps dined at Scoffers for their wedding anniversary last year and Paps said that Mum never complained once about the food, wine and most of all, the service. The place had to be good and to be honest I had fuck all experience of anywhere else save the spicy chicken takeaway in Bricky High Street.

We sat around a candlelit table with a neat white cloth and as Akeisha was sampling her meal of lamb, baby potatoes, mint sauce and veg, I was staring at the candle reflection in her eyes. I was seriously overawed. If Noel had witnessed this he would've slapped me on the back of the head and told me to stop going on like a pussy... But I couldn't help it. We didn't speak much while eating our dinner, I think we both felt a little awkward seeing one another again after a break but her little smiles and glances gave me confidence.

It was when our dessert of rich chocolate sponge and ice cream was served that I decided to present my gift. Earlier, I had tried to wrap it up with last Christmas's wrapping paper but after about ten attempts and my bin overflowing with paper, Davinia decided to help me out. No need to say she done a wicked job. She even tied a cute red bow around it. If Noel saw it he would have gave me a right hook and booted my balls from Bricky to Brick Lane.

'My Valentine's Day gift,' I said, all proud like. Other diners turned around to look at us and they smiled. I bet they wouldn't have smiled if they knew I was a shotta. Burn them.

Before she accepted it she gave me a cautious look. I'm sure she was about to protest but she checked herself, looked around and instead offered me a sweet smile… As she unwrapped my present I never blinked. I felt all good. She opened the velvet box and there it was, the gold bracelet, all nine hundred and ninety pound's worth. It wasn't chunky or blingy, like what ghetto people normally wear, but lady-like and elegant. The candle light glinted off the surface of the bracelet and onto Akeisha's face. For a moment, she held it within her hands, not quite believing what I had given her. She then half stood up, leant towards me and kissed me on the mouth. No tongues but on the *mouth*. She even closed her eyes for a split second. I wanted so much to sample her right then but I had to keep control. Mentally, I kicked the settee image of her naked toned legs out of my mind. It wasn't easy.

'I'm—I'm stunned, Dennis. I really didn't expect this… Thanks so much, Dennis. I hope it didn't cost too much? You didn't spend too much, did you?'

I don't think she realised it was sixteen carat. But the look on her face told me that the nine hundred and ninety pounds I had shelled out was worth it.

'And I have something for you, Dennis,' she said. 'Only a card though.'

She went to her handbag and took out an envelope. It was about the size of a DVD case but to think that she went out of her way to buy it especially for me made me feel all tingly-like. She gave me her gift and I saw that it wasn't sealed. I took out the card in an instant, wanting to see what she had written. *To Dennis, the main contender to my heart, perhaps the only contender.* I felt like dancing on the table but instead I returned the kiss. She pulled away after ten seconds and tried her bracelet on. I helped her with it, enjoying the smooth skin of her wrist and left hand. I gave her another kiss. It was kinda funny seeing Akeisha get embarrassed.

'It's funny,' she said.

'What's funny?'

'My mum gave me a bracelet when I was a girl. Nothing like this one, it was wooden… Hand-carved.'

I had to close my eyes for a second. I prayed that my guilt wouldn't show itself upon my face. Why didn't she forget about it? As she said, it was only wooden. She's got something much better now. *Burn* the wooden thing…

'It was given to her by this rastaman,' she went on. 'You might have heard of him, Jah Nelson. He was well known back in the day. He used to go around in his sandals and a walking stick.'

'Yeah, I've heard of him,' I nodded, almost leaping out of my chair… 'I even know him. He's a friend of my paps and mum. He was at their wedding. He blessed me when I was a baby!'

'Anyway, my mum was quite a rebel when she was young,' Akeisha continued, ignoring my name-dropping. 'She grew locks when she was sixteen years old and she was always out at reggae dances till the morning. My grandparents, being Seventh Day Adventists, couldn't tolerate that so they kicked her out. On a downer, Mum went to social services and they put her up in a hostel. It was while she was living there when she met Jah Nelson. Not sure of the details but they met on that march to protest about that fire in Deptford that killed nuff youths.'

'Jah Nelson used to come to my house,' I interrupted Akeisha. 'He used to give me and my sis lessons about black history and shit. He's my sort of godfather. Well, after the official church service he blessed me in his own way.'

I don't think Akeisha heard my last line because as I looked at her she was in deep thought, perhaps trying to put her memories in order so she could tell her tale… It was so frustrating 'cos I wanted to tell her *my* Jah Nelson memories… Better not tell her that he scared the fuck out of me with his missing eye.

'It wasn't a romantic thing with Jah Nelson and my mum, he was so much older than her,' she went on. 'But he counselled her, made her feel good, made her feel strong and proud. He carved her the wooden bracelet before he went away. To Africa I think. The day after she put it on for the first time, she met my paps. So Mum always felt that bracelet was special, almost mystical… She gave it to me when I was about eight. She thought it would offer me some kind of protection, some kinda good fortune. I never used to race without it. But I lost it while running at Tooting Bec track. At the time I didn't even realise it had come off. I was in a right state that day 'cos I know how much it meant to Mum. I didn't tell her for two days but she noticed in the end. She was well upset. Soon afterwards I had my bad leg injury… Mum put it down to me losing the bracelet. She even went to Tooting Bec track to see if it was still there.'

While Akeisha was telling this story my insides were spinning with guilt. How could I ever give it back now? She would see me as bad-mind. I wondered how long she would refuse to see me if she ever found out about it.

'Maybe this gold bracelet will give me the same protection and luck as the wooden one,' Akeisha smiled. 'It's beautiful. I hope you didn't spend too much on it, Dennis.'

She leaned over and kissed me again on the forehead. This time her lips lingered on my skin and a neat shock of pleasure electrified my whole body. Now wearing her gold bracelet, she ate her chocolate and ice cream with a teaspoon. There is something so sexy about buff women eating ice cream. I watched every bite, every swallow and every gulp. I couldn't believe she was with me. Why me? What was she doing with me? Why not somebody else who had a better job and better money? Well, maybe not the money, I had nuff P's.

We took a cab back to her place. Akeisha insisted that she should pay the fare. We didn't speak much. She held me by the hand as she led me to her room. It was like a proper zoo. There were cuddly toys all over the place. Tigers, leopards, frogs, bears, panthers, owls, ponies and even a few monkeys. She had a double bed and the animals took up most of the space on it. On one wall there was a poster of Mary J. Blige. On the opposite side was a pin-up of Marvin Gaye. She had three shelves fixed to another wall and they were full of accountancy text books and those self-help books that black women love so much. My mum has loads of them at home and I know they piss Paps off. They were all about finding the inner you and shit like that.

Beneath the shelves was Akeisha's computer and desk. Next to her mouse was a pair of those Chinese chiming balls. Mum has a pair and when she gets stressed out she twirls them around in the palm of her right hand. This pisses Paps off too 'cos every time they have an argument in the bedroom, Mum reaches for the Chinese balls.

Akeisha's video collection, piled up on her dressing table, was your normal American black coming-of-age shit like *House Party 1* and *House Party 2*. But her musical tastes were different to any other chick I knew. She had shit by Cab Calloway, Duke Ellington, Bessie Smith, Mahalia Jackson, Aretha Franklin, Ray Charles, Gladys Knight and Sam Cooke. My mum would sing that kind of thing on a Sunday morning while boiling the red kidney beans and it fucked everybody off.

Sitting down on the bed, I looked at the photos of Curtis that were all around the rim of her dressing table mirror. I wondered if one day he would call me *Daddy*... Would I make a good father? I will try not to lecture like Paps but I'll keep his education and books thing.

Akeisha took off her suede jacket and placed it in the wardrobe. 'Do you want a drink, Dennis?'

Want a drink! Is she crazy? Have a drink and delay making love. Is she kidding me?

'No thanks, Akeisha. That wine in the restaurant oiled me enough and to be honest it's making me kinda giddy.'

She smiled then walked over to her mini-stereo. She switched it on and pressed the play button... H-Town started singing a slow jam in that over-the-top way of theirs. Why is this happening to me? I asked myself. She then sat beside me and looked at me square on in such a way to make me uncomfortable. I remembered the groping incident in the kitchen. I placed my hands behind my back.

'Dennis, I'm feeling you but you must be yourself,' she said. 'You're very articulate when you wanna be. You're witty and clever and sometimes so cynical you make me laugh like crazy!'

She kissed me on the forehead. 'And you're persistent,' she laughed... 'My mum thought you was nuts the way you called every day and she saw you waiting outside my gates one morning.'

I returned the kiss upon her mouth but I still kept my hands to my side. 'All that got me you though, innit,' I managed.

She then placed her hands on my collarbone and smothered my face with kisses. 'But you gotta learn to transcend Brixton,' she kinda stuttered between kisses. 'Transcend the ghetto. You're not like the rest of them... You don't have to go on like them with their macho bullshit. You don't have to be a shotta to prove how much of a man you are. They haven't got anything else so they trade with their macho bullshit. You're *not* like them. You're different.'

Shocked, I pulled back from her. 'You know?'

'Of course I know! Bricky's a small place. I was bound to find out, Dennis... It's no big deal, Dennis. So you shot herb. So what? My mum smokes it. Nine out of ten people in Angel Town burn it. As long as you ain't shotting harder drugs I'm not gonna get all moral about it.'

We got back to our kissing and her last words seemed to free my hands and they started wandering. She didn't mind. 'It's just that you're better than that, Dennis,' she went on. 'Don't believe what the shitstem has planned for you. I heard you say once that your paps expected you to be a professor or something. You said you can't live up to that. Why not, Dennis? Listening to you makes me think you have all the potential in the world. *Don't* believe what *they* want you to believe.'

To be honest at this stage I was in no fit state to continue the conversation with Akeisha... Adrenaline and all sorts of other feelings were pumping through me and I almost tore her clothes off. She left me for a second to switch off the light and when we finally made love, I made sure that her face was pressed next to mine throughout... I just wanted the sensation of her warm breath blowing upon my neck. I wanted to be close up to any movement of her neck, every taking in of breath and to every sound.

Even when we had finished our lovemaking I wanted to feel her body upon me, her weight pressing down on me. I'm sure she was uncomfortable but she finally fell asleep... But I couldn't sleep. I spent the early hours simply stroking her hair, not wanting the morning to come. Not wanting another day to start. Why couldn't the world just stop for a while? Just to hear her breathe was a pleasure for me. Simply to watch her toss and turn in her sleep was enough. Man! I had it bad.

She got up about 4 30 a.m. and she put her white dressing-gown on over her naked body. She then sat down in the chair beside her bed. I pretended I was sleeping but after ten minutes of this I was beginning to feel cold and neglected, I sat up. 'Something a matter, Akeisha?'

'No,' she answered. 'Just thinking.'

'Thinking about what?' I asked.

'You.'

'About me?'

'Yes, Dennis, and how intense you are.'

'Intense?'

'Yes, Dennis. You gotta let me breathe when I'm with you. You know. In bed and out of it.'

'Did I do something wrong? I haven't done it for a long time. Was I that bad? A bit too rush-like? Was I too eager? I fucked up, didn't I? I fucked up!'

'No, no! You made me feel *so* good and you certainly know how to give a girl your full attention. But afterwards let's just, er, relax. Take it easy... Go to sleep. I'm not going nowhere, Dennis. Now I'm *your* girl.'

'Oh, I get you. I'm kinda smothering you, right?'

Akeisha nodded and then laughed. I got out of the bed, reached for her hand and pulled her back in. She playfully pinched my butt and then rested her head just beneath my throat and collarbone. I couldn't resist the sensation of that so we ended up making love again. This time it was slower, nicer, although I continued the face pressing face thing. She didn't seem to mind. Afterwards, I did allow her to sleep on the bed instead of me but we did interlock our fingers and the feeling was good.

I did crash out afterwards 'cos the next thing I remember was waking up and seeing Akeisha had already got washed and dressed.

'Come on, get up, Dennis,' she said. 'I've got to go and pick up Curtis.'

She threw me a spare flannel and towel. 'It's a bit nippy but I'm gonna take him for his walk in Brocky Park.'

Pulling on my slacks I said, 'Can I come with you?'

Akeisha stopped in her tracks and looked at me hard. 'You don't have to do this, Dennis. Yes, we made love and it was good and you stayed the night… But you don't have to do this fathering thing, Dennis. You've impressed me already.'

'I want to,' I said.

'You sure about this?'

'Yeah, I am.'

'I don't bring people into my son's life if they're not gonna stay around.'

'I'm not going nowhere.'

'Curtis eats, shits and sleeps. In between that he wrecks the flat. And he's my life. Can you be second to that? You're not yet eighteen.'

'Age ain't nothing but a number.'

'You've been listening to Aaliyah too much. This is real life, Dennis.'

'I can only go with how I'm feeling now. Right now, today, this minute, I wanna be with you. No matter what. Simple as.'

Akeisha smiled, walked up to me, cradled my jaw with her palms and kissed me on the forehead... 'You'd better go home and change your clothes.'

An hour later I reached home. I had this fucked-up grin on my face that for the first time in my life had nothing to do with me burning a fat-head. Man! Was I happy. Davinia saw me coming in, quickly realised that I spent the night with Akeisha and burst into giggles. I was too happy to slap or cuss her so I went to my room, closed the door and took out Akeisha's hand-carved wooden bracelet from its secret place at the bottom of my wardrobe. I looked at it for over five minutes and I seriously wondered if its mystical powers were now working for me. 'I ain't never gonna fling you away,' I told it. 'No, man. *Never!*'

Chapter Fifteen

TWO SHOTTAS IN THE DARK

July, 2003

Noel and myself looked well buff at Uncle Royston's wedding. We were both wearing Italian-designed tailor-made suits and our hair trims looked as sharp as a knife in an *Itchy and Scratchy* cartoon. I doubt if there was another pair of twenty-year-old brothers who looked as slick as us at the reception. No, I don't doubt it, there wasn't. Our chicks looked proper sweet too. Priscilla, who had now graduated to the front passenger seat of Noel's new ride, was showing off this pink dress while Akeisha dripped class and buffness in this cream and black outfit. She was soon to be twenty-two and I couldn't believe that Akeisha and me had been going out for two and a half years.

Now working at the Ritzy bar in central Bricky and serving cocktails to wannabe cool white liberals with designer stubble, Priscilla had a bit of a moment in a hair shop in Bricky three days before the wedding. She had bought these hair extensions and Priscilla being Priscilla, when she reached home she decided she didn't like the pink, cherry and red colours. So she took the hair back. Problem was, Priscilla lost the receipt. The Asian man behind the counter was saying she couldn't claim a refund and Priscilla switched big time.

'What do you fucking mean that *I* can't get my money back? *Don't* ignore me! I'm chatting to you. Us black sisters keep your curry backside in a nice house and your women wearing nuff lengths of satin with the amount of P's we spend in your fucking shop! And it ain't like you're smiling at the gates to greet us. No, fucking no! But you smile wide like clown when you see our dollars. We pay for your children to go to them private schools in Dulwich and it's our money you're sending back to your shit poor country in Asia where your brute ugly uncle is trying to milk a maaga cow while wearing a chi chi man dress! So don't fucking tell me this sister ain't getting her money back! See I don't burn down your fucking shop after I get some hardback brothers to loot the damn place! And don't think we don't notice your sneaky looks at our buff bodies. *Forget it* 'cos I'd rather wok a white brother than your curry ass! Now where's my fucking money, you stinking grabilicious short-assed Asian spastic!'

As Noel and I backed away onto the pavement, wondering if the Feds were gonna be called, Priscilla got her money back. The shopkeeper obviously wanted to keep her quiet as other black women in the shop were pondering on what Priscilla said. I guess the moral of that little story is don't fuck with a black woman's hair and money at the same time.

I had to admit that my respect for Priscilla grew over the years. No matter what Noel did, and he done some crazy shit, she stuck by him like a dumb-assed politician's wife sticks to her lame excuse of a man. So on the few occasions she kicked off big time with her mouth, Noel allowed it. He even let her call him *My Boo.*

Noel had finally taken up my advice and got himself a job. It was only as a twilight zone shelf-filler in the same supermarket where his mum, Cara, worked. But at least if he was pulled up by the Feds he could say he paid for his ride with the P's he got from work. Even though his ride was a brand new Peugeot 206. He spent more time choosing the stereo system for the car than the car itself. He had these road jolting bass speakers in the boot and he always cranked it up if he saw any fit chick on road. Noel wouldn't care if he held up a world of traffic behind him if he was chirpsing a chick on road. Only in Bricky.

It was all good though. Noel was giving his mum, Cara, a regular housekeeping money and she now did her shopping in Tesco's or Asda; no more Lidl shit for her. And she didn't have to beg for cigarette money any more. Also Cara now had a bit of a social life. Noel and Priscilla did the babysitting for Noel's younger brothers as Cara went to the bingo on Thursday nights. When Cara won the odd twenty or fifty pound she would spend it on name-brand garms for her younger kids. If Noel had some shotting to do then it would be just Priscilla doing the babysitting duties. Cara and Priscilla got on all good and I reckon that was because they were very similar. Well, not too similar, they just cussed and bad-mouthed with the same Brixtonite intensity. Oh, and they also burned fat-heads together with their rum cocktails and Kentucky takeaways.

At the wedding it was good to see the whole family together after such a long time. Even Great Aunt Jenny flew in from Jamaica to attend and I could see the spirits of Granny uplifted by Jenny's presence. Them two kept going on about Granny's preparations to return to Jamaica for good and she bade some goodbyes to long-time friends. It was all emotional shit. Some celebration dinner was being talked about to honour Granny but no-one could decide what Jamaican restaurant to go to.

Old Great Uncle Jacob was at the wedding too. Felt a bit sorry for him 'cos he was getting proper smashed on Appleton's Special sitting all on his own…

Paps was the best man and there were genuine tears in his eyes when he made his speech. This was all good for Paps 'cos the whole wedding thing made him feel important again. With all his old crew around him, faces that I remembered from the past like Brenton Brown, Yardman Irie, Floyd Windett and his wife Sharon, Smiley and others whose names I couldn't recall, Paps laughed and joked like I had never seen him do so before. Auntie Denise and Uncle Everton were with him and it all became a bit too much for Paps when suddenly he burst into tears. He started to tell everyone

Alex Wheatle

how he loved them so much and everyone was proper shocked. Black brothers from Bricky didn't do that kinda shit in public and I thought women were supposed to do the wailing at weddings.

Although a catering company was hired, Mum busied herself in the kitchen, giving orders, bitching about something or other and I guessed she did this to keep away from Granny… Them two were still not talking much, even though Granny had already packed off some of her shit to Jamaica and was almost gone. I don't understand women sometimes. But after a few glasses of champagne, Mum relaxed with Sharon, Floyd's wife, and them two when they got going managed to get themselves proper smashed. Cara saw what was happening and she joined the entertainment, getting pissed too. I couldn't believe Mum could embarrass us like that but Paps never seemed to mind. He whispered in my ear, 'Isn't it great that your mum's laughing again? I haven't seen her so happy, since…'

He trailed off and as I looked into his eyes, I knew that my parents marriage had had its ups and downs. I hoped he wouldn't burst into tears again and go into that *I love you shit* but now they had seemed to get over the worst. Davinia was proper upset at Mum's behaviour though, especially as Mum, Cara and Sharon sang along to some old school lovers rock tune. Pap's old crew were shouting them on. With apologies to Louisa Mark, this is what they sang.

'IIfff, If only you told me yourselfffff
Only, I, I, I, I, I heard it from somewhere else
Yeah, yeah
I know you're having an affair
And I know who
And I know where
It's that easy-going chick, just down there
She lives at number six, Sixth Street, yeah yeah
Why? Why just down the road from me so I could see.'

By the time the out-of-tune trio got to the last line about thirty other old school wedding guests had joined in and as the cameras

146

clicked and people clapped, it was a special moment on a special day. But there had to be one person who wasn't impressed...

'Dennis! Can't you do something with Mum,' Davinia squawked. 'Look at her! In front of everybody! My friends! Can't you get her into the kitchen and make her drink a strong coffee?'

Baby Sis had just taken her A-Levels and she was confident that she passed them all. She was already thinking about what university to go to and secretly, I was proper proud of her. I'd never tell her of course, that'd make her head swell too much. But sometimes I wished she would stop waving her moral guardian baseball bat shit. It was bad enough with Aunt Jenny being around and funny enough, after Jenny clapped her eyes on her ex-husband, Uncle Jacob, she was going on weird.

'Leave Mum alone, Davinia,' I said. 'When's the last time you seen Mum happy like this?'

'Can't you see, Dennis?' she said. 'Maybe her consumption of alcohol is masking a real sadness. We need to talk about this as a family.'

'Oh, Davinia! Can't you stop your psychobabble-analysis shit for a second? Why don't you go and enjoy yourself.'

'Don't you care, Dennis?'

'Not about your bitching, no.'

Davinia marched off to rejoin her geeky friends. I had already given the guy in her group a fucked-up don't-even-think-about-woking-my-baby-sis look. I knew the type, all polite and shit, says all the right lyrics to Paps and Mum about how he wants to be a fucking biological chemist or something. But deep down he wanted to wok Davinia. Burn him, the glasses he wears and his mum.

As for my uncle Royston he seemed well happy with his bride Joanna. She was a mix-race girl and could drink like him. As for her weight she was a bit of a salad dodger but Royston wasn't the owner of a chiselled six-pack himself. She also burned fat-heads, liked football, knew all the latest Jamaican dancehall moves and, following a serious Jamaican cooking course taught by Granny, she could cook a wicked chicken, rice and peas. Crucial for any woman entering our family. So she was an ideal choice. My only niggle about Joanna was the cheap bling she wore. It made her look like a skettel but apart from that she was cool.

A slow jam came on the sound system and as I watched my two eleven-year-old cousins, Natasha and Natalie, take to the empty dance floor to perform some kinda waltz, I looked for Akeisha.

We now had been tight for a sweet two and a half years and now I was spending my weekends at her place. Her parents didn't seem to mind and they were away most weekends anyway. She was working in the accounts department for some aerospace firm and was quietly saving up and dreaming to get her own place. I offered to help save with her but she was determined to do that shit on her own. Twice she was offered a flat by Lambeth Council but Akeisha turned them down, not liking the locations or the tower blocks that were offered. 'What's the damn point of moving from one ghetto to another?' she said at the time…

We didn't really go out much, preferring to stay indoors at weekends, playing strip chess, watching DVDs, chilling with music as she sipped red wine and I burned a fat-head, making love to music.

Any board games we played were serious events and Akeisha would sulk for ages if she lost at Monopoly, Ludo, Draughts, Connect Four or something. If she caught me cheating she would punch me like a man in my chest and even sometimes on the forehead. I guess it was down to her competitive spirit.

Because of spending so much time with Akeisha I started to get into jazz musicians like Miles Davis and John Coltrane. Whenever I tried to play their CDs in Noel's ride he would press the eject button, fling them over his shoulder and say, 'Don't pollute my car stereo with your ancient school shit, bruv! That's chi chi man music.'

'Yeah,' Priscilla would nod. 'What kinda fucked-up weird shit is that? You're getting ancient before your time, Dennis.'

Unable to tolerate that kinda humiliation, I bought my own ride. Even though I didn't need their P's, Mum and Paps helped me pay for my little Vauxhall Corsa. I put a nice stereo in it, Jamaican boxing gloves that hung from my rear-view mirror and I banned any brother from smoking cigarette in my ride. I allowed the occasional fat-head but no cancer sticks. Fuck that. I didn't want Akeisha or Curtis sniffing in that shit when they were in my ride.

I was still shotting, making around four hundred P's a week. Noel and me had about fifty, sixty regular clients and we paid people like security guards at the Brixton Academy to give us a spot outside the place so we could sell our shit. Things were rolling neatly. My only little worry was that Courtney Thompson and his fucked-up beard crew started to run a few things in Bricky. They had protection shit going on with a number of shops and businesses and word on road was they wanted to control some of the Bricky drugs market. It was kinda lucrative 'cos anybody who wanted to score in the Dirty South immediately thought of stepping to Bricky. Some shottas left Bricky because of Courtney's crew but fuck if Noel and me are gonna run like pussies. Why the fuck should we run from Courtney Thompson? The man got jacked for his packed lunch at school!

My parents were now happy with me 'cos I was still working at Everton's garage and I started to go college on a day release course to study mechanics. I found it interesting but I wasn't loving it. In bored moments I would take out a book about Caribbean history and study that. *The Iron Thorn,* a book about the Jamaican maroon wars that Akeisha bought me, was a favourite of mine. Akeisha encouraged me to read more but I don't think she meant to read in class and there was absolutely no fucking way I could read with her in bed beside me. Impossible.

If the weather was sweet on Sundays or a bank holiday I'd drive Akeisha and Curtis to the south coast or somewhere, usually leaving about six in the morning to beat all the traffic. It felt good playing Paps and on a few occasions I brought up the idea of Akeisha and I bringing another baby into the world. I felt old enough at twenty but she trampled the idea saying she wanted to get settled first in her own place and shit. But it was an education watching her raise Curtis. He wasn't allowed to watch any TV. Talk radio was OK, for according to Akeisha and her mum it made him pay attention to what was being said. *Working Curtis's attention span* became a familiar phrase for me. We talked and read to him constantly and all this seemed to be working 'cos Curtis was another Davinia in the making. He was way ahead of any other kid of his age I knew. Scary shit.

So as I took Akeisha in my arms for the last dance at my uncle Royston's wedding, I was well content. I closed my eyes, thinking to myself life don't get much better than the shit I had. But I was interrupted by Noel.

'Hey, Dennis,' he nudged.

'What is it? Can't you see man's dancing with his chick?'

'It's important, bruv. Trust me.'

'I don't care what it is! Bin Laden could be outside with his brothers and his fucked-up beard. But I'm still gonna finish my dance with Akeisha…'

'Yeah but you two can finish that off tonight. Man needs to talk.'

'Man needs to dance! You know how it's been fucked up today, Noel. With all the family and shit, doing introductions and shit. I haven't had no time with my chick.'

'Dennis, stop swearing!' Akeisha rebuked. 'Why is it that when Noel's around you swear more?'

'Well, tell Noel to find Priscilla and dance with her.'

'She's outside with your paps, Sharon, Everton, Cara, Denise and all of them,' said Noel. 'They're all burning fat-heads. Even Royston wants your paps to build him a fat-head that he can burn before he sets off on honeymoon.'

'Burning!' I raised my voice. 'If Aunt Jenny catches them they're all gonna catch a fire.'

Akeisha pulled herself away from me. 'Five minutes, Dennis,' she said… 'You two lovebirds chat if you have to. I'm gonna get myself some curried goat.'

'Can you get some for me?' asked Noel.

'You've had two plates already!' replied Akeisha.

'Yeah, I know,' said Noel. 'But I don't get invited to weddings that often. In fact this is only my second one. Brothers ain't walking down the aisle too much with their chicks. Simple as. So man has to eat tonight and sample all the food he can 'cos who knows when the next wedding will be? You get me? Get me a chicken pattie too and some of them cheesy biscuits. Oh, and some of that potato salad shit.'

Standing with her hands on her hips, Akeisha glared at Noel.

'*Please*,' Noel remembered.

I watched Akeisha laugh and shake her head before she walked off towards the kitchen. Damn! She could walk sexy! Naomi Campbell, run and collect your motherfucking P45!

I turned my attention to Noel. I wasn't the happiest, smiliest hyena in the pack... '*Burn* you, Noel! All day I've been trying to have some time with Akeisha! And now you proper fucked up my dance with her.'

'Don't worry about it, bruv,' Noel said. 'You'll get to wok it later on.'

'Fuck you, Noel!'

'Why you swear so much when I'm around you?' Noel laughed.

'Fuck you!'

'Anyway, lover boy, I just got a call from Nathan,' said Noel.

'This conversation's gonna be dead quick time if you call me lover boy again... Simple as.'

'Oh shut the fuck up, Dennis, and stop being a fucking pussy! Now listen up, lover boy.'

'Nathan called?' I said. 'We haven't done business with Nathan for ages. What does he want? Did you know his fucked-up, traitor brother is high up in the Feds? He's even got a ride with all sirens and shit! No, Noel, we have to burn any dealings with Nathan. Fuck him and his Fed brother...'

'He wants three ozes.'

'Three ozes!'

'Yeah, he wants to start shotting again.'

'He wants to start shotting and his brother is a Fed? That's fucked up, Noel. Tell Nathan to get a job checking illegally parked cars or shit like that... His parents would be proud if he done shit like that, more proud of him than the other son.'

'No, it's all good, Dennis,' Noel argued. 'Nathan has left home.

He lives with that long-face girl, Stephanie. Stephanie Davies. The junz bitch who used to go to Stockwell youth club and she honey-trapped this fuck-off-faced short brother from Harlesden. You know the weird brother, the one where you're not sure which one of his eyes is looking at you. He was mercy-woked by Shyanne Moore after a burning session at Blackie Norton's gates… Them Harlesden boys are all weird.'

'Don't remember this guy from Harlesden or Stephanie Davies,' I said.

'You must remember, she's got man hands. Proper huge. Like them old school Jamaican plumbers. She can merk a man with a single slap.'

'Oh yeah. I remember her. Fuck! Why did Nathan move in with that? The government need to have a full enquiry into that messed-up decision. That bitch should be giving kids free rides on Blackpool beach or carrying Jesus into Jerusalem. Have you seen the size of her feet? Think a fucked-up Charlie Chaplin with even bigger feet and you get the scene. Fuck my days! Her feet are big.'

'Correct! That's the bitch. Anyway, here the coup,' Noel continued… 'Nathan don't chat to his Fed brother. Them two fell out. I think it was because Nathan went to his gates while some of his Fed brothers were there and Nathan, forgetting himself, started to build a fat-head.'

'They fell out?' I asked.

'Yeah,' Noel replied. 'Proper fell out. So it's all good. He wants the food in three days time so you're gonna have to contact Dryneck.'

'Hold on a minute,' I said. 'We sure we wanna deal with Nathan?'

'Why not? OK, we had to pound him a couple of times but he come through. He showed us love and the P's, which is the important shit.'

'He might be an undercover Fed? You never know, bruv.'

'Don't be a fool, Dennis. You think the Feds are gonna give two black brothers a job in the same station? You ever seen two black Feds in the same ride? You ever seen two black Feds ride on horses together? Besides, Nathan's too dumb, even for a Fed.'

I thought about it. No, I had never seen two black Feds in the same ride. And Nathan is a damn fool.

There were still stacks of beers and drinks on the tables near the kitchen so I walked over to them and grabbed two for Noel and myself. I offered Noel his drink. He took a glug and said, 'So are you on this, lover boy?'

'Yeah, I am,' I answered. 'But Nathan will have to wait. My great aunt Jenny is here and 'cos Mum didn't get no time off work I have to drive Aunt Jenny around in my ride. And next Saturday my granny is leaving for good. So man has got family commitments, you get me? Tell Nathan he will get his three oz of food in over a week, say ten days. I still can't see why you interrupted my dance with Akeisha? You could have waited.'

'I wanted to tell you about this shit before I drink too much.'

'You're a joker, Noel. Anybody would think you get jealous when I'm dancing with my chick.'

'Fuck you! I ain't no fucking chi chi man!'

'Alright! It was a joke! Calm down. Anyway, this Nathan thing sounds all good.'

'OK,' Noel agreed. 'Deal done. Now let us sample more food.'

I looked up and Akeisha was walking towards us with two plates of food. She offered one to Noel and she started to eat from the other plate. 'Where's mine?' I asked.

'You didn't ask for any,' she said.

'I don't believe this!'

With Noel's giggling sounding in my ears I went to the kitchen to get my curried goat. I returned to a table where Noel and Akeisha had parked themselves and thought to myself it was a good day.

Six days later. Most of my family were having dinner in this Jamaican restaurant called Bamboula's on Acre Lane in central Bricky. We proper packed out the place… It was good to see Great Uncle Jacob there, Aunt Jenny's ex-husband. I only chatted briefly with him at the wedding but I had cool memories of him giving me sweets when I was young and telling me Bible stories. Throughout the dinner, Aunt Jenny glanced at Uncle Jacob suspiciously but he didn't care. It was clear that the old man was very close to Granny and she was proper happy for him to be there. Davinia was glad to see him and talk to him too. She always got on better with old people than she did with her own age despite her attempts to appear cool with her geeky fucked-up friends.

Great Aunt Jenny called the meal *Hortense's Last Supper in England* but it was Paps, Mum, Auntie Denise and Uncle Royston who persuaded everyone to come. There were secret riffs, arguments, ism-schisms and all kinda hating shit going on in my family so the achievement of twenty-three of us sitting down to dinner was a proper good one. Even Mum came and after the awkward how-nice-it-is-to-see-you-after-such-a-long-time shit, Mum complained about the cleanliness of the wine glasses. After that it was all good.

Granny got very emotional and told us all the story about her arrival in London almost forty-three years ago. As usual she made us all laugh when she said that her husband Cilbert thought that the smoke coming out of terraced houses was the result of untold men working in untold factories.

'But what do me have for the forty-three years since me come here?' lamented Granny, becoming misty-eyed. 'Not too much.'

'You have the love and affection of all of us,' said Paps. 'Just by coming here all those years ago you have given us opportunity. Opportunities that still don't exist in Jamaica even now. We might whinge, moan and complain about this country but at least it gives opportunity.'

Even Mum nodded to that thought. Aunt Jenny hugged Granny and I just had to big-up the way them two wiped away each other's tears, fixed each other's make-up and adjusted each other's hair.

Following the meal, every one of us went up to Granny and gave her a hug. She had now stopped crying and her smile and feistiness returned. When I reached her she whispered, 'Me want you to keep your promise, Dennis. If you have a boy-child me want you to call him David.'

'Of course, Granny. No worries. And if I am blessed with a daughter I'll call her Hortense.'

I could feel her cheeks opening into a bigger smile upon my

shoulder and she said, 'Let her dance, Dennis. Yes, let her be free and dance.'

It was hard to imagine that when Granny was the same age as me she was living in the Jamaican bush, stripping corn, feeding chickens and shitting in a pit. I will miss her tales and I hope my memory serves me well enough so I can tell her stories to my kids.

I went to bed that night thinking who's gonna be the one to nag us to attend church as a family? Who's gonna be the one who makes rum punch at Christmas? Mum tried to make it once and it was a disaster. Who's gonna be the one to shut up Paps when he gets in lecturing mood? Who was gonna dance in my front room like Bojangles when Davinia passes another set of exams? Who was there to ask if I wanted some advice about chicks and sex? Where could I go if I wanted some quiet, to get away from my parents and Davinia for the odd weekend? I thought about all the other third generation Jamaican kids out there of my age and whether they missed their grannies if they moved back to the Caribbean or passed away. What do you do about that missing link in your life? Why is it easier to talk to grannies about your worries and strife than your own parents? I started to miss her more than I ever realised.

Next morning it wasn't my alarm that woke me but a call from Noel. I didn't want to answer it but he would carry on ringing me all day if I didn't pick up. 'Have you called Gloria?' he wanted to know.

'No, not yet, bruv.'

'Your granny's gone, yeah?'

'Her flight is this morning, Paps drove her to the airport.'

'Then what are you waiting for? Call Gloria.'

'What's the rush?'

'I wanna use half of Nathan's money to pay for my ride to clear MOT. Also Mum wants to pay her mobile bill and do a bit of shopping. Oh, and she's getting her weave done next Friday and you know the hairdresser's ain't cheap.'

'Stop sweating, bruv. I'll call Gloria before I go to work.'

I slipped out of bed, went to my chest of drawers and pulled on a pair of my Pierre Cardin boxers; since I had been going with Akeisha I preferred to sleep naked. Sitting back down on the bed, I grabbed my phone and thumbed in Gloria's number...

Over the last three years or so we met in supermarkets, bingo halls, wine bars, bowling alleys and even one time in a leisure centre's squash court for us to do trade; proper distracted by her fine legs she beat the fuck out of me in squash... She always came to our meetings very well garmed, she would rant about her politics for a bit, count the P's in that bank teller way of hers and drive off in her sky-blue Audi sports.

'Hi, Gloria, what's gwarnin?'

'Dennis? So early?'

'I wanted to call you before I step out to work.'

'Is that right?'

'Yeah. How's things?'

'You know, this and that,' she replied. 'Getting peed off with my boss telling me to remind customers of our exceptional deals on house insurance, blah fucking blah.'

'Why do you stay working in the bank? Seems like you've hated it for so long?'

'Stability, I guess. And I've built up quite a substantial clientele for my other business. Anyway, I will soon head west.'

'Head west?'

'Yeah, America.'

'America?'

'I'll tell you more about it when we meet. What can I do for you?'

'I need six green Aussies.'

'Each baggy green wrapped up like Christmas prezzies?'

'Yeah. Neatly, with a bow and shit.'

'OK, no worries, mate.'

Gloria's attempt of an Aussie accent was shit.

'Where shall we meet?' I asked.

'You're lucky, Dennis. I have quite a lot of green Aussies walking around butt naked in my depot. We'll meet this evening. 8 p.m. The underground car park at Asda's in Clapham Junction. I have to do a little shopping this evening. I'm gonna try and cook a lasagne for Dryneck.'

'Lasagne? Shouldn't you try rice and peas or something?'

'I can never get the hang of rice and peas, I always flood the rice. Anyway, enough about my culinary skills.'

'The usual rules?' I asked.

'Yes, the usual rules. You should know me by now, Dennis. I'm a creature of habit.'

That meant that she would only deal with me, nobody else was allowed to come along. We had been buying all types of cannabis off her for over two years and she still didn't trust me enough to bring Noel. Mind you, Noel did scare the fuck out of most white women.

At first, I was surprised that it was Gloria who did most of the selling but it made perfect sense. I guessed Dryneck bought the stuff from a port of entry somewhere and he passed it on to Gloria to do the retail shit. What Fed is gonna stop and search a stunning wokable blonde who looks like Lana Turner? Dryneck and Gloria didn't make most of their income from the likes of me, but whole-selling to city types, business men, celebrities, anti-Nazi long-haired freaks and white liberals who went on legalize drugs marches; strangely, the one time I got involved with one of those marches I was just about the only black brother there. All these trying-so-desperately-to-be-cool freaky white people were coming up to me, saying things like *cool* and *aaaiiigghhhtt*! It was fucking horrific. And when I think about it, what the fuck was I doing on a legalise cannabis march anyway? If weed was legalised there'll be no more shottas and I'd be out of a sweet little earner.

One look at Gloria and there's no way that dopeheads won't agree to pay the set price because as most of her customers were men, they thought they might get a wok out of it. Pussies! For whatever reason, Dryneck had Gloria under one piece of heavy lock and 'cos he was ugly as shit I never worked that one out.

Noel and myself were now careful of who we sold our weed to. Noel worked the snooker halls of south London, the rave clubs, wine bars where they played loud R&B music, gigs at venues like the Bricky Academy; he was bold enough to walk up and down the queue outside. He sold mostly to white brothers. They didn't sweat you about the prices and offered you less grief than black brothers. As for me I had a sweet customer base at my college. White girls mainly who were studying shit like administration, media, IT and how to be a legal secretary. I guess they bought the skunk 'cos they wanted to impress their cousins who lived in boring fucked-up places like Leatherhead and Sutton. I could just imagine them saying *This is Brixton skunk, girlfriend. From Brixton!*

Again, no negotiations on price, no arguments, they just bought my shit without so much as a peep to check my merchandise. My skunk *was* proper good though. Students are always bitching that they're broke but they always had enough dollars to buy my food. Easy money.

Now and again I would get invited to the odd white people party but burn that shit. White people love to sit down, get drunk, dance badly and pass their fat-heads around where untold acne-fucked-up mouths pollute the spliff. Well fuck that! No one was gonna put their lips around my big-head.

Also, I done a bit of trade with some of the white chicks who brought their rides to the garage. I'm not sure if my boss, Everton, knew what was going on but I could have handed out invoices for skunk as well as six-month car services. There were only a few black brothers who we sold to and Noel and myself knew them since school days. Nathan was an example of that. Selling blatantly at youth clubs, on road and other places where the brothers hung out was even too dangerous for Noel. We left that shit for the young pups coming up.

The jacking of shottas in Bricky increased and I kept on hearing that Muslim crews like Courtney Thompson's were trying to muscle in on the skunk and coke trade all over the Dirty South. They can call themselves whatever religion they like but at the end of the day a thug who specialises in jackings might be wearing a rasta tam or a skullcap with a fucked-up beard. Money's the main religion in Bricky, simple as.

Sitting in my ride I watched Gloria's Audi sports enter the

basement car park of Asda's at 8.10 p.m. She wasn't usually late. It was kinda windy in the car park and the shape of the place made car engines sound louder than they were. The ceiling was low and I felt a little claustrophobic. I walked over to Gloria's ride and, spotting me, she opened the passenger side door. As I filled the seat she lit a cigarette and turned down the volume of her car stereo... Judy Garland was belting out some song and for a moment I thought of Granny.

Gloria was wearing a navy blue trouser suit and a white blouse. Her blonde hair was wrapped up in a bun and apart from her ride, the only clue to her wealth was the expensive-looking watch that she wore around her left wrist. Her lipstick was murder-red and the fragrance she wore I couldn't recognise but I knew it was pricey... I wasn't in awe of her no more. Why should I be? I had Akeisha.

'So how's it going, Dennis?' she asked without looking at me.

'All good,' I replied. 'All good.'

'That means you're still with Akeisha.'

'Yeah, she's some girl.'

'You'll have to introduce me to her sometime, Dennis. Whenever we meet she's all you talk about.'

'Am I that bad?'

'Yes,' Gloria answered instantly, now looking at me.

'What about you and Dryneck?'

She gave me a hard stare but it soon softened. 'We're cool. As a matter of fact we're getting out of this business and heading for the States. It's getting too hot in south London.'

'Really?'

'Really, Dennis. Dryneck is getting too well known. And I think those Muslim boys have their greedy eyes on him.'

'They're all front,' I said. 'They ain't real Muslims, they're wannabes. They think brothers will be more frightened if they can drop shit like *I knew bin Laden's cousin so if you don't pay we're gonna bomb your ends motherfucker and superglue a hand grenade on your mum's back.*'

'Then if they're not Muslims who's doing most of the jackings, Dennis? Who's targeting all the dealers and demanding protection money? It certainly ain't a gang of Christian boys who wear crosses and look like fucking Charlton Heston.'

I thought about that for a minute. I knew the answer to Gloria's question but couldn't bring myself to admit it. It was brothers like Courtney Thompson who had mothers who attended Christian churches. Their parents were West Indian and they probably still got brushings from their parents if they left their dirty plates in the sink. Somewhere along the line, they swapped their Bibles for Korans.

'You need to be more careful than ever, Dennis,' Gloria added. 'You and Noel.'

'We'll be safe, Gloria. We're careful of who we shot to. So what you gonna do in the States?'

'I can do more than selling skunk to white men in grey suits and black guys who don't wear belts in their jeans,' Gloria answered. 'I'm a talented girl, Dennis. I can whistle through my fingers, ride a horse, light a fire with two sticks, shoot a bird, set type and be a babysitter to my nieces... That's probably the hardest thing I do, babysitting.'

'Babysitting?'

'Yeah, it's put me off having my own. Screw that for a walk on the boards... Those little shits fuck up a woman's figure and take up too much time... And I really like my quality time. Dryneck won't want any babies affecting that and I feel the same way.'

'So where are you going in America?'

'Los Angeles. Don't laugh, Dennis, but I wanna be an actress. A *big* actress. I've been going drama school for the last two years. I've already done a few adverts, you know, a walk on, background kinda thing. Done a bit of glamour too. Now I've got enough saved up to have my crack in the States. If Catherine Zeta-Jones can make it on her minuscule talent, then so can I. But this chick ain't gonna fuck a has-been actor to get there...'

'Well, you've got the hair, Gloria.'

What a fucked-up comment. It just kinda came out. I felt like a prick but Gloria smiled... 'If I don't make it in Hollywood then I'll be the world's most glamorous bank clerk,' she laughed.

'So what's Dryneck gonna do while you're chasing your dream?'

'He said he'll come out with me but that's as far as I know. He might move on, I dunno. I never quite understand men, especially Dryneck. I can only hope that he stays around. We'll look good on the red carpet together...'

'Don't understand men?'

'Yes, Dennis. Plain women know more about men than beautiful ones do. Dryneck has a saying, a career is wonderful but you can't curl up to it on a cold night. He's always saying that.'

'I'm gonna say the same shit to Akeisha.'

Gloria laughed out loud. This white guy walked passed us and he offered me a fucked-up stare. Burn him!

'The thing is, Dennis,' Gloria continued, 'our generation don't wanna spend time building careers in administration, banking, civil service and crap like that. I fucking hate it, Dennis. *Boring!* That stuff was alright for our parents but *not* us. We spend most of our free time reading all those Z-list celebrity mags and we think the people we read about have a better life than ourselves.'

'Don't they?'

'Well, yes is my answer. That is why I *have* to do something else. Even if it means risking all. My older sister lives in a council flat in Roehampton with three kids. Her man left her when she was pregnant with her second one. As soon as she gets home from picking up the kids from school she cooks dinner and she likes to finish that at 5.30. So she can sit down and watch her soaps. Then she puts the kids to bed and reads her celeb mags, dreaming of appearing on *Footballer's Wives*. When I have a conversation with her the subject matter ends up on *Big Brother*. As if I really give a fuck!'

'Er, Gloria, you told me to say something and stop your flow if you start ranting about shit.'

She laughed out loud again and then kissed me on the cheek. 'You were raised well, Dennis. You must have been a good kid. You know how to prick a balloon gently! You know what, all I remember as a kid was my freckles coming out on my face every spring and they never cleared up till Christmas. It's funny, my big sister was always regarded more prettier than me. I was always jealous of her but look at the silly cow now.'

She bent down and beside her feet was a Crew Clothing shopping bag. She passed it on to me. I looked inside and the merchandise was packed in kitchen foil. It gave off the same fragrance that Gloria wore. Smart chick. I had a sneaky look at her nostrils and I could tell she had been snorting some shit. Gloria always chatted too much when she was on charlie.

'Five hundred for that little lot,' she said with a grin.

I took out a wad of P's from my inside jacket pocket. It was bound with an elastic band. She took it from me and immediately put it in the glove compartment. Maybe she now trusted me enough not to count it, or she was pressed for time. 'I enjoy our little talks, Dennis. Hopefully we'll meet again before we fly out. Perhaps dinner? I'll pay.'

'Yeah, I can do that.'

'Bring that girl of yours along, you got me intrigued about her.'

I climbed out of the car as Gloria looked into the rear mirror and applied a little lipstick... Man! They should make a TV drama about her. *The Shotting Blonde*.

After calling Noel I drove up to his ends 'cos he wanted to sample the skunk. Cara and Priscilla were watching *The Bill* when I came in with my bag of skunk... They both offered me a *I know what shit you have in the bag* glance as I made my way to Noel's bedroom. Noel's three younger brothers were playing quietly in the hallway, the oldest was now twelve and the other two were eight and six. They had a Game Boy between the three of them and it was creepy how they were so silent when Cara settled down to watch her soaps. 'Hi, Cara, Priscilla,' I greeted. 'Hi kids.'

'Hi, Dennis,' the oldest boy, Chris said. The other two ignored me.

'What's gwarnin?' Priscilla greeted without looking away from the TV.

'Hello, Dennis,' Cara said, refusing to divert her gaze.

Noel had a tiny bedroom, just big enough for his single bed

and a chest of drawers. I always took the piss out of it, saying he must be careful when he puts the key in the lock 'cos he might bust the window. His expensive garms were on coat hangers, hanging from the curtain rail. Rap magazines littered the floor and DMX was getting rid of some angst about living in Yonkers from a mini-stereo upon the chest of drawers. Noel himself just had a white vest on and I had to admit he looked a lot better than Bruce Willis. He was looking out of the window, burning a fat-head in that casual way of his. White brothers would pay a lot of P's to learn how to look as cool. Asian guys would pay even more.

'What's gwarnin, Noel?'

He turned around. 'Yeah, things are good.'

I placed my bag upon his bed. 'Well, six little green Aussies,' I announced… 'Get your scissors, scales and your bags.'

For the next hour we cut up the skunk, weighed it and put it in our little button bags. After more than a few years of doing this we were quick, efficient and neat.

'Just gonna give a bag to Mum,' Noel said.

I followed him into the front room. Cara and Priscilla were still watching TV. Noel passed on the skunk to his mother and she looked at it and scowled. 'Can't you ever give me high grade, baby?' she said. 'I'll smoke this but it knocks me out. Don't expect me to iron your jeans tonight, baby. Anyway, I could do with a good night's sleep. When you go to the kitchen, baby, make Mummy her drink. Thank you, baby.'

'Of course, Mum.'

Sitting beside Cara with her arms folded was Priscilla. She offered Noel an evil look. 'Don't I get a bag?'

'Unless you have ten pound you don't,' Noel replied.

'That's bad-mind, Noel.'

'No it ain't, it's business.'

'But I'm your girl.'

'So. Do I ask you for a free drink when I link you at the Ritzy bar?'

Priscilla thought about. 'Er, no.'

'Case dismissed,' said Noel before we returned to his room.

He sat on his bed and called Nathan on his new mobile. 'Nathan, what's gwarnin?'

Noel put his phone on loudspeaker. 'Yeah, bruv. I'm good, still. Got my food?'

'Yeah, bruv. You have our dollars?' Noel asked.

'Of course, bruv. When you gonna bring the food?'

Noel looked at me. 'I'm doing something with Akeisha tomorrow evening,' I revealed. 'Can't put it off. Tell Nathan we'll bring his food the day after.'

'We'll bring your food the day after tomorrow,' Noel said.

'That's all good,' Nathan said. 'You'll both be coming, right?'

'Yeah,' replied Noel. 'You know the score. When we're dealing with more than one green Aussie the both of us are on the pitch, you get me?'

'Yeah, I get you.'

'So where you wanna link?' Noel asked.

'I'll be at my girl's sister's gates the night after tomorrow… I'm helping her move in some furniture. Flaxman Road ends. You know the sports centre.'

'Yeah, I know it.'

'We'll link in the car park there. My girl's sister's flat is just around the corner.'

'That's good,' agreed Noel. 'See you about nine. If you're late we'll be missing.'

'Don't worry, bruv. I'll be there.'

Noel killed the call. Then he remembered something. 'Oh, shit! My mother's drink!'

He ran out to make Cara's gin and tonic as I wondered what it would be like to grow in a family like Noel's. I came to the conclusion that I'd be similar to Noel, just more cynical.

Flaxman Road was more or less the Camberwell end of Coldharbour Lane on the ghetto side… It was in Bricky and within range so we didn't mind driving there for the link. I did kinda protest about supplying Nathan with food 'cos I didn't really need his money. But

Noel bitched again about how he needed some quick P's for his ride and Cara's hair.

'Can't she wear a wig for the time being?' I suggested.

'Fuck you, Dennis! Would your mum wear a fucking wig! No, bruv. She's gonna buy some decent hair. Simple as.'

Two days after I bought the food. It was one of those sticky July nights that flies and shit love. Noel had his car roof open and the air conditioning on at full blast… He was wearing a white vest and I had to admit, his new thick gold chain looked good against the black skin of his neck. He had a half-smoked fat-head in the corner of his mouth and he was bopping his head to some rap by DMX, his favourite rapper… Priscilla wasn't with us. She was babysitting while Cara went to her bingo. I was wearing my Jamaican football shirt and my Chicago Bulls baseball cap. I had the passenger-side window wound all the way down and I was proper liking the breeze licking my face.

We headed to Flaxman Road via Angel Town and Loughborough and it was still light enough to see the buff girls on street and the rude boys on road. When it's a hot day Bricky is always vibing and the chicks look their best wearing their multicoloured weaves, crop tops, gold studs in their bellies, hipster jeans or short denim skirts. Man! Black ghetto chicks know how to walk sexy.

We pulled up in the Flaxman sports centre car park just after 9 p.m. There were only about seven parking bays available and we filled the last one. The sports centre itself was the kinda place where poor brothers worked out and ugly chicks did aerobics… Shottas and white people who had a decent job wouldn't be seen dead in the place. By now the sun was casting long shadows and from the council estates that surrounded us, you could hear hip hop and bashment music blowing over from every block.

Noel switched off the engine as I climbed into the back seat. The passenger seat was now awaiting Nathan. I began building a big-head as Noel relit his. We watched a salad-dodging white girl walk past us while towelling her head. The sweet smell of skunk filled the ride and Noel wound down his window all the way. Someone was looking at us through the large window of the sports centre but we didn't give a fuck…

'He's late,' said Noel. 'Why are brothers always late?'

He switched the car battery on and pressed play on the car stereo. DMX's 'Look Thru My Eyes' spat out from the speakers. The heavy bassline vibrated the ride and I thought that one day Noel would duppy his battery doing this and he won't be able to start his car. The track was starting to fade when we saw Nathan appear in front of the windscreen. He was all smiling and shit, as if he was just about to wok a girl. A bit of sweat was wetting his temples but it was still humid… Noel opened the door for him and he sat down in the passenger seat. He seemed very lively. Too happy? Almost anxious, looking this way and that. I put it down to the fact that he hadn't been shotting for a while. Maybe it was just excitement that he was getting back in the game.

'What's gwarnin?' he greeted, looking more around him than he was at Noel.

I sensed something wrong.

'Where's the P's?' asked Noel.

Nathan produced his biggest smile yet. From his jacket pocket his left hand emerged with four hundred pounds. He gave Noel the money. Nathan had this strange expression going on. I couldn't quite read it and before I could, seven shadows suddenly darkened the front windscreen and the side windows of the ride. I looked out of my window and there was a gun pointing at my head. This brother with a messed-up beard beckoned for me to get out of the car. Noel had to do the same. Nathan got all apologetic like. He was shaking his head, 'They made me do it, bruv! They made me do it, bruv.'

Nathan splurted. Fucking pussy. He disappeared around a corner. I had a body rush of fear charging through me. Courtney Thompson was looking at me with hating eyes… 'Let Nathan go,' Courtney said. 'He won't say nothing.' A gun held by another brother was pressed against the back of my head. A similar pistol was now trained on Noel's forehead. Noel's face was changing into all kinds of expressions. I wondered if he could tolerate this shit.

No was my answer. He was gonna switch. I had to do something. Rage was polluting him fast, it was in the eyes. I had to calm him down before he got himself shot.

'Just cool, Noel. Cool.'

'Peel them,' ordered Courtney Thompson. His burning eyes never left my face and I guessed this was more about me than it was about a jacking. He was wearing this white dress thing, a brown skullcap and the hair beneath his chin was now untamed. To me it still looked fucked up to see a brother I used to go school with dress in that way. I wondered if he was the last brother I would see from my schooldays... I glanced through the window of the sports centre. No one was there. Where's the fucking receptionist? Someone must be witnessing this shit?

They took our P's, our skunk and our mobile phones. They even swiped Noel's half-smoked big-head. They pulled off my Jamaican football shirt and my head got caught in the collar. In their aggression, they ripped the seam from the collar to the right sleeve. My granny bought me it for Christmas last year.

'Couldn't do it on your own, could you, Courtney?' Noel raged. 'You fucking pussy.'

Courtney still glared at me as a gun butt struck the back of Noel's head. He fell to the ground.

'Just cool, Noel,' I said. 'Cool!'

Nike-clad feet began to wade into Noel's body. 'You fucking pussies!' he screamed. 'PUSSIES!'

I moved forward but was dragged back. 'Noel, it'll be alright, bruv. Trust.' I felt a gun butt strike my neck and I almost fell over. I glimpsed Noel. It wasn't gonna be alright. The Nikes were now aimed at his face... It was sickening to watch but I couldn't turn away. I tried to move forward again and I received a gun butt in the temple. I momentarily lost my sight and I dropped to my knees. Someone then booted my backside and I stood up again... I tried to say something to Noel with my eyes but he was no longer looking at me.

'WHAT ARE YOU?' one of the attackers shouted at Noel. 'WHAT ARE YOU? MUSLIM OR CHRISTIAN?'

'Fuck you! You fucking pussy! Go wok your mum!'

The words barely came out of Noel's split lips. I now felt tears on my own face... 'Noel, bruv. Just...' I tried yet again to wriggle myself free but something blunt hit my right cheekbone. I didn't even see what it was. Courtney Thompson was still glaring at me, not even bothering to look at Noel's battering. I got another gun butt. This time in my face. I was now on my knees. The inside of my head felt hot.

The Nikes never stopped. Kick after kick. I was thinking that boots to the face in real life sound nothing as loud as they sound in a movie. Noel's resistance was now over. His nose was pumping blood and his eyes were now swollen and closing... Blood was now spotting the concrete.

'MUSLIM OR CHRISTIAN?' one of them yelled. 'Say MUSLIM and we'll stop.'

Noel shook his head. Even now he wasn't gonna give them the pleasure. I wished he would just say it, murmur it. Just so the beating could stop. 'I'M A MUSLIM,' I shouted. 'Satisfied? Stop beating him, bruv... I'M A FUCKING MUSLIM!'

'I want *him* to say it,' said Courtney Thompson in a low voice. 'Then *you*. You'll get your turn.'

The kicking continued. All over his body. There were no more yelps of pain. It would have been kinder to just pull the trigger, simple as. I hardly noticed the tears dripping off my chin. My best friend laying still in front of me, trying to curl himself into a foetus position, trying to protect his head. And I could do nothing. If someone studies my DNA long after I'm dead, they'll see that image. Kick, kick, kick. A fist opened my eyes. Courtney Thompson still staring... Courtney Thompson still hating. For a short moment I thought *burn* all the religious shit out of it. This was just about sex. Me being more wokable to women than him. It was in his eyes. Maybe he was impotent or something?

They all started on me. I felt yet another gun butt behind my left ear. I could hardly focus my eyes but there was a figure in front of me. Right up close. It was Courtney... He was proper hating. His eyes wouldn't leave me alone. 'All this 'cos I could've woked Tania

Blake?' I said. 'And trust me, Courtney, she was proper begging for it.'

'He won't say nothing,' he said to his crew. 'No, he won't say nothing.'

Courtney punched me on the side of my face. I was bordering on unconsciousness but he placed his right hand beneath my chin and raised my head. 'There are two types of people in this world. Those who know where your girl, Akeisha Parris, lives… And those who don't. Angel Town! Second floor. Need I go on? You two look so kinda together, especially when you go out as a family with her son, Curtis.'

By now I knew it wasn't worth saying anything. I just hoped I would leave this place alive. Noel's body was crumpled on the concrete. He wasn't moving. But at that moment I saw something in Courtney. Something deep and troubling Something that he could never reveal. I was in a fucked up state but I saw it. It was a wild guess but it was there in his eyes. Could he be a chi chi man?

'From this day onward, you're paying tax,' continued Courtney. 'A hundred notes a week for the privilege of shotting in Bricky. You pay or we pay a visit to Akeisha. Simple as. And I would enjoy woking her.' He turned around to his crew expecting some kind of applause, some kind of salute of how *manly* he'd just been. I searched his eyes and I was convinced he was a shirt-lifter. Attracted to me.

My mind began to play tricks on me. I had just recalled the time Noel nicked from a corner shop for the first time when Courtney kicked me in the jaw. It's funny what you remember during shit like that and the last thing I recall is that Courtney was the only one in his crew not wearing Nikes. He was wearing these black brogues and I thought it just didn't go with his white dress thing. It's a fucked-up memory but that's how it was.

Chapter Sixteen

THE LION OF JUDAH VERSUS THE CRESCENT MOON

Waking up in a hospital bed, I focused and saw my family around me. Mum was closest, sitting on a wooden chair. She was holding her handbag tight and it was obvious she had been crying. She looked so tired. It was only when I turned my head to look at her that I realised my head was wrapped in bandages. A banging ache made me grimace but I still managed to give a weak smile for Mum. She returned the smile and leant towards me. She placed her hands around my cheeks and chin and she started to cry again. Her lips were trembling as they touched my forehead. I couldn't really call it a kiss but a vibe of warmth and familiarity went through my body.

I glanced further along the side of my bed and there was Paps and Davinia. Paps look was one of relief and anger. It seemed he had been controlling his fury for quite a time. Davinia seemed to be in shock. Her mouth was slightly open and she couldn't take her eyes away from my head. A nice sensation filled me, knowing my family were around me, but it quickly turned to dread. The ever-present image of Noel laying lifeless on the concrete pounded my senses like a Lennox Lewis combination… Kick after kick. His face gradually getting messed up before my eyes. Kick after kick.

'Noel?' I spoke, barely having the energy to get his name out.

Mum then placed her arms around my shoulders and gently put her head upon my chest. She looked towards the bottom of the bed as she cried. I looked at Paps and he was desperately trying to avoid my gaze. Davinia covered her eyes with her palms, turned sideways and started bawling. She wasn't holding back and I have never seen her like that before or since.

'Noel?' I asked again.

I knew the answer but I wanted someone to confirm it. I searched my paps' eyes again and this time he had the courage to look at me full on. I felt a horrible pang in the pit of my stomach and this weird feeling in my throat. There was a pause as Paps collected his thoughts. He then scratched the side of his nose and rubbed his forehead with the palm of his hand. He took in a breath and said, 'They tried so hard to revive him on the scene but he was dead on arrival… He had a blood clot in the brain. I'm so sorry, Dennis.'

A single tear ran down Paps' left cheek but he didn't wipe it away. It just went down to his jaw and there it stayed for a while. I felt empty, like someone had stuck a hoover to my spirit and whatever sweet vibes of life I had were sucked away. I wanted to be duppied like Noel. Wherever Noel was I wanted to take my sad black ass there so he could take my place here. I felt like a cheat, a fucking cheat! Why Noel and why not me? Courtney Thompson hated on *me*. He had no issues with Noel. If I wasn't there it would have been an everyday jack, simple as. Noel would have lost his skunk, his mobile and his Nikes but he would have lived.

Tears were flowing but I still kept looking at Paps. I knew he had been where I now was… He had faced his maker when he was flung over a fourth floor tower block balcony by a Bricky crime lord. It was only now that I finally understood why he never wanted to talk about that night. Fear of what feelings you may bring to the surface… Pure undiluted dread. I guess it's difficult for men to accept that sometimes we can't face up to shit.

Things are sometimes too scary. I wondered if he felt like a cheat for escaping death.

Mum kept crying and Davinia refused to reveal her face. Paps took a step forward and reached for my left hand. He gripped it tight and I maintained eye contact with him. But suddenly the hand he was holding turned into a fist. I wrenched it free and punched the wall behind me. Why Noel and why not me? Mum's wailing got louder and Davinia, unable to take the stress of the situation, about turned and marched off.

'I'll better go get her,' said Paps.

He hobbled after her and it was only then that I realised he was using his walking stick.

It felt good to have Mum so close to me. I wondered why was it that she only showed her love for me when someone pounded the fuck out of me? I began stroking her hair but she just kept on crying. Of course, she wouldn't let me see her tears... Memories of Noel were filling my brain at rapid speed. I realised that the thing he craved the most was his mother's love. Simple as. I wondered if Cara ever stroked Noel's hair. I wondered how many times did Noel fall asleep in her arms. I'm sure she did love him. In a fucked-up kinda way. But did Noel know that she loved him? I really hope he did. Why Noel and not me?

Mum wiped her face before she turned to me. Even on a day like this she was wearing make-up and her newly-permed hair was now messed up. 'When we got the call we thought you was dead,' she said in a voice just above a whisper. 'It was Cara who called us. She was very calm. Almost dream-like. The police had found Noel's car.'

She trailed off. Obviously, describing the discovery of our bodies was too much for her. 'You have already had two x-rays,' Mum revealed. 'There is a swelling of your skull at the back of your head and you will have to remain under observation for a while. You've been unconscious for hours. We was frantic with worry because there was concern that you might slip into a coma...'

I wasn't really listening to Mum. My mind just kept on repeating the same question... Why Noel and why not me?

'The consultant at first thought you had a stress fracture but after the second x-ray he said it was just a swelling. But it has to be monitored.'

I thought Mum felt better talking about my medical condition. I guess it was easier to talk about what the fuck's wrong with me than talk about Noel and what a huge loss we had all suffered. Guilt pressed my next question. 'How's Cara, Mum?'

She glanced behind her as if she wanted Paps to deal with the question. But he wasn't there. 'She was bearing up well until she had to identify the body,' Mum answered. 'I don't think she was taking it all in. I phoned Sharon and Floyd and they are now looking after her and the kids. Cara's mum is on her way down from Thornton Heath too.'

The tears started again and Mum just buried her head into the bed covers. I looked up and saw Paps returning. He was without Davinia.

'She's getting something to drink,' he said. 'She's very upset.'

Paps sat on the bed and looked at me. I felt he was trying to read my thoughts.

'What piece of fucking shit did this to you and Noel, Dennis?' he said. Now his fury was obvious. His words were spoken softly but they were loaded with venom and a hunger for revenge. Would he round up his old bredrens and hunt for Noel's killers and my attackers? 'Did you recognise who did it?'

For some reason I thought of Akeisha and Courtney Thompson's threat. Then I wondered what would Noel do if he was in my place and I was dead. He would take Thompson out. Simple as. Merk the fake Muslim, no doubt about it. That was Noel.

'I didn't recognise them, Paps,' I finally answered.

Paps offered me a long hard stare. He knew I was lying. 'I want you to think about this very hard, Dennis. Noel is dead and you could have died too. Noel needs justice and so do you. Try and think, Dennis. Did you recognise who did this?'

I held Paps' gaze and after a few seconds I shook my head. 'No, Paps. All I know is there was about seven or eight of them.'

Paps was brewing but he managed to control his anger as he

said, 'The police will probably question you tomorrow. Maybe before that time something will jog your memory. After all, you have suffered concussion.'

'Yes, Paps. I'll try and go over what happened.'

Davinia returned drinking from an apple juice carton and Paps stood up. 'Do you want a hot drink, Carol?' he asked Mum.

Mum nodded, her face still buried in the bed covers. Paps patted me on the shoulder and limped along the hospital corridor. If I can withstand an interrogation from him, I thought, then the Feds will be no worries.

Two hours later, Paps had taken Davinia home but Mum still remained. To be honest she was getting on my nerves a bit. Fussing about is the bed comfortable? Are you hungry? Shall I go home and cook something special? Was I thirsty? Shall I bathe you? Shall I buy a pair of pyjamas? It was a relief to see Akeisha enter the ward and sit on my bed. She kissed me on the left cheek and offered me a huge smile… I glanced at Mum and I could see she was put out a bit.

'I'm so relieved you're alright,' Akeisha said. 'Thank God!'

'He's not out of the woods yet,' Mum interrupted. 'He has to stay here under observation for a few days yet.'

'Well, when you come out you can stay with me for a while until you get back on your feet,' Akeisha said.

That last sentence improved my recovery no end but judging by Mum's expression there was no way I could agree to it. 'Mum's already took time off work to look after me when I come out,' I revealed. 'I'm sure I'll be alright anyway.'

'He needs his rest now, Akeisha,' Mum said in her over-polite voice. 'Needs his sleep.'

'I'm OK, Mum,' I said.

I began to think that Mum was trying to compensate for all those years when she wasn't home when I arrived back from school. She needn't feel bad 'cos I preferred it that way. When Mum was home all she did was nag my black ass.

Akeisha kissed me again and gave me a hug. I felt good, very good, but Noel won't have that sensation any more. He will never feel the tingle of Priscilla's lips on his forehead. He will never wake up in Priscilla's arms. He will never...Why Noel and why not me?

With Akeisha's arms around my neck and feeling the warmth of her skin next to mine, I came to a decision. There was no debate in my mind and there was no way I could allow Courtney Thompson to have a threat over me or Akeisha. *Burn* him! No way he's gonna trouble or hurt Akeisha. I won't let it happen... I'll have to merk him, duppy him, simple as. He duppied my bredren and as long as I could remember Paps was telling me not to trust the Feds. They couldn't be trusted. So I ain't gonna tell them shit. Noel hated the Feds so he would have agreed with me.

Granny always used to tell me that when the West Indian cricket team was in their prime, they targeted the captain of the opposing team. If they could humiliate the captain, the team would lose confidence was the idea. Courtney Thompson's the Muslim crew's captain. What did Robert De Niro do when the local mafia don tried to sweat him for P's in *The Godfather 2*? De Niro's character took full responsibility and duppied the white-suited don, simple as. Courtney has to be merked, no doubt about it and the responsibility is mine... When I recover I'm gonna stalk the motherfucker. Find out where he steps, where he prays to his Muslim God, where he chills, where the fuck he buys his crisps, where he shits, where he buys his fucking batty paper. I'm gonna blaze him like a Capleton song. His mother will be shopping at motherfucking Morleys for her black garms shit and she'd better buy a new pair of fucking glasses so she can recognise her pussyhole dog-heart son. Noel would have done the same shit for me. And I ain't saying dog to nobody. Not even Akeisha... It's for her anyway, it'll keep her safe. Nothing's gonna happen to her. *Nothing! Trust!*

Next morning two Feds appeared by my bed. One was a woman, the other a guy. It was the guy who came with the notepad and shit. He wasn't that much older than me and he looked a little nervous, chewing his pen and shit. I ain't gonna tell him a fucking dog! He probably lived in somewhere like New Malden. Fuck him and his mum! The woman looked too confident, too assured. She was thirty-something, attractive but businesslike. She grabbed an extra chair from the hallway and brought it up close. She probably grew up around black people, somewhere like Streatham. Maybe she woked a black brother once in her teenage years but was too ugly to keep him. *Burn* her anyway! I ain't gonna tell her shit.

The other Fed pulled the curtains around my little space. Paps was sitting at the end of the bed. He had his screwface on. His walking stick was propped up against the wall; I noticed he had decorated it in red, gold and green tape. Mum had gone for a walk, she didn't want to hear the *details* of my jacking. The Feds introduced themselves. They were so polite I kinda thought for a minute that my black ass had turned white and I was on a Caribbean Sandals holiday. I thought of that old school *Smile Orange* film that Paps loved so much. The Feds finally got down to business.

'Did you recognise any of them, Dennis?' the woman asked, her head tilted at an angle.

'No.'

'Not even vaguely?'

'No.'

'How many were there, Dennis?'

'About seven or eight.'

'Were they all black?'

'Yes.'

There was a pause. Paps was giving one of his suspicious stares to the male Fed. He ignored Paps and carried on writing.

'Can you tell us what they were wearing?' the female Fed went on.

'The usual garms. Baggy jeans, sweat tops, name-brand trainers. A couple of them were wearing hoodies but everyone wears them.'

'Anything distinctive, Dennis?'

'Three or four were wearing skull caps. They had guns.'

Shit! Didn't mean to reveal that. The Feds looked at one another. The male Fed scribbled furiously in his notepad. Paps stood up and switched big time. 'What are you gonna do about it?' he yelled. 'I've heard about this! There are Muslim gangs marauding all over the place in Brixton! Killing people and doing these violent religious conversions! Armed to the fucking teeth!

What the *bloodclaat* you gonna do about it! This ain't the first time! You know it's going on! Outside schools and youth clubs. Dreads in my day didn't go around killing people all because they weren't rastas! They didn't ram their beliefs down people's throats. If we had issues with society or the police we fought them man to man! We didn't kill innocent people in the name of religion. What the *raas* you doing to prevent this fuckery? Or are you too busy trying to catch drivers without MOTs? Is this gonna be another Stephen Lawrence episode? SAME OLD FUCKING BABYLON! SAME OLD FUCKERY!'

The male Fed got even more nervous and I almost laughed to myself. It was good that Paps still had some of that old revolutionary 1981 Brixton uprising shit in his blood... The woman turned to Paps. 'Please, Mr Huggins. I understand your anger but I want to assure you that we are doing everything in our power.'

I glanced at Paps and he sat down. He looked kinda embarrassed, shame-faced even. The female Fed looked at Paps and satisfied herself that he wasn't gonna have another outburst and carried on. 'Were your assailants wearing any distinctive jewellery, necklaces or anything of that nature?'

'Can't remember.'

'Can you recall if any of your assailants had facial scars?'

'Can't remember.'

'In your own time, Dennis, can you tell us what happened?'

'Me and Noel drove up to Flaxman Road ends 'cos we was about to link with a bredren. We parked at the sports centre and all of a sudden we saw pure man. Two of them had guns. They ordered us out of Noel's ride, jacked us of all our money, our mobiles and shit and then they started pounding Noel. They kept on kicking him. They wouldn't stop. Just kicking. Kicking...I couldn't do anything about it. A gun barrel was pressed to the back of my head. They kept on...Kicking.'

My headache suddenly got worse. I had to close my eyes for a second but that was no escape... Noel's merked body was in my head in full fucking colour. I struggled to get my black ass in control 'cos I didn't want to bawl in front of any motherfucking Fed. 'Then they turned on me,' I went on. 'Simple as. Don't remember nothing else.'

'What did they take?'

'Our money, mobiles and stuff. Didn't I tell you that already? They even took my Jamaican football shirt!'

'Anything else?'

Maybe this Fed bitch knew what was going down with these so-called Muslim crews jacking shottas and shit. But if she thought I was gonna say, yeah, they jacked our weed, then she might as well direct her questions to the moon.

'Nothing else!' I raised my voice.

The male Fed looked up, his pen all ready-like. He communicated with his eyes something to the bitch Fed that I couldn't read but the questioning only went on for another five minutes. It was only at the end of the interview that I realised Paps was in floods of tears.

They released me from hospital four days later. Mum came to pick me up but I desperately wanted to stay with Akeisha. Not wanting to cause any fuss I didn't say anything... I called Akeisha constantly instead on her mobile. 'Are you alright? Are you safe? Is there anyone hanging around your gates? Has anyone been following you? Don't step out too late on road. It's too dangerous out there. Don't walk on road alone.'

At home I was treated like a prince. Mum cooked my favourite meals, bought me DVDs, CDs and she had prepared the front room for me. She didn't want to climb the stairs all day to see how I was. It was all good 'cos I had the TV remote control to myself. But I couldn't get away from thinking why was my Noel dead and my black ass living? By my second night back home, I was too depressed to watch any TV or even listen to music. I burst into tears like a pussy and Mum thought about sending me to a private counsellor. We was offered the services of a Fed counsellor but Mum burned that idea.

Akeisha came to see me every evening about 9 p.m. after she put Curtis to bed. Laying together on the sofa-bed, we spoke of our future plans together and where we would like to go on holiday. We settled on Crete 'cos there was so much history there and Curtis would get to hear and watch those cool stories about the Minotaur. But when Akeisha left about midnight I would sink into depression. On the third night I wanted to climb the stairs with my sleeping bag and sleep in my parents' room. I got as far as the staircase landing but I stopped myself 'cos of my pride. I ain't no fucking pussy.

For untold hours at night I had to face the returning image of my best friend's unmoving body laying on the concrete of some ghetto car park. I could even visualise the dirty crisp packets, the stamped-on cigarette butts, the flattened drink cans and a couple of empty Ribena fruit juice cartons that were littered on the ground. My headaches came and went.

On the fourth morning out of hospital Mum took me to my doctor. I was given pills to help me sleep and other pills to help fight my paranoia; I had developed some kinda fucked-up fear of anyone who approached our house. On one morning I scared the shit out of Davinia when she entered the house. Anyway, these tablets put me in some weird trance-like state but at least they made me tired and I slept a little... Sometimes I couldn't walk in a straight line and I pissed myself twice... Proper embarrassing but Mum was cool. She cleaned me up like I was a baby. But I was sober enough to make sure my teeth were cleaned and I was wearing something decent for when Akeisha visited. I started to get out of my sofa-bed at 8 30 p.m. just to step to the window and watch her arrive at 9 p.m. If she was more than a minute late I would call her frantically and ask where she was. 'Where are you? Are you OK? Is anyone following you? Hurry up! Paps or Mum will drive you home and you really should come in a cab.'

God! Did I live for those moments when Akeisha and I cuddled up on the sofa-bed and she would just look at me, caressing my face. And she would break out into a smile... Her visits kept me from being suicidal. She kept me sane. Just. But why Noel and why not me?

Noel's funeral was days away. The Feds were keeping his body doing all kinds of forensic shit on it to see if they could pick up any clues. I don't know what they found but they said Cara could collect

the body tomorrow. All I could think about was I have to make
sure that I don't go through with this shit again with Akeisha. I
have to merk Courtney Thompson.

The funeral itself was a fucking nightmare. At least my black
ass made it. So many people came up to me and offered their
condolences but I don't remember their faces or who they were.
I was in some kinda fucked-up world where I imagined around
every corner I might be pounded by black brothers. I hated being
scared but I had no choice but to stay close to Mum. I was still on
medication and Paps argued that the funeral would be too much
for me but I didn't want my last image of Noel to be of him sparked
out on the concrete.

When I caught the eyes of Cara at the service, anger surged in
me and I wondered what I could do for her. Or if I was honest, I
wanted her stamp of approval for my vengeance… But I wouldn't
ask for it on the day when she laid her son to rest. I did have a
chance to see Noel before he was buried. Cara, Priscilla and
Mum had dressed him in his favourite baggy jeans, sweat top and
baseball hat. He looked peaceful. Like he was simply asleep but in a
coffin. It was only when the coffin was lowered into the ground that
Cara totally lost it. Screaming she was. You could see the strains,
muscles and thin bones in her neck. I've never seen someone open
their mouth so wide. Mum, Priscilla and Auntie Sharon tried to
console her, but Cara just screamed louder. They had to pull her
back so she didn't fall into the grave. I felt I had to do something
for her. Had to…

'MY BABY! MY BABY! MY BABY!'

As I heard and took in every fucked-up scream, my decision to
merk Courtney Thompson just hardened. Nothing else mattered
to me. I would do any shit to make sure I ain't standing at no
motherfucking graveside and watching Akeisha lowered into the
dirt. Fuck that. After I finish my revenge then God can do what
he pleases with me. I didn't really give a shit no more. I was in hell
anyway so bring on the fucking devil, Lucifer or Old Screwface as
Granny used to call him.

Akeisha ushered me into the back of Mum's car after the funeral and I sat and held her hand. I looked at her and she asked me, 'How you feeling?'

'Good,' I replied. 'Noel's at a better place now. He's left us to carry on to live in this fucking *hell*. That's what it feels like to me, a fucking *hell*.'

Kinda shocked at what I said, Akeisha gave me a tight hug. I think it was the first time and only time that I really frightened her. Mum turned around and offered me a disapproving stare. I didn't care anymore. I knew what I had to do.

Five days after Noel's funeral I had recovered enough to link up with Gloria Grahame... We met in the SW9 bar in central Bricky and we found a quiet corner. She bought me a Red Bull and vodka and she asked if I wanted anything to eat. I declined but she ordered some kinda veggie burger for herself. I watched her eat and drink her red wine and she didn't smudge her red lipstick once. But she did leave her mark on the glass.

'I need a gun,' I whispered.

'Are you sure, Dennis?'

'I don't wanna argue about this, Gloria. Can you get me a gun yes or no?'

'Well, it's not my thing, Dennis. That's Dryneck's domain...'

'Then tell him I need a gun.'

'You can't kill all of them, Dennis. It won't bring Noel back.'

'I don't wanna merk all of them. Just wanna duppy one of them. The pussyhole leader.'

'Whoever you kill will not bring Noel back.'

I had to check myself as my voice was getting louder. I dropped it to a whisper again... 'Look, they merked my best friend and they threatened to merk Akeisha... These pussies are not joking, Gloria. It's their leader or me, simple as. He's gonna come for me or Akeisha when he realises he will never get no pussyclaat P's from me. He's gonna have to merk me so he can keep face. That's the way it goes. Ghetto rules. Only one brother gonna be standing and don't give me that shit on black on black murders that you love to go on about or I will fling World War One in your face – mass white on white murder. Don't fuck about with me, Gloria. You and Dryneck can get me a gun if you want to. I know Dryneck has his own arms. You can either deal with me or I'll go to someone else. So, can you get me a gun yes or no?'

She took a sip from her wine and for the first time since I've known her, Gloria looked vulnerable, scared even. She took another sip and played with the fork in her hand. The veggie burger thing was half-eaten. She looked at her plate then flicked her eyes up to me. She put her fork down on the plate and then lit a cigarette… She blew her smoke towards the ceiling.

'Then I can't say no,' she finally said. 'If someone killed Dryneck I'd wanna kill them so the answer is yes.'

'OK, that's all good.'

'We had to move, Dennis,' Gloria said. 'One night we came back from the theatre and there was a crowd of them in the forecourt of the estate. They stared at Dryneck and he had to reveal his gun. That didn't deter them though. They kept on staring. I must admit I shit myself. We knew then that our time was up. Time to get out of the game. We moved out a few days later and we're renting a place in Purley before we head west at the end of the year.'

To be honest, I didn't care about whatever crew threatening Gloria and Dryneck… At least Dryneck had a gun to protect himself and his girl. I didn't have shit.

'When can I pick the gun up?' I asked.

'I'll call you.'

'How much?'

'On the house.'

'I want instructions, all the shit.'

'Don't worry, we're careful with all that kind of thing.'

'Nothing too big,' I said. 'I wanna put it in my inside pocket of my leather jacket. I wanna know all about the safety catch and that shit.'

'Don't worry, we'll get what you want. But you must get rid of it. Not in a council bin or any place like that. In the Thames. For all our sakes that gun can't be found once you have used it.'

'I hear you.'

There was a pause as I drained half of my Red Bull and vodka.

Then after a while Gloria smiled. 'Dryneck asked me to marry him.'

'You serious?'

'Yeah, can you believe that? I said I'll think about it.'

'What's there to think about? Don't you love him?'

'Yeah, I do. But people wouldn't rush into marriage if they had to pay the same amount to the minister as the divorce lawyer.'

Gloria's remark relaxed me a bit and made me laugh. But I wanted to get back to business.

'You'll call me right?'

'I promised, didn't I,' Gloria answered.

'Don't be stalling me hoping that I'll change my mind.'

'It'll be about a week,' she assured. 'You're getting a clean gun, Dennis. That takes days to arrange.'

'Just don't make it too long.'

'As long as it takes, Dennis.'

I finished my vodka and Red Bull and stood up.

'Dennis, be careful.'

'Call me soon,' I said as I left the bar.

I didn't have the gun yet but I decided I was gonna start scouting for Courtney Thompson's black ass. Brixton mosque should be a good bet on a Friday morning.

Chapter Seventeen

STAKEOUT

Next Friday I got up early. It was before 7 a.m. and when Mum saw me she thought I was going to work. Everton had told me to take as much time as I wanted to recover. So I wasn't going to the garage.

'So where are you going?' Mum wanted to know.

'For a drive,' I said, avoiding her eyes. 'Some fresh air.'

'Are you sure you'll be OK driving, Dennis? It's only been two days since you was on medication.'

'I'm good, Mum. I just want some fresh air. It's better in the early morning.'

'Why not go for a walk?'

'It's alright, Mum, I can drive. In fact I was thinking of driving to the park and then walk.'

'If you are sure, Dennis.'

I made myself a strong coffee and put a teaspoonful of honey in it. With that I had three slices of toast. I was still eating the last slice as I headed out of the front door. 'Bye, Mum.'

'Take care, Dennis.'

I got in my ride and finished my toast. I pulled my Chicago Bulls baseball hat down to almost cover my eyes. Then I switched the engine on and tuned into Choice FM. I turned the volume down from what was usual for me and the DJ was saying it was gonna be a hot day. I drove off and headed for the mosque in Gresham Road, central Bricky. I pulled up about sixty yards away from the mosque, parking on the opposite side of the street. Adrenaline was flowing through me but fear had yet to grip me. I found it ironic that the Fed station was only another thirty yards further on from the mosque.

Some worshippers had already arrived for morning prayers and men were mingling around in front of the mosque in their bright garments and strange hats; why were the hats all too small? Children were also there with their parents. The women looked elegant and mysterious in their long dark robes and Noel once joked to me how does a Muslim brother know if the girl he's chirpsing is buff or not?

My eyes were focused on every new arrival and every departure. If a bus shielded my vision then I'd get out of my ride for a better look. I didn't want to miss Courtney Thompson and his crew. I got back into my ride when I realised that he might arrive from behind me and spot me.

By 8.30 a.m. the traffic was building up but I remained where I was. Tension was building inside of me and every black brother I saw under the age of twenty-five was a potential enemy.

By 8.45 a.m., I finally saw Courtney Thompson and his crew climb out of a BMW and a Lexus. My mouth went all dry-like and fear suddenly filled me up like a bitch injection… In my head I saw the shit getting kicked out of Noel and I wondered if it would be my black ass next? My black ass might be lowered into the dirt. Mum would be making sure that the tablecloth being used for my wake was spotless. Paps would be wondering why did God spare him and allow his son to die.

The rides couldn't park outside the mosque so the drivers had to park somewhere else. Courtney's fucked-up beard posse were all dressed in white and beige and all of them were wearing some kind of hat. It looked like they were wearing some kind of black slippers too. I recognised at least three of them. *Fucking pussies!* Again, I saw in my inner vision the savage kicks that merked Noel.

I shook my head to rid myself of the picture and concentrated my sight once more…

Then I saw Courtney's crew approach the entrance but three older guys confronted them and an argument took place. I noticed that the older men were not wearing anything on their feet. From what I could make out the greybeards would not allow Courtney and his crew to enter the mosque. From where I was I could hear raised voices, some in Arabic. *'Ackroog! Ackroog!'* Jostling and pushing was going on. Courtney himself was gesturing wildly with his hands, obviously fucked off. But it didn't matter how loud he shouted or how mad his body language was, the elder Muslims wouldn't let him in. *'Ackroog! Ackroog!'* I sat back down in my ride, closed the door and laughed out loud. On my stereo Jay-Z was rapping about some dirt off his shoulder.

Moments later, Courtney pulled out his mobile phone from a pocket and called somebody. Then my own mobile sounded and it nearly made me jump out of my black skin. What the fuck?

'Hello?' I said cautiously. My hands were shaking. My heartbeat pounded… I thought about starting the ride in case I needed a quick getaway. How the fuck would Thompson know my number? I only got this new mobile the other day and I hadn't put any numbers in it yet. Be logical, Dennis. It can't be him. Be cool. Don't panic and chat normally.

'It's Mum, Dennis. Where are you? Something the matter?'

'I'm just pulled up outside Brockwell Park, Mum.'

'Are you OK?'

'Yes, Mum.'

'If you start to feel dizzy you come straight home. Even leave your car where it is and one of us will come and get you.'

'No need for that, Mum. I feel OK.'

'You sure, Dennis?'

'Yeah I'm sure, Mum. I'm gonna park somewhere and go for a walk in the park. I might try swimming later on.'

'Well you look after yourself, Dennis, and if you're feeling dizzy you call me or your father straightaway. Oh, and park your car legally, Dennis. You know what Lambeth parking wardens are like.'

'Yeah, Mum, they're brutal.'

'Have you got the doctor's number in your mobile?'

'Er, yes, Mum.'

'OK, Dennis. I'm just walking into my office now. It's your dad's day off today so if you need anything, he's there. Bye.'

'See you later, Mum.'

Just as I killed the call, the Lexus and the BMW arrived outside the mosque. Courtney and his brethren climbed into the rides as they shouted badwords at Muslim elders... Other male worshippers emerged from the mosque and they were gesturing with their arms for Courtney's posse to move the fuck away. I thought of bouncers at the Ministry of Sound nightclub and laughed to myself again. *Pussies...*

Should I follow them? Do I have the nerve? Of course I should track their black asses! You think Noel would have pussied out? Noel would have stepped up to the mosque and shanked Courtney right there and then.

I kept a safe distance as they turned left into Bricky High Street. As usual in rush hour the traffic got vexed and the pavements were proper heaving with pedestrians... The traffic lights seemed to stay red for ages at the crossing to Bricky underground station. Hundreds of people were getting on and off buses and for a moment they filled my vision. But I could just see the BMW about thirty yards away. Above, the clouds were parting and it looked like the Choice FM DJ was right about the weather. Noel loved days like this when he would cruise in his ride and feast his eyes on buff chicks, halting traffic as he chirpsed girls walking by. I won't hear Noel's deep laugh again while he's doing shit like that. Thompson has to be merked.

I followed the BMW and Lexus up Brixton Hill and after turning left into the South Circular, they made their way into Palace Road council estate. I was surprisingly calm. But I had to be careful now, not too much traffic on road. Don't want them pussies to turn around and see my black ass.

They pulled up outside a shop within Palace Road estate and two of them got out. The flat we used to live in was just a three minute walk away. There's probably refugees living there now. Stay focused, Dennis!

Remaining a safe distance away, I parked and just watched. A mother walked inside the shop with her two kids. Older kids were performing wheelies on bikes and one fell off... The others laughed out loud. Shouldn't the brats be in school? No, it's the summer holidays. Dennis, don't get distracted. Focus on the cars.

Courtney stayed in the BMW. He was in the back seat. The mother with the kids came out with a newspaper and was lighting a cigarette and if I smoked cancer sticks I would have lit one too. I should've burned a fat-head after breakfast to help relax me.

After a couple of minutes the two fake Muslims who went to the shop returned carrying bottles of drinks, crisps, other sweets and cigarettes. The two rides performed U-turns and headed in my direction. It caught me off-guard and I had to move *Mission Impossible*-quick. I ducked before they went past and my heart did some pole-vaulting shit but I soon regained my composure. When their rides passed mine, I could hear hip hop music blaring from their windows. Yeah, fear was in me but I had control of it.

Executing a frantic three-point turn, I tracked them to the back streets of Streatham. I looked into my rear-view mirror and realised I was sweating and gripping the steering wheel too tight. Relax, Dennis. Relax. I pressed the play button on my ride stereo. Mya was singing 'Taste This'. I could picture Akeisha singing in a MTV Base-style video. Then the screen suddenly went blood-red. When it cleared Akeisha was laying on the ground. She had been shot through the head. Courtney appeared on screen with a smoking gun in his hand. He was laughing manically. Laughing. He didn't stop laughing.

I shook my head madly to rid myself of the image.

They climbed out of the rides on Faygate Road and I watched them from about a hundred yards away... I wiped my face and concentrated my eyes again. I don't think they suspected a damn thing. *Pussies*. My heartbeat gathered pace as I saw Courtney Thompson climb out of the BMW. He was wearing this gold-coloured skull cap and he was smoking a cigarette. If I don't merk him I hope cancer duppies his wannabe bin Laden ass.

They all entered a house and my eyes were focused on that front door for another two hours... Nobody of the original crew departed but others arrived, some in Muslim-type clothes and some in normal garms. What is this place? A recruitment centre for terrorists?

I recognised at least one of them. Didn't know him by name but he was a shotta from Black Prince Road, Vauxhall ends. A tall, messed-up face ugly brother. Maybe he was paying his tax 'cos he was only in the house for five minutes. *Pussy.*

3 p.m. At last some movement. Courtney and his crew come out from the house. They were still wearing their bright garments and too-small hats. They climbed into their rides as I started my engine. They headed to Brixton Hill and I followed them as they turned into New Park Road. I was quite calm and kept a safe distance. They drove into New Park Road council estate, Brixton Hill ends and I considered if I should follow them in. And then I remembered that Courtney's mum still lived in the estate. I parked fifty yards away from the estate entrance. I started on another pack of cheese and onion crisps as Tupac rapped about 'No More Pain'.

Five minutes later I saw the BMW and the Lexus emerge from the estate. Courtney wasn't inside any of the cars. What do I do? Just wait? When I get the gun I don't wanna merk him near to where his mother lives. Can't do that shit... No, I'll just wait and see where he goes.

Wait I did. I was proper determined. Tupac kept me company in the late afternoon and early evening. I got my reward at 8.30 p.m. when I saw the BMW return. Sure enough, the ride picked up Courtney and they drove out of the estate and headed for central Bricky. I was about ten car lengths behind as we passed Bricky Town Hall. The usual winos and drunks were mingling around Windrush Square and I noticed the weather was still warm enough for drinkers at the Bug Bar to sample their shit on the outside seats and benches. Some drunks were flat out on the grass. *Don't* get distracted, Dennis. Focus.

The BMW drove along Bricky High Street but they didn't turn into Gresham Road as I expected them to. I felt a pang of hunger but I had no more crisps. The empty packets were now surrounding my feet and I only had half a Lucozade bottle left…

Just as I was thinking that Noel would have loved to own that BMW, it now turned right, towards Angel Town. I drove one-handed as I clicked open my glove compartment. I had a black metal bar inside there. It was Noel's. I speeded up as images of Akeisha filled my head. I glanced at the metal bar, then looked ahead of me and back to my weapon. I wound down the driver-side window all the way. Then the BMW turned off towards Loughborough Junction. I heard myself breathing out hard but my heart was still pumping. I closed the glove compartment and slowed down a bit. I wondered if they saw me in their rear-view mirror. Tupac was chanting 'Heartz Of Men'.

I watched the blue BMW pull up at the feet of one of the white-coloured council tower blocks that dominated this part of Bricky. I was about seventy yards away and I parked my ride and turned off my engine. It was only Courtney that got out of the Bimmer and he made his way to a white council block. From where I was I could see the balconies of the block where Courtney headed so I got out of my ride and just looked upwards. The sun was setting in that direction so I put my sunglasses on. Meanwhile, the blue BMW pulled away. They still hadn't seen me. *Pussies.*

Two minutes later, Courtney appeared on the fourth floor balcony. He walked along and then rattled a letter box. Moments later, this white girl opened the door. I didn't see much of her, just half a face, one leg and one arm. I bet she had a Croydon facelift. Courtney glanced behind him before entering and closed the door behind him. Bang went my chi chi man theory.

I'll merk him there, I said to myself. Before he gets in the lift. Yeah, next Friday. I just hope that white bitch is a regular Friday night wok for him. I've done all my scouting and shit. Fuck! Was it this easy to stalk somebody and they don't know shit? I'm gonna blaze him, duppy his motherfucking wannabe-a-terrorist ass. But I still need somebody to justify it. I'll see Cara after the weekend.

Yeah. See how Cara is. Haven't seen her since the funeral. I haven't even seen Priscilla and checked on how she is.

I returned home. I needed to wind down. I found Paps reading his newspaper. When he saw me he placed his newspaper on the floor and he glared at me. I was about to leave the room but he said, 'Sit down, Dennis.'

I sat down and I felt more nervous than I had been following Courtney Thompson. Sweat returned to my forehead with a vengeance. 'In the hospital,' Paps began, 'when you was interviewed by the police, I was wrong to make my outburst. Wrong.'

'Yeah, so?' I said. I didn't want the conversation to last more than a minute. I wiped my face with the palm of my hand.

'We have to trust the police, Dennis,' Paps said.

'You what?'

'Trust the police. Yes, it might sound hypocritical but it can't be a "them and us" situation for ever. We have to work together, trust each other. Too many black kids are getting killed and the killers are going free all because no-one in the black community will talk.'

'You've changed your programming,' I remarked.

'Dennis, I feel you're hiding something.' Paps' voice was now deeper, more serious. I was trapped in his angry gaze.

'No I'm not,' I answered.

'Are you sure you didn't recognise any of your attackers?'

'You calling me a liar?'

'No, I'm not calling you a liar. But I think you might be scared to reveal who did this to Noel and you. It's quite understandable, nothing to be ashamed of.'

'I'm not scared, Paps.'

'So you don't know who did this?'

'No, Paps!' I was shouting now.

'Don't you want these people to get caught?' Paps asked.

'Of course I do! I don't know who it was! And you're a hypocrite! All my life you've been telling me stories how the Feds were corrupt, how the Feds planted evidence, how the Feds framed black brothers, how the Feds pounded you in cells. And now you're telling me we have to work together? You never trusted them and I don't. Simple as. Got nothing to tell them anyway.'

'Yes, I am a hypocrite!' yelled back Paps. 'But please, Dennis… If there is anything that you know can help the police you have got to tell them… The police are *not* the enemy here.'

'I don't know anything else. *Nothing* to add!'

Paps picked up his walking stick, glared at me for half a minute and then limped out of the room. He slammed the door behind him in disgust. I didn't care. I had to merk Courtney Thompson. Anyway, back in 1981 Paps and his crew duppied a Bricky crime lord. He didn't go to the Feds when Auntie Denise was kidnapped… So *burn* Paps and his hypocrisy.

That night I went to Akeisha's. I wasn't good company and I didn't play with Curtis like I normally did. I didn't really want to speak to Akeisha's parents either. I just crashed out on Akeisha's bed and tried to sleep for a while. Despite closing my eyes all I could see was Akeisha getting shot by Courtney Thompson and Noel getting kicked to death.

Akeisha woke me up with a kiss and we made frantic love like it was the last time we would ever be together. Usually we worried about Akeisha's parents hearing us but this time it was so intense. We didn't care, or I didn't care. Throughout, my face was within an inch of hers and I was just kissing her on the lips repeatedly, looking into her eyes. I kept on thinking what would become of me if Courtney Thompson merked my girl? I was bordering on insanity now so there wouldn't be much hope for my state of mind if my worse scenario actually happened.

After we made love we were laying in the bed, wrapped together. Her left cheek was pressed against my right cheek. I liked it like that. As usual I was holding her too tight but I liked that too.

'What you scared of, Dennis?'

'What do you mean?'

'You were shaking earlier when I hugged you and you've been preoccupied about something.'

'It's the medication I was on. Even though I stopped taking all the tablets I still feel drowsy.'

'No, Dennis. This wasn't drowsy. You're scared of something.'

'Yeah, maybe.'

'You'll be alright now, Dennis. You got people who love you and will look after you. You're safe now.'

'I'm not scared of that, Akeisha.'

'Then what?'

I sat up and looked at her. Then I cradled her jaw and cheeks with my palms like the way my mother always did to me. 'You can read me good, Akeisha. Yeah, you're right. I am scared. Proper scared. Scared of losing you.'

She smiled and kissed me on the lips. 'You're being silly,' she laughed. 'I ain't gonna leave you! No way! Ain't we been tighter than we've ever been? Stop sweating, Dennis! This girl's not gonna go walking out or go missing on you. And I can't wait to go Crete with you. Everything's gonna be alright.'

She kissed me again. She didn't understand what I meant but she seemed so happy that I was with her. I wanted so much to be honest with her but I didn't want to fuck up the moment or the vibe by admitting I was losing my mind 'cos I feared she might be merked. So I laid back down, hugged her tight and pressed my cheek against hers. I wished I could stay like this for ever. I wished Noel was by my side on my mission. With him it would be easy.

The following Sunday Mum roasted a big leg of lamb and cooked rice and peas. She also prepared side dishes of salad and shit, bought some wine and invited Auntie Denise, Uncle Everton and the twins over. We dined on plates and drank from glasses that Mum normally had displayed in the front room cabinet. She even made an attempt to make Granny's rum punch and I had to admit it wasn't that bad. Paps said it was excellent but he had Brownie points to gain. Mum ignored Paps and everybody else as she catered for all my needs. Davinia, smart as she is, noticed this but didn't say anything. Mum was being so nice to me it was embarrassing… Paps and myself were hardly on speaking terms but that was all good. It meant I wouldn't have to suffer another interrogation for the time being.

As Mum was serving the dessert of apple pie and custard I

received a text. It was from Gloria. All it read was *got it, can you talk?* Gloria was always cautious like that. I excused myself from the table and went to the toilet. Our toilet was so clean and smelled so good you could invite your complaining fussing auntie in for a chat and not feel bad.

I called Gloria. 'Can I pick it up now?'

'I'm at the South Bank,' Gloria said.

'Can't we link up? Now like?'

'If you have to, Dennis.'

'OK, where you wanna link?'

'Well, I've got to drive home and pick up your goods. Give me an hour and I'll meet you in the Sainsbury's car park in Nine Elms.'

'Shizzle my nizzle!'

'You what?'

'Oh, nothing. Just something that Noel used to say. It means everything is cool...'

'OK, Sainsbury's car park.'

'Be there.'

I killed the call, flushed the toilet and when I returned to the front room, I wolfed down my apple pie and custard like I was Homer Simpson.

Mum was vexed about me leaving when guests were here but I just wanted to take ownership of the gun. I still heard her nagging when I shut the front door behind me. I didn't care.

Gloria was five minutes early and when she spotted me she even left her ride and climbed into mine. She had never done that before. She was carrying a shopping bag and when I looked inside it there was something bulky wrapped in kitchen foil. She took off her sunglasses and looked at me. 'I didn't expect to be delivering this kind of thing when I started in this game,' she said... 'But this is your property now. If you use it or don't use it, you have to get rid of it. *Properly*. I don't want you ringing me up saying that you wanna give it back. Dryneck told me to make that very clear...'

'I hear you. Everything there? Instructions and shit?'

'Everything is there, Dennis.'

She opened the passenger door and prepared to leave. But she thought about something and sat back down, pulling the door closed. 'Would it sound racist if I said I hate those fucking Muslims? You know, the ones that wanna kill white people? 'Cos that's what they mean when they say they want jihad against the west. Is it my fault that my race has had the better of it in the last few hundred years?'

'Look, Gloria,' I replied. 'Don't really want to get in this argument again. All I know is that I have to deal with Courtney Thompson... Simple as. This ain't no religious mission I'm on. I ain't no *raas* Crusader and I ain't doing my mission for Christian kind and shit like that. I still think of Thompson as the ugly motherfucker in school who didn't have no bredrens and loved his fried chicken and crisps... Thompson and his crew merked my best friend and threatened to duppy my girl. His reasons were stone-cold money and rep. So I'm gonna merk Thompson. Call it personal, simple as.'

'Then know this, Dennis. If Dryneck didn't hate those Muslims so much then he wouldn't have got you what's in that bag. He was totally against getting you the gun.'

Gloria opened the door and was gone. She didn't even look back and her steps were no longer elegant or sexy but angry. I nodded. At least she was honest.

She had placed the shopping bag in the feet position for the passenger seat. I crouched and started to unwrap the kitchen foil. And there it was. A black gun. It looked new and it felt greasy to the touch. There were instructions with it in English and in German. Stapled to the instructions was a polythene bag that contained seven bullets. A chill went down my spine as I realised the seriousness of what I was about to do. But my resolve hardened when I remembered the suffering wailing of Cara at Noel's funeral. Courtney Thompson has to ketch a fire, as Granny would have put it.

The following Thursday night, the day before I planned to merk Thompson I arrived at Cara's flat at just after 10 p.m. Cara herself opened the front door. She was wearing a sky blue dressing-gown. Her hair was all over the place. Her eyes were half-closed and I couldn't tell if she had been drinking or if she was tired...

She let me in and I have never seen the place so clean. There was a whisky bottle and a lemonade bottle on the coffee table and a pint glass that Noel had kidnapped from a pub. The ashtray was full of big-head butts. I could hardly sleep without thinking of Noel so what must it be like for her?

'How you doing, Dennis?' she asked.

Many people had asked me that question since Noel's death and in reply I was always polite and said, I'm OK. Like fuck I was OK! But I didn't have to put a gloss on it for Cara. She knew better than anyone the shit I was going through. The lack of motivation to get up the next morning to deal with the living, the "can't be bothered" shit. I hadn't brushed my teeth for three days and worse of all, I hadn't wiped my white Nikes clean for a bitch of a long while.

'Fucked up,' I finally answered. 'I feel like a ghost, a duppy… Like I ain't part of the real world no more. You get me?'

I dropped myself in an armchair and looked at the TV. Cara was watching the BBC 10 o'clock news and had turned the volume down. Cara laid down on the sofa and looked up at the ceiling. 'I dunno how I feel,' she said. 'All I know is that it just hurts. *Fucking* hurts. People tell me I will feel better. But I don't wanna *feel* better. Fuck that! If I'm gonna grieve for the rest of my days then let it be.'

She closed her eyes and this pained expression she had made me get up out of my chair and go towards her. I squeezed her left shoulder and she opened her eyes and I guess if she had any tears left, she would have cried. Suddenly, she started singing…

'Love and hate can never be friends
Here I come with love and not hatred
Surely goodness and mercy shall follow I all the days of my life
There'll be no one who'd wish to be with no evil man
Cos there'll come a day they'll be whipped by the Father's hand
Live up roots children
Live up rasta children
My head is anointed and my cup runneth over…'

Cara trailed off and opened her eyes. 'I used to love singing in church, Dennis. I used to love singing full stop. But when I had Noel I stopped going church. My mum was so disappointed in me. She'd thought I'd have a white wedding one day, live in a three-bedroom house, have a garden where I'd grow my own greens and cabbages, bake cakes for the church's day out to Blackpool, you know, all of that fuckery. But it didn't happen. The song I just sang, Dennis, was a big hit for Dennis Brown back in the day. Did you know you was named after Dennis Brown, Dennis?'

'Yes, Cara.'

'Your mum and everybody else has been brilliant with me, Dennis. So kind. But my reality is that *they* can't make me feel better. Only singing does that. My mum's gonna take me back to the church. It's where I belong. A lot of my generation has forgotten that and we haven't passed it on to our children. I'm feeling guilty now 'cos I hardly took Noel to church. I don't know what went wrong. When I was a little girl I used to be in the choir. I felt like a big star. I could play the piano too. At school me and my friends wanted to be in a lovers' rock group. Both of my parents warned me that nice Christian girls should stay away from reggae. But I didn't listen and I used to sneak out to clubs, raves and go bluesing... That was the start of my fallout with my parents. But Mum's been brilliant over the last few days. She told me to sing whenever I want to. She knows it's good for me. I bet you didn't know that old Cara could sing, Dennis...'

'A bit. Mum said something about it a few times. Even Mum sings Dennis Brown tunes in the bath.'

For the briefest of moments there was a hint of a smile upon Cara's face. 'Yeah, your parents loved Dennis Brown. Everyone did,' she said.

She trailed off again and this time there were tears in her eyes. For the next five minutes I hugged her and cried with her. Then I dried her tears and said, 'If you had a chance, Cara, to face Noel's killers, what would you do? What would you do, Cara?'

She thought about it for a long time. Then Cara's sadness turned to anger and I saw her face change from being broken to one that burned for vengeance. 'I'D KILL THEM BLOODCLAAT! THEM

KILL ME FIRST BORN AND ME BORN AND GROW AS A CHRISTIAN GIRL BUT ME COULD NEVER FORGIVE THEM. THEM FUCKING PUSSY'OLE KILL ME FIRST BORN! SO LORD GIVE ME STRENGTH TO KILL THEM TOO!'

I left Cara's flat that night knowing what I had to do.

The following evening I parked my ride on Minet Road. It was about a thirty-second sprint away from the council block where Courtney's white bitch lived. It was just after 6 p.m. and even though I didn't expect Courtney for another two hours or so, my shirt was sticking to my skin and my heart was racing.

I placed the gun in my right jeans pocket. The pockets were deep so no-one would see it... I had already loaded the gun and as I climbed out of my ride I looked at the people on the street going about their everyday business. I realised they could be potential witnesses and in my head I could see Fed blue and white tape all over the damn place.

Walking over to the tower block where Courtney's ho lived I kept my eyes on the fourth floor balcony. There was no movement from the front door. I reached the block and I wasn't sure what to do with myself. There were still people about. Some were waiting for the lift and some were getting out of it. I decided to go on little walks to and from the lift but that made me too nervous. I just felt that everybody was looking at me.

In between the council blocks there were spaces of greenery. I headed to one of those and just crashed on the grass. I thought I'd relax myself by building a fat-head but I even had trouble doing that. My fingers and thumbs were shaking. Shit! It was only 6.30 p.m.

Burning the fat-head made me feel better. My hands stopped trembling but I got a sudden attack of the munchies. I had to get something to eat. The nearest shop was on Loughborough Road, about fifty yards away. But if I went inside the shop I might miss Courtney. Fuck it! I had to get something to eat.

Went to the shop. Bought two packets of chocolate biscuits. Went back to my place on the green, eyes proper checking everything. Finished the biscuits within minutes... Had the munchies bad.

Built another big-head and this time I managed to roll it to my liking.

7 p.m. Felt a bit more relaxed. Thought of good times with Noel and all the pranks we got up to at school. Then I decided I'd better move into position for when Courtney turned up. If he turned up. Do I want him to turn up? Yeah, I do... Of course I do. *Don't* pussy out now, Dennis. *Do* this for Noel and Cara. Let the game begin.

Near to the lift was an emergency staircase and I sat on the first landing of that. I could see the road because the window on the first floor of the landing was smashed and I could see anybody who walked towards the lift. My only worry was that I couldn't see people coming out from the lift. I would just have to take the chance.

7.30 p.m... My hands were proper clammy. Sweat was dripping from my forehead. I couldn't keep still and I must've sat down and stood up about fifty times in the last half an hour. Can I do this? Remember Cara. Her tears, her fury, her need for vengeance. Courtney threatened to merk Akeisha. Remember that too. God! Preparing to kill a man ain't easy. Granny would think I took a walk with Old Screwface and sold my soul. Whatever happens she must never know. Got to control my fear. Should I wrap another big-head? No, Dennis. Ready or not... Do this shit.

7.48 p.m... The blue BMW turned into the road of the white tower blocks. I could hear hip hop playing from the car stereo. My gun was in a Sainsbury's plastic bag and I took it out from my pocket. I crept down the flight of concrete steps. The BMW pulled up. A car door opened and closed. I could recognise Busta Rhymes' voice on the car stereo but I hadn't a clue what he was rapping about. Busta's rap was always too fast for my liking. I didn't hear Courtney's steps. He must be wearing trainers. But I sensed him. My eyes were darting everywhere. Beads of sweat dropped on the gun. My breathing accelerated... I heard the BMW pull away. Busta Rhymes faded.

Then I saw him amble into the entrance of the block. Right in front of me. I pointed the gun at him and he stared at the gun barrel. He stopped walking. Then he stared at me. I slowly walked towards him and he backed off. His head made a movement to his left as if he was looking for an escape. Then his head made a movement to his right. He looked at me again. Proper scared he was. Disbelieving he was… His hands were slowly moving upwards to cover his face and then he made a rapid movement. That's when I shot him. Not sure where I hit him but he dropped to the ground. I've never heard a noise so loud. Like a firecracker it was. He was still moving on the ground and I raced up to him. I loomed over him. I held the gun with my two hands and I searched his eyes. The gun was beginning to feel heavy. Courtney's eyes were pleading, begging. The rest of his face expressed his pain. Severe pain. But he merked Noel and threatened to merk my Akeisha. I couldn't allow him to get up. I shot him twice again in the chest. There was more blood seeping from his back than his front. His eyes were now half-closing. That's what I was waiting for. Now I had to move…

Running as hard as I could, I got back to my ride. There wasn't a lot of space to get out of my parking position and as I reversed I hit something. Had to get away. I dropped the gun on the floor of the passenger side. My heart was still racing and the temptation to drive fast was overwhelming but I just about managed to keep control. I headed to Clapham. Tupac's 'Tradin War Stories' was playing. Got on the A3 and passed through Wandsworth and then Putney. Felt a bit calmer. Headed to Richmond and parked my ride on a street there. The gun was back in the plastic bag and in my pocket. I climbed out of my ride and I noticed I had broken the passenger side rear brake light. I walked towards the river as the insides of my stomach felt like Fatboy Slim was mixing it.

There was a pub located on the river bank and I headed for that. People were enjoying the warm evening and the sight of three black brothers laughing and drinking with white people made me feel like I didn't stick out too much. There was a path that ran parallel to the river and I walked along that. About a hundred yards away from the pub I hurled the gun into the Thames. I walked on another fifty yards or so, sat down on a grass verge and built a big-head. As I torched it, I realised I had taken away everything Courtney Thompson had. Every potential wok, every child he might father, every pleasure, every Sunday dinner, every joke he might crack, every smile, every laugh and any hot tune he might nod his head to… I took that all away from him. I drove home with guilt seeping into my bones… Tupac was chanting about how Shorty wants to be a thug.

Akeisha would be safe now. Courtney's bredrens wouldn't go after her now that their leader is duppied.

The next few days I hardly ventured out of my bedroom. I complained of headaches and dizziness but the truth was I didn't want anyone to see the guilt in my eyes. Mum was still being nice to me and Paps still wanted to know if I could identify Noel's killers. But it was Davinia who noticed my fucked-up mind.

'Dennis, I think you should go and see a counsellor,' she said to me one evening as she brought my dinner to me. 'You're on the verge of a breakdown.'

'I'm alright, sis,' I lied. 'It's just these headaches.'

Courtney Thompson's murder was reported in the local press but there was no sign of it in the national newspapers or television. My mind began to play tricks on me and I started to imagine that every caller to the house was a Fed or that my murder of Thompson would be staged on *Crimewatch*. I had to get out of this bedroom. But what if Courtney's crew suspected me of merking him? They might be looking for me, they might start tracking me. I need to defend my black ass. Need to chat to Gloria again. One last favour. I called her when no-one was at home.

'It's me, Dennis.'

'It certainly is! I never thought you'd do it. How are you?'

'Not good.'

'Did you get rid of it?'

'Of course.'

'Where?'

'The Thames.'

'Good!'

'I need another, Gloria.'

'Why?'

'Self preservation. Shall I say that some fucked-off brothers might be looking for me. If that does happen I want to defend myself.'

'I see your point. Give me four days.'

'OK.'

'Same rules as before.'

'OK.'

'You'll have to pay for it this time.'

'No worries.'

Gloria killed the call. That evening I told Mum that I wanna get back to some kinda normality and that I would return to work in five days time after I finished my latest set of tablets. She kissed me on the forehead and gave me a hug.

Five days later I was returning to work. Mum had made me a packed lunch of corned beef sandwiches, crisps and two apples. My sandwich box was sitting on my passenger seat and as I drove to Everton's garage, the rush of wind that came through my driver-side window felt good. I then stopped at a traffic light and I briefly glanced in my rear-view mirror. Someone was flashing me. It was the Feds. The lights had turned to green but I didn't see because I closed my eyes momentarily in dread. My heart dropped. I pulled over just a little way beyond the traffic lights and the Fed car parked immediately behind me. A male Fed got out of the car and approached me. For a short second I considered driving off at high speed but I didn't give it serious thought.

'Your brake light is not working, sir,' the Fed said. 'Are you aware of that, sir?'

'No, officer.'

'Would you mind stepping out of the car, sir? Just a routine search.'

I climbed out of my ride and I asked the officer if it was alright if I called my boss, Everton, at work, for I didn't think I'd be coming in today. The feeling I had at that point was an empty one, a weird one. As if this *was* how it was meant to be. I had to *pay*. The officer looked at me strangely and then he was joined by the other officer and they started to search my ride. The brand new gun that I bought from Gloria only two days ago was in the car glove compartment, bullets and all. If they had asked me to confess to the Courtney Thompson murder I would've done. But they didn't.

Chapter Eighteen

DAVINIA

July 2006

So here I am in Pentonville prison. They gave me five years bird but I got some of that chopped off for good behaviour. It hasn't been too bad apart from the start of my sentence. 'Cos I come from the Dirty South, I had east, west and north London brothers trying it on with me. I had a few fights, got mashed a couple of times, pounded head a couple of times and I won some respect. Looking back on my early bird I felt kinda lucky that I didn't get burst… You might be in prison but there's still a chance of being shanked and burst by a hot-headed brother.

There was a bit of beef between rastas, Christians and black Muslims but nowhere near as bad as what we all heard was happening in Belmarsh prison. I only lost privileges once when I pounded the fuck out of this new cell-mate I had. He refused to clean up his shit when he pissed all over the toilet seat and left his scum in the sink… I got two weeks solitary. I didn't really bitch about my punishment but I always bitched about the fuck all chances I had to visit the prison library… Sometimes the waiting time could be weeks before you had the chance to read another book. In my letters to Akeisha and Paps I asked them to send me certain books but most of what they sent never reached me.

They're not interested in making people better inside here. Screws have this power over you and they're happy to express that shit. It ain't no surprise that so many guys in here reoffend when they get released and I reckon they return to crime 'cos they're made to feel like dumb pussies inside prison. Simple as. To survive in the outside world you gotta be strong and be rooted and ignore the fucked-up behaviour of the screws. I was lucky 'cos I never forgot what my parents had drilled into me from an early age. I *knew* I had something worthwhile to give to society. I had shamed my parents enough by being inside so I had to do something.

Since doing bird I've passed my A-Level history and English literature. Mum and Paps were proper proud about that and when Davinia last came to visit I told her I was now the brains of the family. Davinia is visiting me today and there is only three weeks of my sentence to serve. I write to Akeisha once a week and although she begged with me to send her a visiting letter, I refused. It was bad enough trying to do my bird here but if I saw her in the flesh and then I was escorted back to the cells, it would do my fucking head in. She understood in the end. It took me four months to agree to see Mum and I made Paps promise that he'd never tell Granny about my prison term. I was *not at home* whenever Granny made a long-distance call from Jamaica.

In those first months of my sentence I had to admit I felt serious guilt about merking Courtney Thompson. I thought about his younger two sisters and brother and I couldn't help but remember the times when Courtney's mother and my granny chatted to each other at church. But it so easily could have been my mum or Akeisha's mum grieving. Cara was still proper sad and she'll probably stay that way till the end of her days. I kept on asking myself why life had lost its value with my brothers and myself? How did Courtney and myself get into a state where we wanted to merk a brother or a school colleague?

At the end of the day though, I know even though I'm only in here for gun possession, I'm a murderer. I guess I'll have to carry that till they burn my black ass at the crematorium. I thought about death a lot in my cell and the scenes of Noel's murder and burial were constant visitors to me at night. No way they'll lower my body into the earth! Fuck that! They can cremate my black ass.

Davinia had grown into a good-looking woman and as she sat opposite me I had this feeling of pride and nice vibes for her. Inmates around me openly admired her but she was used to that by now. In all my time in prison she had never talked down to me, lectured me or failed to visit when she said she would.

'Hi, Dennis,' she said. 'How you keeping?'

'Same shit, different toilets,' I answered. 'You're putting on weight and didn't I tell you not to come here wearing your fucking crop tops?'

'Well, if that's your response I must look good!'

'Anyway, I'm looking forward to getting out of this shit. I can't wait.'

'Nor can we.'

'Anyway, what's gwarnin with you? You gonna take a gap year from uni?'

'No, I wanna get my education out of the way. I'm going on a week's holiday to Tunisia with friends from uni and then I'll be preparing to return to Loughborough.'

'What's a matter with you, Davinia? Why don't you take off travelling and shit for a year? See Granny in Jamaica or something. Life is to be enjoyed as well as all that studying shit you do. Ain't you tired of that? Do you have some kinda fucked-up allergy to having fun?'

'No, I don't. Like I said, I wanna get it out of the way.'

'*Boring!* Typical Davinia. You'll be a doctor of sports medicine soon or whatever it is one day and you'll be the most sad one.'

'Boring maybe,' she snapped. 'But where did an exciting life get you? And what about you with your studying? And the Leicester thing? Are you thinking of studying there?'

'First of all I study in this motherfucking place 'cos if I don't do something with my head I'll go all cuckoo on your ass. And I already told you why I wanna move out of London. I won't be able to concentrate on my shit if I'm in the Dirty South. There's this brother I met doing bird, a good bredren who helped me out in my first few months. He's bonafide and his peeps live in Leicester. If I'm in Bricky I'll be looking over my shoulder everywhere I go. I know Akeisha's still there but to go back to Bricky might pull my black ass in the shit again. I'll be down at weekends to visit Akeisha, Paps and Mum.'

'Well if you are in Leicester we could meet up during the week for lunch. Loughborough ain't too far away. You could pay me to do your assignments!'

'Burn you, Davinia. I can do my own fucking assignments. And as for meeting up, yeah we could but I don't wanna waste my lunchtimes with you.'

'Dennis!'

We laughed but after the joke faded I looked into Davinia's eyes. We were silent for about a minute. 'You think I can do it, Davinia? Go on to Car mechanics or something? Not too many options for a man with a gun possession conviction, are there? *Shit!* Will the pussies let me do it? Fuck! If they do I'm gonna be more like Paps and Mum than you! Imagine that shit. Me in a fucking training class! Can you see my black ass in that kinda situation?'

She nodded… 'Yes I do, Dennis. I hate to admit it but I didn't believe it when Mum told me you passed your A-Levels. God! My brother who was always chasing the next buzz and excitement! Passed his A-Levels! It took a while to sink in. Some of the family's good genes finally found their way to your brain! But seriously, if you want to go any further you've got to put the work in. There are two fundamental differences between me and you – I'm better-looking and you're bone idle and easily influenced, prone to peer pressure. Wait a minute, that's three!'

'*Burn* you, Davinia.'

We laughed together and there was something reassuring about laughing with my sis. It wasn't always like that. During my first three months doing bird Davinia visited me and all we would do is have a fucked-up grim pulling face contest. But she saw it through with me and she always took the piss out of me as she's always done before she left. I liked that, it gave me a vibe of something normal in this fucked-up place.

'You *can* do it,' she said, getting all serious again. 'This is still a racist society and in it black women are tolerated more than black men... I know that now. Many victories have been won, by our parents' generation and Granny's generation. But there's still a few more battles to be fought. So, Dennis, every test you pass, every examination you pass and every progress you make is a small victory and a kick in the teeth for the people who hate us.'

For a few seconds I just had to sit there in admiration. Man! I was so proud of her but I still wanted to tease her like I always did. 'Davinia, shut the fuck up! Don't start your preaching, Martin Luther King shit. Save that for nigger moments in uni.'

'Why is it that whenever I try to be serious with you, you throw it back in my face? I'm getting fed up of it, Dennis. Sometimes I dunno why I come here...'

'Why you come here? 'Cos having a banter with you is the only normality I get in this fucked-up place. I look forward...'

Weren't meant to let that shit spill out. We looked at each other as I trailed off and Davinia kinda blushed. We both felt uncomfortable.

Before Noel died I never told him what he meant to me. I ain't gonna make the same mistake with other people who are close to me. So I might tell Davinia what she means to me when she's about sixty. I thought I'd better change the subject to stop Davinia looking at me with a fucked-up smug grin.

'So Mum and Paps are really selling the house?' I said.

'Yes. Mum's dragged Paps to Purley for the last two weekends. She's set her heart on moving there. I don't think Paps has much say.'

'Mum will never change,' I laughed. 'I guess it's the end of an era. We're all leaving Bricky. What year did Granny settle here? 1961?'

'No, it was 1960,' Davinia corrected me. 'July 1960. She arrived with her husband Cilbert, Great Aunt Jenny and her husband Jacob. Even on the day before she left Granny said to me she still misses Cilbert. It was a big deal me going to Loughborough University but can you imagine what it was like for them leaving Jamaica and coming to London?'

'Scary.' I replied. 'Fuck my days! Forty-six years ago she came here and now she's back where she started.'

Davinia was looking away from me but judging by her expression she was thinking of a sweet memory of Granny.

'So you think you and Akeisha can make a go of things once you get out? Will she move to Leicester after a while?'

'None of your damn business! Why you wanna know? When you showed me that pic of that sad ugly brute that you went out with you didn't take no notice of what I said. You ignored my advice when I said he looked like the kinda brother who would rub up women on packed tube trains.'

'Screw you, Dennis! He treated me with respect. Not like those other Bricky boys…'

'He had to treat you with respect. A wok from you is probably the only wok he'll get in his sad, ugly fucked-up life.'

'Dennis!'

'Alright, alright. I'm just playing you! With the Akeisha thing, well. I'll have to take every day at a time. Well, you know how I feel about her but I can't move back to Bricky. So many brothers who have finished their bird go back to their ends and end up doing the same shit. They get pulled back into the game. Fuck that.'

'It'll be sad if you two broke up.'

'We're not gonna break up. I'm not going to New Zealand, Davinia, just Leicester. Anyway, I want you to visit Akeisha and give her something.'

'Give her what?'

I leaned in closer to Davinia and spoke softly. 'Go to my wardrobe and at the bottom of it there are quilt covers and sheets. Look under all that and there is this special jewellery box. Inside that is a wristlet, a wooden bangle. I want you to give it to Akeisha as soon as possible.'

'Why can't you give it yourself?' Davinia asked. 'You're out in three weeks.'

'Believe me, Davinia. I have tried so many times to give her that bracelet. But I just couldn't.'

Davinia was proper confused. 'Why?'

'It's a long story, Davinia. Just promise me that you will give it to her...'

'I still think you should do it yourself.'

'Davinia! Can't I ask you to do one fucking thing?'

'OK, OK, I'll do it. God! What's the big deal? It's only a wooden bangle! It's not like it's twenty-four carat gold or something...'

'Davinia! *Give* it to her and then say I was sorry for not passing it on to her earlier.'

'Alright, Dennis. No need to look at me in that tone of voice. I'll give it to her tomorrow.'

'Thank you. Trust! I will remember this favour. Maybe I'll fix your ride for free one day.'

'Did you steal this thing from her?'

'Kind of.'

'When?'

'Before she even knew me. Like I said, it's a long story.'

'Dennis!'

'But I'm gonna be truthful with her now, Davinia. Gonna tell her everything... I have to 'cos I wanna spend the rest of my days with her.'

'What else is there to tell?'

'What is there to tell? Nuff tings, Davinia. You just make sure you give her the bangle.'

Davinia looked at me and placed her left hand on my right wrist in an act of reassurance... 'I will, Dennis.'

'Then I think it will turn out all good.'

EPILOGUE

October, 2006

At St Pancras train station, a boy was eating a red apple while he was waiting patiently with his grandmother. They both stood outside a shop that was at the base of the stairs leading up to the platforms. Akeisha was buying magazines, drinks and nibbles for her journey and upon her left wrist was her wooden bangle. She stepped out of the shop, struggling to carry the items she had just bought while pulling her cabin case.

'Got everything?' Akeisha's Mum asked.

'Yes, Mum.'

'Apart from your good sense!'

'Mum! Don't start. We have gone through this nuff times and I'm not gonna argue with you in front of Curtis.'

'I'm not arguing, Akeisha. I'm just speaking my mind. Aren't I allowed to even do that?'

Akeisha didn't answer her mother. Instead she kneeled down to meet Curtis's eyes. He was now six years old. She zipped up his jacket and stroked his cheeks… 'You behave for Granny and Granpa while I'm away for the weekend, OK. Be good for them.'

'Yes, Mummy.'

'Next time I go to Leicester, you'll be coming with me. I promise.'

'OK, Mummy.'

Standing again, Akeisha smiled away her mother's glare. 'It's gonna be alright, Mum. Trust me on this. Dennis is a decent guy. It was the environment that shaped him how he was. Now he's out of that environment he can be what he really wants to be.'

'I hope so for your sake.'

'You raised me to be independent, Mum. Make up my own mind on things. Dennis is working at a garage up in Leicester and is going to college in the evenings. What else does he have to do to prove himself?'

'By keeping himself out of trouble not just for a couple of months but for years and years.'

'He will, Mum.' Akeisha glanced at her bangle. 'Anyway, I'm sticking to my decision. Curtis and me are moving up to Leicester in the new year. Come on, Curtis, you can see Mummy getting on her train.'

Walking up the stairs with purpose, Akeisha laughed when she noticed Curtis jumping up the steps, trying to keep up. He had left his grandmother still standing at the base. 'Come on, Granny,' he urged. 'Don't you wanna see the long trains?'